'Tamsin is an enormously talented writer. This is a beautifully atmospheric and magical novel, which young readers and grown-ups will love.'
LUCY CUTHEW

'A middle-grade book perfect for dreamers of all ages.'
ANDREINA CORDANI

'A warm, sensitive story with an original take on valuing and channeling one's emotions.'
KIRSTY APPLEBAUM

'This book is wonderful, drawing on the myths and legends about the beautiful Shetland Isles and the wonders of Mother Nature's most unpredictable creation – weather.' NETGALLEY

'I would recommend this book to all middle grade readers and anyone who loves myths, legends and all those who look up at the clouds and dream.'
NETGALLEY

'The story is exciting, charming and full of emotional
intelligence.' AMANDA CRAIG, *THE NEW STATESMAN*

'Mixes whimsical magic and characters with
real-life emotion.' *THE HERALD*

'An enchanting, action-packed story that's funny,
light and easy to read.' *THE NATIONAL*

'This story is bursting with themes of weather weaving,
myths and legends, nature, love, grief, and family. It is such
a magical tale, but it is so rooted in the everyday
here and now.' *READINGZONE*

'This magical, highly original story of a girl who learns to
control the weather will blow you away with its drama,
warmth and wit – and the lovely little Nimbus will make
you long for a cloud friend of your own!'
ANNA WILSON

'Crackling with the best kind of storm magic and rich with invention.' AMY WILSON

'A storm-swept adventure brimming with wild Shetland magic. I loved it!' ALEX ENGLISH

'I adore the way this book is so original and at the same time ties in traditional myths and storytelling. Such a good balance: this is going to be a favourite book for a LOT of children.' JENNI SPANGLER

'A tender story of family with a whiplash of thunder.' JASBINDER BILAN

'*The Weather Weaver* crackles with stormy magic. A masterfully written, utterly spellbinding adventure that swept me away from the very first page. Tamsin has a rare gift for crafting mesmerising worlds so real and tangible that they stay with you long after the last word has been read. An electrifying and assured debut that is destined to become a modern classic.' DAMARIS YOUNG

HAVE YOU EVER WONDERED HOW BOOKS ARE MADE?

UCLan Publishing is an award-winning independent publisher, specialising in Children's and Young Adult books. Based at The University of Central Lancashire, this Preston-based publisher teaches MA Publishing students how to become industry professionals using the content and resources from its business; students are included at every stage of the publishing process and credited for the work that they contribute.

The business doesn't just help publishing students though. UCLan Publishing has supported the employability and real-life work skills for the University's Illustration, Acting, Translation, Animation, Photography, Film & TV students and many more. This is the beauty of books and stories; they fuel many other creative industries! The MA Publishing students are able to get involved from day one with the business and they acquire a behind the scenes experience of what it is like to work for a such a reputable independent.

The MA course was awarded a Times Higher Award (2018) for Innovation in the Arts and the business, UCLan Publishing, was awarded Best Newcomer at the Independent Publishing Guild (2019) for the ethos of teaching publishing using a commercial publishing house. As the business continues to grow, so too does the student experience upon entering this dynamic Masters course.

www.uclanpublishing.com
www.uclanpublishing.com/courses/
uclanpublishing@uclan.ac.uk

WINTER'S KEEP

TAMSIN MORI

Cover illustration by David Dean

With interior illustrations by Hannah Blackman-Kurz

uclanpublishing

Winter's Keep is a uclanpublishing book

First published in Great Britain in 2023 by
uclanpublishing
University of Central Lancashire
Preston, PR1 2HE, UK

Text copyright © Tamsin Mori, 2023
Cover illustrations copyright © David Dean, 2023
Interior illustrations © Hannah Blackman-Kurz, 2023

978-1-915235-05-3

1 3 5 7 9 10 8 6 4 2

The right of Tamsin Mori and David Dean and Hannah Blackman-Kurz
to be identified as the author and illustrators of this work respectively
has been asserted in accordance with the Copyright, Designs
and Patents Act 1988.

Set in 10/16pt Kingfisher by Becky Chilcott.

A CIP catalogue record for this book is available from the British Library.

Printed and bound in Great Britain by Clays Ltd, Elcograf S.p.A.

For Cat – wise witch and treasured friend.
Long may we cackle together!

One

EYES ON THE SKY

GRANDPA had let Stella borrow his big binoculars today, on the condition she take good care of them. She pulled the lens caps off and brought them up to her eyes, then fiddled with the dial, bringing the glittering waves into sharp focus. Grandpa was right. These were next-level powerful! She could even make out the mainland – a misty smudge on the horizon.

The view abruptly disappeared in a grey haze and she lowered the binoculars. "Nimbus! I can't see a thing if you're right in front of me." She ruffled the little cloud affectionately and he turned a cheery yellow. "Go on. Go play up there," she said, pointing to the slope above Grandpa's cottage.

She refocused the binoculars on the high tide line just below the cliffs. *Wow!* She could see individual strands of seaweed. *I NEED binoculars like these.* She scanned from one end of the beach to the other, taking in every detail.

Still no sign of the sea witch.

Stella sighed. It was probably a good thing, but still . . .

She wanted Heather to *know* that Velda's reign had come to an end. No more storm clouds would be stolen from their novices. All the trapped storm clouds would be set free. It might not make a difference to her – but then again, it might.

Tamar didn't think so, but she hadn't seen how *human* the sea witch looked after the battle. "Do you think she could turn back, Nimbus?"

Stella glanced across as her cloud tumbled down the slope, then flew back to the top to do it again – more interested in having fun that worrying about the sea witch.

She smiled. *He looks so happy.*

It hadn't taken him long to shake off the stress of the trials. For Stella, it wasn't so easy. She'd come so close to failing. Even though they'd proved everyone wrong, the fear of losing Nimbus still buzzed in her bones.

She understood the desperation Heather must have felt when her cloud was ripped away from her. Stella didn't *think* she'd have turned sea witch if Nimbus had been taken, but you never knew.

Nothing would bring Heather's cloud back. But seeing the storm clouds released . . . Maybe it would help?

Stella lifted the binoculars again and looked towards the western horizon.

"What are you searching for, little star?"

Dad's voice, behind her.

"Anything unusual or untoward," she said, without turning round.

"Care to be more specific?"

"No."

Mum and Dad weren't meant to be here any more. 'Just for the weekend' they'd said when they arrived at the Gathering, but that was before they'd seen weather magic. Now they kept finding excuses not to leave.

Stella knew they just wanted to make sure she was safe, but it was frustrating. She lowered the binoculars, self-conscious now she was being watched.

Dad sat down beside her, stretching his legs out and turning his face up to the sun. "If this weather is your doing, keep it up," he said. "I haven't seen a bonnier day in a long time."

"I've got one cloud, Dad! I can't control everything. This is just . . . summer."

Mum came striding up the path behind them.

"Come on, you two. Chop chop! We're off to Lerwick."

"Oh, Muuuum!"

"None of that. We're visiting estate agents," said Mum briskly.

"We can't camp at Grandpa's forever."

"Mum, you can't just come back here and boss me about! You're getting in the way of my training."

Mum raised her eyebrows at Dad. "Only a week, and she's had enough of us already!"

Stella knew she was meant to deny that, but it was sort of true. Tamar had promised to teach her weaving after the Gathering, but they hadn't even been able to start, yet – not with Mum and Dad around.

"Won't you get fired if you take any more time off?"

"We're leading the research team," said Mum. "They can hardly fire us."

"But don't they need you there?"

"They'll cope. Besides, if *you* need me, I know who takes priority!"

"I don't need you. I've got Grandpa."

Mum's mouth tightened, but Stella clenched her jaw, unrepentant.

Dad hopped to his feet and put a hand on Mum's shoulder. "Come on. Let's leave Stella here, go and find ourselves a nice little flat in the centre of Lerwick. What do you say?"

"What?! No!" exclaimed Stella, getting up quickly. "It's got to be here! Near Grandpa. And Tamar."

Feeling her agitation, Nimbus flew towards them with a warning rumble. He swooped around Dad and came to a smart stop between them. Stella reached out to soothe him.

"Seriously!" she said. "Can you imagine Nimbus living in town?"

Mum looked warily at the small thundercloud. "Dad's teasing you, love," she said. "There's an old croft up for sale about half an hour's walk from here."

"Oh! Phew." Stella scrunched her nose up at Dad. He was such a wind-up sometimes.

"You sure you won't come with us?" asked Mum.

Stella shook her head. "I want to see Tamar."

* * *

As Mum and Dad made their way down towards the jetty, Stella put the lens caps back on Grandpa's binoculars and stashed them safely in her bag. Maybe he'd let her keep them on long-term loan? As long as she was careful with them.

"Come on, Nimbus," she said, swinging the bag onto her shoulder. "To Tamar's! You know the way."

The little cloud turned a loop of delight and sped away along the cliff path.

He's been missing training too, she realised.

No wonder, really. He'd been so well behaved with Mum and Dad around, but she could tell it was an effort; too much making himself small and lurking in corners.

"I'll race you there," she called, jogging to catch up with him.

Nimbus turned a cheeky sunset orange and put on an extra spurt of speed.

A whole day of freedom. At last!

Stella pushed open the door of the croft. The front room was stacked with half-emptied crates, bales of cloth, and boxes of buttons and fastenings – Tamar's shopping haul from the Gathering. She obviously hadn't finished unpacking.

"Tamar? Are you here?"

Please be here.

There was a clatter in the larder and Tamar appeared, her face crinkling in a wide smile. "Hello, stranger! I was starting to think you'd given up weather weaving!"

Stella grinned. "Not likely."

"Where have you been this past week?"

Stella huffed. "With Mum and Dad. They want to spend every minute with me before they have to go back to work."

Tamar shook her head in disapproval. "Don't they realise you should be training?"

"I did try and tell them," Stella shrugged. "Still, we've got the whole day, today."

Tamar nodded and rubbed her palms together. "Better make the most of it then! So, are you ready to try spinning?"

"Yes!"

Finally! Stella raised her eyebrows at Nimbus. *You up for it?*

Nimbus bounced once, then scooted along the top shelves. They were stacked with reels of magic yarn – a whole rainbow of them. Stella grinned, her heart skipping with excitement. Spinning the magic your cloud collected was the first step in learning to weave. And weaving meant: invisibility cloaks, never-empty purses, flying carpets. All the magic Tamar had originally promised was nearly within reach.

"Can I make an invisibility cloak?"

Tamar frowned slightly. "Let's not get ahead of ourselves."

"But you said—"

Tamar cleared her throat loudly.

Stella bit her lips together and nodded: *I'm listening*.

Tamar pursed her lips and took a deep breath. "Spinning needs real focus – cloud and weaver in perfect harmony. It takes—"

"Calm control?" Stella interrupted eagerly.

"Exactly." Tamar smiled. "Now, I know calm is not Nimbus's forte, but—"

"We passed the trials, didn't we? Even with Velda breathing down our necks."

"That you did," Tamar nodded. "That you did."

"Have you heard anything? About the storm clouds? When they're letting them go?"

Tamar shook her head. "Nothing certain yet. But as soon as the council set a date for it, they'll let us know." She turned towards the fireplace and edged through a gap in the stacks of crates and boxes. Stella followed.

On the far side, the spinning wheel and stool stood before the fireplace. The low table had been shunted aside. A cup of tea steamed gently and a plate of shortbread had been laid out ready.

7

"You knew we were coming!" said Stella.

Tamar shrugged. "Hoped, rather than knew. Herbie saw your parents setting off without you. He's been keeping an eye out for you."

Stella smiled. Herbie was Tamar's house cloud – not great at weather magic, but friendly company and handy as cloud cover. She quite liked the idea that he'd been quietly watching over them.

"You sit there," said Tamar, patting the little three-legged stool. "And Nimbus, you over here," she said, pointing to the other side of the spinning wheel.

Stella sat down and put her foot on the little pedal under the wheel. She pressed it experimentally and the wheel whirred into life. Nimbus sprang backwards.

"Oops!"

Nimbus gave a reproachful rumble.

"Stop it, both of you!" said Tamar. "Stella, keep your foot off the pedal until we've got Nimbus set up. And Nimbus? We'll have no grumbling, please."

Nimbus turned an apologetic blue.

Stella tucked her feet under the stool. *Sorry, Nimbus. My fault.*

"Shall we try again?" said Tamar. Nimbus bobbed his assent and Stella nodded.

Tamar pointed to a little hole in the wooden contraption on the far end of the wheel. "Nimbus, thread yourself through here."

Stella looked at the row of little metal claws that waited on the other side and winced. "It's not going to hurt him, is it?"

"Of course not," said Tamar. "The spinning just puts a twist into the magic – turns it into workable yarn. It's no worse than braiding your hair."

Stella's scalp tightened. Mum had insisted on braiding her hair this morning, so she looked 'a bit less feral', and her scalp still smarted from it.

Nimbus backed away.

Tamar looked at Stella's tight braids and gave a rueful smile. "Maybe that wasn't the best analogy?" she said.

Stella shook her head vehemently.

She tried to imagine what being spun might feel like for a cloud. It couldn't be that bad? None of Tamar's clouds seemed to mind it. She gave Nimbus an encouraging smile and nodded at the hole Tamar had indicated.

"You won't know until you try!"

Two

SPINNING MAGIC

NIMBUS hesitated for a moment, then extended a thread of mist through the hole at the side of the spinning wheel. Tamar pointed and the fine line of cloud followed her finger along the little line of hooks on the far side. Tamar attached it to the far end of the reel.

"Doesn't he need to go round the wheel?" asked Stella in surprise.

Tamar shook her head. "No. Self-spinning clouds do that, but it's a bit trickier. For now, all he needs is to let go of the magic. You're going to help him by running the wheel. Alright, you can press the pedal now, Stella. But *slowly* this time. Nimbus, you'll feel a slight tug. You pull back to twist the magic, then move forward to wind it onto the reel. Back and forth, back and forth." She waved a hand to and fro, as though conducting.

Stella looked at her cloud and tried to think calm thoughts. *Ready? We'll go really slow, okay?* She pressed gently on the pedal and the wheel began to move. The whirly bits came to life.

Nimbus pulled back, the fluffy line of mist twisting tighter and tighter until it became a fine shining cord.

Tamar gave a nod and Nimbus moved towards the little hole. Silver yarn wrapped rapidly around the reel.

We're doing it! We're spinning magic! realised Stella, with a thrill of excitement.

Nimbus glowed in response and poured faster through the little hole. The spinning wheel wobbled, making Stella jump.

Careful, Nimbus. Calmly, remember?

Nimbus pulled back a little and the line of mist stretched thin again.

Calm definitely wasn't his strength, but he was learning. *For me*, thought Stella, with a sudden swell of gratitude. She kept the pedal rocking to and fro and slowly moved her hand like Tamar had, letting Nimbus know when to pull back, when to move forward.

The wheel spun with a soft hum, and the magic flowed onto the reel in a mesmerising spiral – it sparkled and shone, like a line of sunlight on fresh snow.

Tamar watched them for a minute or two, then nodded, satisfied. "Looks like you're getting the hang of it."

* * *

Now and again, Tamar came and swapped the reel for a new one. Each time, she clucked with approval and gave Nimbus a little pat.

How much magic could one small cloud carry? It seemed endless. Stella had finished her tea and all the biscuits. She glanced up at the clock – a whole hour they'd been at it, and he was still going. The regular motion of her cloud and the soft whir of the wheel were hypnotic. Stella's thoughts drifted back to Heather.

"I think you would have liked her," Velda had said. Not that you could trust anything that Velda said, but—

She was yanked from her thoughts by a sharp rattle. Stella snatched her foot off the pedal. The wheel rolled to a stop. A loose end of magic fluttered from the reel.

Oh, no!

"Tamar, the yarn broke!"

"Don't worry," said Tamar. "Nimbus is empty – that's all."

Nimbus jolted in the air, almost like a hiccup, and bolted towards the door.

"Where are you going?" exclaimed Stella.

"Off to gather more," said Tamar, opening the door for him. Nimbus shot outside.

Stella stared after him. "I didn't even get to say 'well done'."

"He'll be back," Tamar reassured her. "Clouds are always a bit jittery when they're first emptied. I suspect it's like being very thirsty – desperate for a sip of magic."

Tamar picked her way across the cluttered room, lifted the last reel of magic off the spinning wheel and peered at it.

Stella's knee bounced involuntarily as she waited for the verdict.

Tamar turned it round a couple of times, tucked the loose end in, then nodded. "Not bad at all, for a first go!"

Stella grinned.

Tamar handed her the reel of yarn. "Your very own hand-spun magic."

Stella took it and turned it around, like Tamar had. The magic had looked perfect flowing onto the reel, but up close, it went from thin, to thick, to thin again. Her smile faded.

There were bobbly bits! It looked nothing like the fine silky thread on Tamar's reels. She pulled a face. "It's not meant to be lumpy, is it?"

"No, but that's just practice," said Tamar, with a smile. "Anyway, lumpy magic's more fun. Adds a touch of the unexpected to whatever you're weaving."

Stella clutched the reel to her chest and nodded. She ran her fingers over the yarn, the tingle of magic prickling against her fingertips. "How soon can we start weaving?"

"We've already started!" said Tamar. "Spinning is the first step. Now, let me show you where you can keep your yarn stash." She headed over to the shelves and pointed up at a gap near the top.

A low set of wooden library steps waited beneath it. "Do you want to do the honours?"

Stella nodded and climbed up. When she reached the top, she spotted the handwritten label pinned to the shelf: *Stella & Nimbus*.

She knew we'd do it!

For all her huffing about 'calm' and 'focus', Tamar hadn't doubted them at all.

Stella stood the reel above their label, feeling a glow of pride. She was sorry Nimbus wasn't here. It felt like a big moment. As she glanced towards the door, her gaze landed on another label a little further along the shelf: *Heather & Fury*.

It was a stark reminder. The sea witch had once been Tamar's apprentice too.

Until her cloud was stolen . . .

She wobbled on the top step, and Tamar reached out to steady her.

"Fury," said Stella. "That's what the Heather's cloud was called?"

Tamar nodded. "Couldn't argue with it. It was well-named. A thundercloud through and through." She pressed her lips together.

The fate of her last apprentice was still a very touchy subject. When the Ice Weavers declared Heather's cloud unsafe, Tamar had agreed. If she hadn't, Heather might still be here now, rather than prowling the depths of the sea.

Stella looked at the small stack of reels above Heather's name;

most of them silver, some shimmering with hints of purple, blue and scarlet.

"You taught her to spin before she'd taken the trials!" realised Stella, with a sudden pinch of jealousy.

A door closed behind Tamar's eyes. "I told you. I rushed her training."

"Did you teach her to weave, too?" persisted Stella.

"No!" scoffed Tamar. "We'd barely even started spinning. We stopped, after it cost me a spinning wheel."

Stella climbed down carefully. "What happened?"

"What do you think happened?" snapped Tamar. "Heather got frustrated, so Fury exploded my spinning wheel. All for half a reel of unusable yarn. That red one, see? Tainted by wild lightning. Can't weave with that. That was the last time I let them spin."

Stella stared up at it.

Tamar turned away, clearly eager to end the conversation. She pulled a heavy leather-bound volume off the bookshelf and began to leaf through it.

Stella stared up at the name card on the shelf. It made it feel so real. Heather had been here, in this croft; an apprentice, just like her . . . Until Velda, the leader of the Ice Weavers, separated her from her storm cloud, and everything had gone terribly wrong.

Velda had come so close to taking Nimbus, too.

Would I have turned into a sea witch, if Nimbus was taken?

Stella thought back to her encounter with the sea witch and

15

shuddered; green scaled skin; needle teeth; hungry eyes; the hissing whisper of her voice, poisonous with accusation.

Stella eyed the small stash of yarn. "'I'll have what is mine'," she remembered. "That's what Heather said to me, before she went back to the sea."

"The Haken," said Tamar, without looking up. "She might have been Heather once, but she's the Haken now. She made her choice."

Stella folded her arms. It grated on her, Tamar refusing to call Heather by name.

"But what if she's not a sea witch any more?" she retorted. "After Nimbus fired lightning at her, she changed. She was a girl! Like me."

"She's *nothing* like you!" said Tamar. "She never was. And becoming a sea witch? That's not something you come back from. Don't fool yourself. There's nothing human left in her. She's the Teran's creature now."

Stella sighed. Maybe it *was* just wishful thinking.

Except . . . Sea witches never returned to land. Tamar had told her that.

"What did she mean, she'll have what is hers?"

Tamar shook her head. "She meant her cloud. She still can't accept that he's gone."

Destroyed, remembered Stella, unsettled by the thought. She suddenly wished very strongly that Nimbus were here, not out gathering magic.

"Anyway, enough now!" said Tamar. "The past is the past. Today is about you; your first weaving project. It's meant to be fun!" She waved the book at Stella.

Stella nodded. There was nothing she could do about what had happened to Heather. It wasn't like they could go back and change history.

* * *

Tamar put the weaving book on the kitchen table and flipped it open. "Thirsty towel?" she suggested. "They're a nice easy starter project."

Stella recoiled. "Anything but that."

"I don't know what you've got against them," said Tamar. "They're endlessly useful. Especially when you've got a cloud who entertains himself by raining on you." She raised her eyebrows.

Stella shook her head. "I don't like that they can move. They're creepy!"

She pulled out a chair and ran her finger down the the index page. The first section was titled *Household* and included patterns for thirsty towels, weather bags and self-cleaning clothes. Her eyes widened as she got further down the page – *Wealth* had never-empty purses, sun gold, moon silver.

"What's moon silver?" she asked.

Tamar wrinkled her nose. "It's a dirty trick, that's what it is. Silver made from moonlight. It disappears in daylight. Mainly, it's used by tricksters and charlatans, keen to avoid settling their debts. I don't approve of it myself."

Stella continued to read, with a growing sense of wonder. She stabbed a finger at a pattern near the bottom of the page. "That! There. I want to make that!"

"Invisibility cloak," read Tamar. "And what does this say, right here?"

Stella looked at the subtitle: *Advanced patterns.*

"But . . . Please? I've always wanted one. Ever since I knew they existed."

Tamar shook her head firmly. "One day, but not yet. You need perfectly even thread to accomplish invisibility. Yarn like yours?" She snorted. "You'll end up as a disembodied arm, or foot, or head. No. For now, pick something with a little movement to it; something a bit more forgiving of those lumps and bumps."

Three

MIDNIGHT TAILOR

STELLA heaved a sigh and ran her finger back up the list to *Beginner patterns – practical magic.*

"What's a sea shawl?"

Tamar leant to look over her shoulder. "Hah! That might be just the thing!"

"What does it do?"

"Calms the sea," said Tamar. "There used to be huge demand for them, but I haven't made one in ages. These days, fishermen tend to rely on fancy gadgets and gizmos, rather than entrust their lives to magic."

"Fishermen?" Stella's eyes lit up. "I could make one for Grandpa! As a present."

Tamar rolled her eyes. "Yes, I suppose you could. But you'll need to learn to use it first. You don't gift a magical item to *anyone* until you know it's working properly. Clear?"

"Clear," confirmed Stella. She chewed on her lip as something else occurred to her. "Could you use it as protection against a sea-witch attack?"

Tamar frowned. "If you or your Grandpa *ever* spot any sign of the Haken, the first thing I want you to do is run and find me! You remember the signs?"

"'Anything unusual or untoward'," droned Stella. "You've told me enough times."

Tamar tutted at Stella's tone. "It pays to be vigilant. Forewarned is forearmed."

"But a sea shawl might be useful, just in case?"

Tamar pursed her lips. "I suppose so."

"One of those then," said Stella decisively.

Sooner or later, the sea witch would be back. Stella knew it. And though she hoped Heather still had something human in her, she wasn't banking on it.

Tamar flicked forward to the correct page and tapped a finger on the sun symbol in the corner. "It's a summer weave. Perfect. So, let's see now . . . five pounds of seaweed, a puffin's growl—"

"I'm not hurting puffins!"

Tamar gave her a startled look. "You don't have to! They growl all the time – you just need to get the yarn close enough to absorb the sound."

Stella smiled. *Puffins! I'll finally get to see puffins! Right up close.*

Tamar's finger stopped on the last ingredient and she tutted.

"Midnight sunbeams," read Stella.

"Mm. At least you've picked the right time of year for it," said Tamar. "You'll need gloves though, for collecting them."

"Magic gloves?" asked Stella, her eyes shining.

"Yes, magic gloves," replied Tamar, standing up. "Now, tell me you're not one of those girls who's afraid of creepy crawlies?"

The sparkling gloves Stella had been picturing abruptly turned into earthy gardening gloves. She frowned. "I don't mind bugs," she said. "Crickets and beetles are alright. Woodlice are weird, but sort of cute. The only thing I hate is spiders – big scuttling ones, especially."

"Oh, for goodness' sake!" exclaimed Tamar. "Here I was, about to introduce you to one of the most skilled weavers in the islands, and you go and describe him as scuttling!"

All the tiny hairs on the back of Stella's neck stood on end.

What kind of spider was Tamar talking about?

She could put up with the skinny ones that hung around in corners minding their own business. It was big busy ones she couldn't stand; the kind that wait until you're all relaxed and then dash out from under the sofa, making you snatch your feet up. Just the thought of it made her twitch.

Seeing Stella's face, Tamar relented. "It's alright, I don't expect

21

he'll mind. I'm sure he's been called worse. He's a charming character. You'll see."

She went over to the far side of the room and reached up to the small gauze of cobwebs in the corner of the ceiling.

Stella shuddered. Mum sometimes got her to help clean cobwebs out of high corners with the long-handled broom. She hated it; the constant irrational fear that the spider would come running down the broom handle.

Tamar turned back towards her. Perched on her palm was the biggest spider she had ever seen. As Tamar came closer, Stella's throat tightened around a squeak. She hurried to stand up and moved behind her chair.

The spider's abdomen was green, patterned with narrow curling lines of silver. Its long legs were black, speckled with tiny silver dots. It looked distinctly poisonous.

Right now, it was sitting perfectly still on Tamar's outstretched hand, but she didn't trust it one bit – better to be on her feet, in case she had to make a dash for it.

Don't you move!

"Well, you haven't run away screaming," said Tamar, "so that's a start." She set the spider down carefully. His legs flexed as he settled on the table. They were long and many-jointed. Every fibre in Stella's body vibrated with the urge to run away.

"Not so bad, is he?" said Tamar. "He's a sweetie once you get to know him."

The spider's bright eyes shone like tiny black pebbles. Stella could see herself reflected in all eight of them. She shivered.

Tamar was watching her closely.

This was a test, Stella realised – a test to find out how much she wanted to learn weaving.

I can like spiders, she told herself.

Stella swallowed hard. She could do this. She could! *Just as long as he doesn't move.*

"He's a very, er . . . impressive-looking spider," she said, finally.

"You hear that, Sid? 'Impressive' – that's better than 'scuttling', isn't it?"

Stella glanced at Tamar and then back at the spider. "Sid?" she said, in a doubtful voice.

"Yes, Sid," said Tamar. "What's wrong with Sid?"

"Nothing," said Stella. "Nothing's wrong with it. He just looks like he might have a bigger name than Sid."

Tamar shrugged. "It's not his full name, of course. That's such a mouthful. But given that we're doing formal introductions . . . Stella, I'd like to introduce you to Sid, officially known as The Mythic Tailor of Homespun Magic and Master Weaver of Coincidence. Coin-SID-ence, you see? Or Sid, for short," said Tamar, looking very pleased with herself.

Stella's heart raced – normally when you meet people for the first time, you shake hands, but she did *not* want to touch Sid. He was too big; too spidery.

The spider stood up on his four hind legs and performed a graceful bow.

Stella stared. "He can understand you!"

Tamar shrugged. "Of course. He's a loom spider – magical. You can tell by the silver. Any spider that spends long enough on a weather-weaving loom absorbs a little magic; Sid more than most. Show her, Sid."

Sid flexed his legs and tilted his body. Stella tensed, but he'd only moved to show off the filigree of silver on his back.

"Well, are you just going to stare at him, or are you going to greet him properly?"

To avoid any sort of contact, Stella bowed, keeping her eyes up in case he decided to leap at her. "Pleased to meet you, Sid," she said in her politest voice. "I'm Stella, Lightning Weaver."

The spider bobbed its head. Lifting one of its front legs, he appeared to blow a kiss to her. Then, with a soft patter, he rotated on the spot until he was facing Tamar. He raised his two front legs.

"You heard, then?" said Tamar.

The spider scampered towards Tamar and Stella's grip on the back of the chair tightened. He was fast. Very fast.

The spider waved his long spindly legs in a complicated and oddly elegant motion. It looked a bit like a flamenco dance.

"Well, fairly urgent, yes. As soon as you can. You tell me?" said Tamar.

The spider swayed from side to side and then raised one front leg.

"Perfect!" said Tamar. "You're a sweetheart."

"Better than we could have hoped for," she said to Stella, with a smile. "I'll pop him back now. It'll be at least day of spinning for him, but he reckons your gloves will be ready by tomorrow night."

Tamar carried the spider gently back to the other end of the room and reached up high to put him back in his cobweb. Stella kept her eyes fixed on the corner to make sure he didn't reappear.

Tamar rolled her eyes when she caught Stella staring. She beckoned impatiently, then led her out of the croft, onto the bright windy hillside.

As soon as they were outside, Stella gave a massive shudder and brushed imaginary spiders off her arms and out of her hair. Meeting Sid had left her feeling itchy all over.

"Are you quite finished?" said Tamar.

"Look, I know he's magical and everything. It's just . . . urgh!"

"Honestly! There's only so much rudeness a spider can be expected to endure," said Tamar, shaking her head in disapproval. "He's doing us a big favour making those gloves. And in double-quick time, too. I've known him for decades and he's not always this accommodating, so count yourself lucky!"

"Decades?!"

"Since I got my first loom. He's been with me since the start."

"Sorry," said Stella, with a twinge of guilt. "I will try and get used to him. Promise." She glanced back at the croft. "Can you *really* talk to him?"

"Yes," said Tamar. "I'm not as fluent as I'd like to be, but he's quite easy to understand. He speaks a rather charming version of the standard spider semaphore. You saw all that leg waving? It's a kind of sign language."

Stella nodded, thinking back to Sid's behaviour.

"People can talk very expressively with just two hands," Tamar continued, "so you can imagine how eloquent and complex spider conversation is. Happily, since Sid is a fairly sizeable spider, he's easy enough to understand – though I'm aware he has to speak slowly and clearly for my benefit. If you ever see him talking with another loom spider, those legs of his are a blur." Tamar trudged to the end of the house and disappeared round the corner.

Stella hurried after her. "Can you talk to all spiders?"

Tamar gave a short laugh. "You won't get much conversation out of a standard spider – juicy flies, web patterns, wind direction; that's about it. Terribly repetitive."

"But you *can* talk them?"

"To an extent. The only ones I struggle with are money spiders. They talk so fast, and their legs are so short. Not their fault, I realise – possibly I need glasses . . ."

"Can I learn it too?" said Stella.

"Certainly," said Tamar, chuckling to herself. She opened the door of the lean-to at the back of the house. "Warming up to spiders now, are we?"

Tamar disappeared inside the little shed. There was a clatter and a series of heavy thumps as she moved things around.

"What kind of gloves is Sid going to make me?" said Stella, changing the subject.

"Gossamer gloves," said Tamar, reaching out to hand Stella two large buckets. "You can't weave a sea shawl without sunbeams.

Midnight sunbeams, to be precise. The easiest way to gather them is with gossamer gloves – Sid's speciality. It's about time you had a pair. They're essential kit; help you handle all the special yarns: sunbeams, moonbeams . . ." She raised her eyebrows at Stella and grinned.

Stella stared at Tamar, her mind boggling. "Lightning, too?"

"If you're careful," said Tamar, then frowned. "But don't try that on your own."

Four

THE CLOUD
COVENANT

TAMAR bolted the shed door and tramped away up the grassy slope towards the broch path. Stella followed, the metal buckets catching in the long grass and bumping against her leg. "Why do we need these?" she called.

"For seaweed!" called Tamar. "That's your first task. Collect enough seaweed to fill both buckets. We'll head down to the bay by the broch – good pickings there."

Stella glanced up. Still no sign of Nimbus. She sighed.

Empty of magic! He'd probably be gone for ages.

As they reached the crest of the hill, Stella paused and looked back at the sea. Sunshine glistened on the waves, lighting a golden path to the horizon. Stella imagined being able to roll it up and take it home – a sparkling sheet of gold. Maybe that was how Farah made the sunshine scarf?

I never got it back from Magnus after the Quest! she realised, with a creeping sense of guilt. It was precious – she knew that much – something to treasure. *I hope he's kept it safe.*

"Do you think I'll get to see Magnus, when we go to see the storm clouds released?" she said, trotting to catch up with Tamar.

Tamar raised her eyebrows. "Probably. His mentor Silvan will certainly be there. I'm afraid it's not going to be anytime soon, though." She shook her head.

"What? Why not!"

They'd promised! The council had *promised* they'd release all the storm clouds.

"The elders are taking their time about it – dragging everything out."

Stella's heart sank. Peter's little sister, so many other apprentices out there, all waiting for their storm clouds to come home. It was awful to think about. And it felt like her fault . . .

We got everyone's hopes up.

It wasn't fair! They'd exposed how Velda was trapping storm clouds, proved it was wrong, but nothing had changed.

"Don't they realise all the apprentices are waiting?"

"Of course! They're just being cautious, as usual. Besides, Velda may be in disgrace, but she can still spread indecision like a maestro."

"There isn't anything to decide! The council overturned the Storm Laws, didn't they?"

Tamar nodded.

"So, they just need to let them go!" exclaimed Stella.

Tamar shook her head. "The safety of the weather weaving community, remember? Serve and protect – all that nonsense. Velda knows exactly which buttons to push. She's got them terrified of what will happen if all the storms are unleashed at once; claims they'll rage around wreaking havoc. Though I suspect that's a bunch of tosh. It's probably got more to do with Velda's fear of the good folk," said Tamar.

"The Trows?"

Tamar nodded. "The council were meant to be guardians of those gems. By using them, Velda broke a sacred agreement."

"What was the agreement?"

Tamar smiled briefly, as though she approved of the question. "The Cloud Covenant," she replied. "Aeons ago, the Trows had their own version of weather magic – they'd use gems to trap clouds, just as Velda's been doing. Unlike Velda, they'd let them go again when they'd got what they needed – catch-and-release weather magic. Regardless, the weather weavers didn't approve of the good folk trapping clouds – quite rightly – so they negotiated an agreement. They promised to supply the good folk with unlimited weather magic, if they gave up using their gems."

Stella hitched the buckets higher as they reached the steep part of the path. Tamar reached out a hand and Stella handed the buckets over gratefully. Tamar carried on down the slope towards the broch. "As a gesture of good faith, most of the Trowie gems were handed over to the council for safekeeping."

"Until Velda started using them . . ."

Tamar nodded heavily. "Big mistake. The good folk are far more powerful than any weather weaver. You do *not* want to annoy them. And they were none too happy to discover that weather weavers had been making use of their gems."

"But it wasn't *us*! It was the Ice Weavers."

"Quite! And right now, the only thing standing between the Ice Weavers and the good folk is an army of trapped storm clouds. You can imagine why Velda's reluctant."

"But the storm clouds can't *stay* trapped!"

"No. We need to set it right."

"I wish you were on the council."

Tamar snorted. "Talking round in circles? Drinking tea until you're sloshing with it? No, thank you. I've done my time on the council."

"Can't you talk to them, at least?"

"I am!" exclaimed Tamar. "Whether they'll listen is another matter."

Stupid. It was stupid. Everyone agreed that trapping clouds was wrong. Nobody on the council could argue with that.

"Why not just let them go? What are the council scared of?"

Tamar scoffed. "Straight-talking. Decisive action. Anything that's not prefaced by a week-long debate."

Stella rolled her eyes. She already knew Tamar's opinions on the council; she'd had to listen to enough of her rants about them.

Tamar sighed. "They're afraid," she stated. "They've always been a bit wary of us Storm Weavers, so the prospect of releasing the very wildest storm clouds is causing them more than a little concern."

Ahead, the great stone tower of the broch was visible now. Stella took a deep breath of salty air. Even from here, she could sense the song emanating from the sanctuary stone inside the broch. It hummed in her blood, lending her certainty.

"We released Tas's storm cloud," she pointed out. "That went alright, didn't it? And if it was okay with one, why not all of them?"

Tamar wrinkled her nose. "But we're not talking *one* storm cloud – we're talking *hundreds*! I might scoff, but the council aren't wrong. If they all ran amok, it'd be chaos. They could disrupt the seasons. And no one can be certain the storm clouds will return to their weather weavers when they're released. Why should they trust people again, when they've been treated like that?"

"If it was Nimbus, he'd fly straight back to me," retorted Stella. "I know he would. Even if it was hundreds of miles." She growled in frustration. "Please, Tamar? You've got to convince them!"

Tamar shrugged. "I'm open to ideas."

Stella thought back to when Tas's cloud was released. It *was* wild – angry and confused. But that didn't last long – not once it saw Tas.

"What about if we bring the apprentices to them?" she said. "Get them to call their clouds, like Tas did. If they were reunited straight away, they'd stay calm."

Tamar pursed her lips and frowned. They walked the last stretch without talking, the silence punctuated only by the crunch of their feet on the crushed slate path and the hum of insects in the grass.

When they reached the foot of the broch, Tamar set the buckets down with a light clang and rubbed a hand over her mouth.

"You might be right. Bring the apprentices to their clouds . . ." She nodded. "I'm going to put it to the council."

Stella's heart swelled with pride. Her idea, in front of the council!

Then, maybe they'll make a decision!

She leant against the curved wall of the broch, its solid presence lending her strength. The sanctuary stone inside held all the weather weavers' stories, overflowing in a constant song. Tamar valued it as a sea-witch deterrent, but Stella just loved the feel of it. This close, the song filled her with hope and courage.

But her doubts lingered.

If it was up to the council, a decision might take years. And would they make the right decision?

"The storm clouds can't stay trapped, no matter what the council decide," said Stella.

33

Tamar patted her shoulder. "One way or another, we'll see those storm clouds released."

"Soon," insisted Stella. "Not in, like, a year."

"It needs to happen by the end of summer," agreed Tamar, "well before winter starts to draw near. If not, I'll do it myself."

"Promise?"

Tamar nodded. "I promise."

Stella leant back against the sun-warmed stone and smiled to herself. Tamar wasn't all wishy-washy when it came to making decisions. Mostly, if you could get a promise out of her, she'd keep it.

Five

SELKIE SONG

STELLA knew how to collect seaweed – she'd helped Gran do it when she was small – but Tamar seemed determined to make it sound far more complicated than it actually was. She'd been talking for ten minutes already and now she'd got side-tracked into reminiscing about recipes.

"—as crisps. Or as a seasoning. Very healthy – high in iron."

Stella knew all this. Gran used to dry seaweed and grind it up to mix into all sorts of recipes. When she was little, Stella could never quite decide if she liked it or not. It was salty and tangy – adding a mysterious sea flavour to whatever Gran stirred into.

"I've done this before," interrupted Stella. "With Gran."

Tamar straightened up, irked to be interrupted mid-flow. "Expert, are we? Tell me what you know about cutting seaweed, then?"

"You don't pull it up by the roots and you never pick too much from just one plant. Leave enough for it to carry on growing."

Tamar snorted softly, refusing to be impressed. "And why are we collecting from this spot, in particular?" She raised an eyebrow.

"Fast moving water, so it's clean. Shallow, so there's lots to choose from when the tide goes out – bladderwrack, dulse, green nori – that's what Gran used to pick."

"Hm! Not bad," conceded Tamar. "I'll leave you to it, then. The tide is on its way out, so you can just work your way down the rocks gradually, but be careful when you get out onto the green, it's—"

"Slippery," said Stella.

Tamar threw her hands up and nodded. "Fine." She smiled. "Two bucketsful. Don't pack them too tight and try not to pick up any passengers."

"Passengers?"

"Crabs, winkles, anemones . . . Passengers!" She turned and stomped away towards the top of the beach.

"Where are you going?"

"Gathering herbs," said Tamar. "Seaweed isn't the only ingredient we'll need, it's just the messiest."

"Hey!"

Tamar shrugged. "Got to be some benefits to having an

apprentice. And if you're going to complain about it, you can collect the herbs too. It is *your* sea shawl, after all."

* * *

Stella had nearly filled both buckets now, and the tide was definitely on the turn. The slope down to the water was shallow, so when it came in, it would come in quickly. She began to pick her way back up the rocks towards the narrow crescent of sand.

She paused halfway back, to trim some strips from a lush patch of nori. Shame about the tide. She didn't really want to stop – she was enjoying herself. It felt almost as though Gran was still here with her, pointing out the smallest freshest leaves, naming each one.

After seaweed picking, she and Gran would always sing songs to the seals. Stella remembered the thrill of the seals' heads appearing above the water to listen. She remembered it so clearly – Gran's warm voice singing the selkie song, the lilting tune in time with the waves – she could almost hear it.

A shiver skittered up her back and she straightened and looked around. It wasn't her imagination. Stella *could* hear it – the selkie song!

But it wasn't Gran singing now.

This voice was lower – humming rather than singing – and there were minor notes that didn't belong, weighting the song with sadness.

She glanced out at the water. Sure enough, two seals had appeared, their heavy heads sleek and curious. Someone else was singing to the selkies . . .

Stella put the buckets down softly on the sand and began to move slow and low towards the sound. Who was singing? Not Tamar, she was pretty sure. She'd headed off in the opposite direction.

It was coming from the next cove. The steep cliff jutted out across the beach. No way round, except back down onto the rocks, near the water line. Stella eyed the approaching waves warily. Did she have time, before the tide came in?

The rocks at the foot of the cliff were large and slick with green. She crept closer on all fours, picking handholds carefully between clusters of sharp mussel shells and trying to avoid stepping in any rockpools. Every nook and crevice brimmed with briny water, bristling with urchins.

Stella lifted her head to peer over the rocks and froze.

The sea witch.

Right there. Waiting for her.

She was sitting in the shallows just a few metres away, a faint smile playing across her pale lips and her eyes fixed on Stella. Her scaly skin glimmered green, catching reflections off the water.

It was definitely her.

Yet she was different than Stella remembered – no more tangle of seaweed in place of clothes – she was wearing a tattered wetsuit. And she looked . . . hopeful. The sea witch raised one spiny hand and beckoned to Stella.

Who is she now? Heather or the Haken?

The water around her was unnaturally still, the waves flattening abruptly as they reached the edge of the cove.

Stella stared, searching for the familiar feeling of threat, but failing to find it.

That doesn't mean she's not dangerous.

Stella rubbed her shoulder absently, remembering the stabbing pain as the spine pierced her raincoat during their last encounter; the heavy ache of sea-witch venom.

Heather watched Stella a moment longer, then turned towards the seals and began to sing softly again, her voice husky and low. Her fingertips stirred the water as she sang, sending small eddies curling across the mirrored surface.

"You know the selkie song," said Stella.

Heather paused, looked across at Stella and nodded.

Stella swallowed.

Heather. She was sure, now. There was no trace of the Haken. "My gran used to sing that song with me," she offered.

"I know. I used to listen. I liked it."

Stella frowned. That was creepy. The idea that the Haken been hiding there, listening to them. It was meant to be a song to call selkies, not sea witches.

And that was ages ago – when she was small. She studied Heather. It was hard to tell how old she was. Stella would have guessed about the same age as her, but she couldn't be – not even close.

"How old are you?"

Heather pinched the scaled skin of her forearm, shook her head and shrugged.

She doesn't know. Maybe sea witches don't age?

The idea of asking Tamar flitted across Stella's mind, but she dismissed it. Tamar would be afraid – afraid that the sea witch was back; afraid that Stella had talked to her. Angry, probably, too.

Stella glanced back across the rocks. Was the tide a little higher already? She couldn't tell, but made a note of an angular rock at the waterline, just in case.

"I heard what you said. On the boat," said Heather. She pressed her lips together and knotted her fingers. "You said you were sorry for what they did to me."

On the way to the Gathering. Stella remembered.

She nodded cautiously. "I found out what Velda did."

Heather bared her teeth in a snarl and Stella flinched. The needle teeth were still the same – sharp and crowded – far too many of them.

"Velda tried to do the same to me and Nimbus," Stella blurted. "But she couldn't. We're Lightning Weavers now."

Heather stood up abruptly, making Stella jump. Her wetsuit clung to her, revealing bony shoulders, stiff as a coat hanger beneath the ragged rubber. She searched the sky, teeth still bared, but there was none of the cold self-assurance she'd had during their battle. She looked like a cornered animal.

She's afraid of us! Afraid of Nimbus! Stella realised, with a small stab of guilt.

"Where is he, your lightning cloud?" hissed Heather.

A twinge of nerves pinched Stella's heart. Heather had tried to steal Nimbus last time, to pull him under the water. She was suddenly glad he wasn't with her.

"Far away. Gathering magic."

Heather's shoulders relaxed, but her eyes still searched the sky warily.

"We won't hurt you," Stella reassured her. "Not unless you're attacking us."

Heather nodded solemnly. She sank lower and lay back in the water, her hair fanning out behind her like a crown of seaweed. "Agreed. Yes. A truce."

It was so strange, seeing her like this; not angry, not fighting. Floating loose-limbed in the mirror-smooth water, she looked almost . . . peaceful.

But had she really changed? How do you ask a sea witch if they're still a sea witch?

Stella gnawed her lip. "You look different than before," she tried. *More human,* she wanted to say, but she wasn't sure how to say it without sounding rude. "Your eyes are different."

"Land eyes," said Heather quietly. "Human eyes."

Stella nodded. "Are you . . . turning human?"

A look of panic flashed across Heather's face. She shook her head vehemently, glancing around as though there might be people listening.

"It's not allowed," she whispered.

Stella wasn't sure what to make of that.

"But you can choose, can't you? You chose the sea. Couldn't you choose to come back?"

Heather shook her head. "I chose the sea and the Teran chose me. No more choices, now." Her voice was toneless as she said it. A simple statement of fact.

"Then why are you here?"

Heather rolled and with one fluid motion, slid through the water towards the rock Stella was crouching on.

Too close!

Stella clambered away; her feet unsteady on the slick stones, until she found her escape blocked by a deep rockpool and an unsteady tumble of slick green rocks. She glanced anxiously back at Heather. The sea witch had stopped. She wasn't following.

Heather looked Stella up and down. "Don't be scared," she said. "Truce, remember?"

Stella nodded, trying to quell the panic that still surged through her veins. She moved carefully along the boulders until she found more solid footing a bit further from Heather, then crouched down again and took a deep breath.

"Why are you here?" she repeated.

Heather sank a little lower and looked at her for a long moment, the surface of the water casting bright reflections over her silvery skin.

"I need your help," she said.

Six

A HURRIED DEPARTURE

STELLA stared at the sea witch. With her mouth closed and her spiny hands hidden beneath the water, Stella could see it again. The girl she'd once been. All alone.

But help her how? To do what? And why me?

Try as she might, Stella couldn't think of anything the sea witch might need that she could help with.

"Why me?"

Heather drifted out into the deeper water, slipping lower until only her head was visible. "Because we're the same."

"Stella? Stella!" Tamar's voice, sharp with worry.

The sea witch's eyes widened. She put a slim finger to her lips and slid beneath the surface.

Stella turned towards Tamar's voice, her heart racing.

Should she tell Tamar? Of course she should. But she knew how Tamar would react.

"I'm over here," she called, forcing a cheerful tone.

Better she doesn't know. Just for now. Not 'til I know what Heather wants.

But Stella wasn't practised at lying. The deception settled like a heavy stone in her stomach as Tamar came into view.

"There you are!" exclaimed Tamar, clambering across the rocks towards her. She looked ruffled. "What are you doing! Can't you see the tide's coming in?"

Stella glanced behind her. Heather was gone. A small wave rolled into the shore, erasing the patch of smooth water. The seals had gone, too – vanishing silently as though they'd never been here. She sighed. "I was just exploring."

Tamar shook her head, angry now that she knew Stella was safe. "Five more minutes, you'd have been cut off! Honestly! I thought you had more sense."

Stella swallowed. She hadn't been keeping an eye on the tide at all – she'd been completely distracted.

Was that what the sea witch wanted? To trap her here? The thought sent a chill down her spine. But she didn't believe it. Not truly.

Heather might not be human, but she wasn't all monster either.

Stella just wished she'd had time to find out what she really wanted.

Her eyes settled on the spot where Heather had been just a moment ago. She'd left something behind. Stella picked her way down across the rocks and held up the large shell.

"It's a conch," said Tamar, unimpressed. "But you're after seaweed. Not seashells. If we're going to get this sea shawl made, you need to keep your mind on the job."

Stella nodded and slid the conch into her coat pocket.

Tamar was already climbing back along the rocks towards the broch, her movements hurried and cross. "Get a move on!" she barked, without pausing to look back.

Stella scrambled over the rocks after her.

'We're the same.'

Heather's words turned in her mind.

What did she mean by that?

* * *

The buckets of seaweed were heavy and the walk back to the croft was long, especially since Tamar was intent on lecturing Stella the whole way about sea safety, like she didn't know!

The more Tamar went on, the more convinced Stella became that keeping Heather secret was the right decision. If she knew, Tamar would only get more worried; more angry.

No. First, Stella needed to figure out her *own* thoughts about the strange encounter.

When they reached the croft, she set the buckets down on the ground and flexed her fingers. The handles had left scarlet imprints across her palms. They stung as the blood found its way back into her hands.

Tamar bent and picked through the buckets. "Should be enough to be going on with," she said. "I'll set the yarn to steep."

"Steep?"

"Soak," clarified Tamar. "In the seaweed. Once it's taken on the right colour, I'll use one of your bottled winds to dry it."

Stella felt a little jolt of pride at that. She was beginning to build up a little weather collection of her own. Nothing like Tamar's collection, not yet, but still . . . It felt good that Tamar had suggested using one of *her* winds.

Stella moved to pick the buckets up again, but Tamar shook her head. "You need to head home."

"What? Why?"

She didn't want to go. They'd missed so much training time already! Who knew if Mum and Dad would let her come back tomorrow, or insist on some family outing?

"Herbie spotted your folks coming home."

"But they're not meant to be—"

"Well, they are. Go on, now. Shoo!"

* * *

As she rounded the corner of the cliff path, Stella spotted Grandpa's boat tied up at the jetty and lengthened her stride.

What were they doing back so soon?

'All day', they'd said. She'd intended to be here waiting for them. She pushed open the front door to a bustle of activity.

Grandpa was dismantling the camp bed she'd been sleeping on in the front room while Mum and Dad were staying. Dad was kneeling on his sailing bag, trying to squish it flat enough to zip closed. Mum was washing socks in the sink.

My socks!

"Mum, you don't have to do that," she protested. "I've been doing the washing with Grandpa. And I've got enough clean ones anyway."

What was the point of Mum telling her to be grown-up and independent if she was just going to come back and take over?

"There you are. Where have you been?" said Mum, squeezing out the socks and pulling the plug.

"Out with Tamar. I told you!" said Stella. "Why are you back? What's going on?"

Mum quickly dried her hands on a tea towel and steered Stella over to the kitchen table. When they were both sitting down, she covered Stella's hands with her own and put on an unconvincing smile. "Now, I don't want you to worry . . ."

Stella's heart quickened and she pulled her hands away. "What's happened?"

"It's nothing terrible – quite exciting really. But your dad and I need to get back to work. Today. Right now, in fact."

Stella glanced at Dad, who gave her a more convincing smile. Mum tucked Stella's hair behind her ear and Stella shook it loose again. "Why? I thought you were going to stay longer?"

It wasn't that she wanted them to stay. She'd been looking forward to them going back to work. But not like this, with hurry and rush and Mum being all weird.

"What do you know about our work?" said Dad.

"You're sea—

"Marine," corrected Dad.

"*Marine* zoologists," said Stella. "Sea slugs and stuff."

Dad nodded and smiled. "We've been monitoring sea temperatures – the effect on sea slug populations – nudibranchs. We've got monitoring buoys all across the North Sea. But today they've reported something exciting. Something unusual."

'*Anything unusual, anything untoward*' – Tamar's words flew through Stella's mind, leaving a faint skitter of warning, like the trail of a skimming stone, but Mum interrupted and Stella lost her train of thought.

"One of the buoys has gone off-line," Mum explained, "but the next three in that sector are showing a large drop in sea-temperature. A big anomaly. If it were just the one, we'd put it down to equipment error, but three of them? Seems unlikely."

"But that's not the good news," said Dad, his eyes bright with barely contained excitement. "There's something big down there. We think the shift in current must be bringing it closer to the surface. We've been tracking it for a while – initially we thought it might be a pod of whales, or perhaps giant squid – they can grow to pretty tremendous sizes. But it's bigger than that; bigger than anything we've seen before. We haven't identified it yet, but the ship's tracking it on radar. It's only a matter of time."

Stella shook her head, the faint sense of worry coalescing into a cold hard premonition. "Don't go."

"Darling, we have to!" said Mum. "This could be huge . . . is huge! Shifting currents, unseen marine life – this is what we do! Opportunities like this don't come along every day. We have to be there."

"I want you here."

Mum put on her best persuading face, but Stella gritted her teeth. "Your work is more important than me, is it? That's what you're saying."

It was low, Stella knew, but she couldn't let them go. Who knew what was down there? Something bad. Nothing good came up from midnight depth.

Mum's face crumpled. She pulled Stella onto her lap and wrapped her arms round her. "We have to, my love. And you said it yourself, this morning: you don't need us here, bossing you about, getting in the way of your training."

Stella swallowed. Why had she said that? She hadn't meant it. She'd just wanted to avoid a boring day in Lerwick, that was all. She hadn't expected to have it thrown back at her the very same day.

"You're happy here, with Grandpa, aren't you?" asked Mum.

Stella looked across the room at Grandpa. He smiled and

she nodded. They were happy, now. Grandpa was the best.

Stella disentangled herself from Mum and moved back to her own chair. She clenched her fists on the table and fixed Dad with a serious look.

"What if it's a sea monster?" she said.

Worry crept onto Grandpa's face. He knew. It *was* possible.

"Then we'll name it after you," said Dad with a smile, finally getting the zip closed and patting the bag in satisfaction. "Stella-saurus."

Mum laughed.

Rage rose in Stella, sudden and hot. She was trying to keep them safe and they were laughing at her!

She stood up, blocking Dad as he carried the bag towards the door. "You're not going! It could be dangerous!"

"Danger is my middle name," said Dad, with a wink. He ruffled her hair and then gently moved her aside to open the door.

Stella cast an urgent look at Grandpa: *You tell them! They'll listen to you!*

But Grandpa gave a slight shake of his head and turned to give Mum a reassuring smile. "Don't you worry. We've been getting on fine here, the two of us. Just be careful, yes? Take care of each other and come back safe."

Mum nodded. She joined Dad at the door.

Dad gave her an encouraging smile. "We'll be back soon, little star. I promise. I love you." He put an arm round Mum and they headed outside.

Stella moved to follow, but Grandpa put a hand on her shoulder and she realised she was outnumbered. Nobody was taking her seriously.

"Fine! Go then!" she shouted after them. "I don't need you anyway!"

Seven

THE BOOK OF
MONSTERS

GRANDPA set a steaming bowl of soup down in front of
Stella and put a small pot of cream in the middle of the table.
He brought his own bowl over and pulled out a chair.

The house was weirdly quiet with Mum and Dad gone. She'd
given them tearful hugs before they left, but she hadn't apologised
for what she'd said. There just wasn't time. They'd barely finished
saying goodbye when a rib had roared up to the jetty to take them
back to Lerwick.

"I wish I hadn't said that," said Stella.

Grandpa nodded. "I know, love."

She leant forward and blew on the soup, raising a small cloud of steam.

"I didn't mean it."

"Of course you didn't. They know that."

Stella took a spoonful of cream and stirred it into the soup, making a pale spiralling whirlpool in the centre of her bowl. "Why didn't you stop them? What if something happens to them?"

Grandpa heaved a great sigh. "Stella, I know we've seen a lot of strangeness lately, but usually the simplest answer is the right one. They'll probably get out there and find it's an equipment malfunction."

"You heard Mum. She said it couldn't be. Not with that many different buoys."

"Still," said Grandpa. "I doubt it's anything to worry about. At best, they'll get to saddle some deep-sea creature with an unfortunate name; at worst, they'll come back disappointed."

"They don't understand what's out there, Grandpa. They might have seen a bit of weather magic, but they still don't get it. They want to believe it's all just made-up!"

"They're scientists, Stella," he replied. "There's no such thing as 'made-up' in their world. Just . . . unexplained; uncatalogued. Did you know your dad has been keeping a journal on Nimbus?"

"What!"

He couldn't do that! Not without asking. Nimbus was her

friend – not some *specimen*!

Grandpa nodded. "It's what they do. When they come across something they don't understand, their first instinct is to study it."

"But what if this *big* thing isn't interested in being studied? What if it's more interested in eating them?"

Stella opened *Shetland Myths & Magic* at the sea-witch picture and studied the monstrous swirl of deep-sea creatures that circled the page.

Grandpa leant over and grunted. "None of those beasties are likely to eat you. Not even sharks." He squeezed her shoulder.

"Sharks eat people," contradicted Stella.

Grandpa shook his head. "Not intentionally. Poor old sharks – you mistake one person for a tasty seal and it's all anyone can talk about." He gnashed his teeth together and smiled.

Stella returned his smile, but she wasn't reassured. She took a spoonful of soup.

'Big', Dad had said, 'bigger than anything we've seen before'. Dad didn't exaggerate – it wasn't in his nature.

It wasn't a shark down there.

She flipped back and forth through the book, failing to find anything that might fit the description. "Did Gran have any books on sea monsters?"

Grandpa hesitated just a moment too long.

"She did! Where is it? We've got to look!"

Grandpa scooped up a spoonful of soup and slurped it. "I'll look for it later."

"No! We need to know now. Please, Grandpa?"

Grandpa heaved a deep sigh and pushed his chair back. "Fine. But after that, let's go and talk to Tamar – see what she has to say." He stood up with a soft grunt. "If anyone's likely to know about deep-sea nasties, it's Tamar."

If Grandpa was suggesting seeking Tamar's advice, he was definitely worried, even if he wasn't admitting it. He headed down the corridor to his room and Stella swallowed. *Deep-sea nasties . . .* He meant the sea witch.

She hadn't decided before, whether to tell Grandpa about Heather. But that made her mind up. There was no way she could tell him. At least, not until she knew more. He'd just go back to being worried, over-protective Grandpa – ban her from talking to Heather; or worse, tell Tamar. She took a spoonful of soup and sighed.

Grandpa came back and set a book on the table: *A Compendium of Sea Monsters: the North Sea and Beyond.* "Just promise me it won't give you nightmares?"

Stella gave him a non-committal smile.

* * *

"What about this one?" said Stella, looking at the illustration with a grimace. "The Marool."

The sea monster leered up at her. It was roughly fish-shaped, but covered with hundreds of goggling eyes. A crest of blue flame leapt from its scaly back.

Grandpa gave it a cursory glance. "Doubt it." He put the soup pan in the sink and turned the water on.

"Are you sure?"

Grandpa didn't seem to understand how urgent this was! Mum and Dad were already on their way . . .

"How big did they say it was?" asked Grandpa.

"Big! Bigger than anything anyone's ever seen before."

Grandpa wrinkled his nose. "Aye, well definitely not that one, then. Look – see that man in the corner of the page? That's for scale. That makes this one about the size of my shed. Smaller than a blue whale or a giant squid." He dried his hands and sat down next to Stella. "Look, we've not found anything that fits, have we?"

Stella shook her head, flipping through the book: Njuggle, Nucklavee, Brigdi, Stoor Worm – all of them pretty fearsome-looking, but none of them big enough. Near the back, she paused. "Where did Mum and Dad say they were heading?"

"The North Sea. Off the coast of Norway."

The room seemed to tilt and Stella's lunch moved queasily in her stomach. She pointed at the last page.

Grandpa leant forward to look. "The Kraken."

The picture showed a mountainous body, surrounded by a mass of writhing tentacles. In the very corner of the page, a huge ship was crushed in its grip, sailors spilling from its deck into the churning water.

Stella raised her eyebrows, but Grandpa shook his head and gave her a knowing smile. "*Architeuthis dux.* That's the giant squid your dad mentioned. That's no myth, that one. I kept an article on it, somewhere."

He stood up and went over to his armchair. After a few moments riffling through a stack of papers, he held up a clipping triumphantly. "Here it is!"

Where myth meets science: origins of the Kraken story.

The black and white photo that accompanied the article looked very much like the monster in the book. "Doubtless terrifying if you meet one in a rowing boat, but not if you're on a socking great research vessel," said Grandpa, closing the book of sea monsters firmly. "Enough catastrophising! Shall I tell you what the most likely explanation is?"

Stella nodded.

"A large shoal," he said, firmly. "That can look like something solid on the radar, until it doesn't. My guess is, your parents will get back to their research vessel, all in a hurry, and find themselves with nothing more exciting than a good fish supper."

Please let that be true.

Grandpa smiled and patted her shoulder. "Just to be on the safe side, we'll go and tell Tamar. Let me wash the dishes, then we'll head up there together."

* * *

"The Kraken? Hah! Ha ha ha ha!" Tamar cackled.

Stella scowled at her. "It's big, whatever it is. Really big.

And it's coming up from way down deep."

"And, let me get this straight . . . You thought . . . you thought your parents had discovered . . . ?" Tamar was gripped by another fit of laughter.

Stella clenched her teeth in annoyance. It wasn't funny! She'd been scared; properly scared. "It's exactly what you said to look out for – 'anything unusual or untoward'!"

Tamar wiped tears of laughter from her eyes. "I *am* keeping watch, you know."

Grandpa snorted. "You didn't spot that sea witch until she was already ashore!"

Tamar looked affronted by that.

"Well, you didn't," added Stella.

"She was being sneaky," Tamar blustered. "Didn't *want* to be spotted. There's nothing sneaky about a Kraken. Besides, I'm not the only one keeping watch! Do you know how many clouds the council have?"

"Lots?"

"Yes, lots! Constantly watching for anything that might disturb all those simple souls who prefer a 'normal' life." She shot a pointed glance at Grandpa, but he studiously ignored it. "Seriously," Tamar shook her head, "I can't believe you thought—" She chuckled again, but contained herself when she saw Stella's expression.

"They've got equipment!" protested Stella. "Scientific equipment! I'm not just making it up!"

Tamar shook her head. "Do you know how long it is since a real Kraken surfaced? I'm not talking about your 'giant squid' variety, I mean an actual Kraken."

Stella shook her head.

"Centuries. The last one recorded was back in the 1600s."

"You're saying they exist," Grandpa stated.

"Of course they exist! But they're deep-sea dwellers. And happy down there! The only thing that would bring one up is a summoning from the Teran. And even then, they can't survive long on the surface."

"The Teran?" asked Stella. *Heather mentioned the Teran . . .*

The secret she was keeping, her meeting with the sea witch, suddenly grew tentacles in her chest. It crawled its way up her throat into her mouth.

"You don't think the Teran might have . . ."

"No!" exclaimed Tamar. "The Teran is the spirit of winter. He's at his lowest ebb right now. Look outside – blue skies and sunshine!"

"What about that sea witch of yours?" asked Grandpa. "Could she summon a Kraken?

"Never," Tamar scoffed. "Summoning a Kraken would take more power than she's ever had."

But Grandpa's eyes were sharp with interest. "Even if she set her mind to it?"

"Pfft, not a chance," said Tamar. "Besides, from what Stella's told me, she and Nimbus did a fairly good job of stripping the

Haken of her powers. Couldn't have mistaken her for a girl otherwise."

Stella glanced guiltily at the floor.

We had to. She was attacking us.

Having seen Heather on the beach, she didn't feel good about it any more. She'd looked scrawny and scared in her tatty wetsuit.

No. Heather hadn't done this.

Grandpa huffed, unsatisfied, and Tamar rolled her eyes. "If it'll set your mind at ease, I'll ask the council to take a closer look."

Grandpa nodded and patted Stella's shoulder. She turned and gave him a hug.

"And that's your cue to leave!" said Tamar. "Stella and I have a busy afternoon ahead of us. We're off puffin-spotting."

Grandpa's mouth dropped open. "Not without me, you're not. Besides, I know the best spot on the island."

Eight

A PUFFIN'S GROWL

THE sandy soil was riddled with holes and peppered with rabbit droppings. The hillside sloped gently down, the grass becoming gradually sparser until it vanished into the beach.

Tamar stood with her hands on her hips, surveying the sandy grass with a critical eye.

Grandpa spread a picnic blanket on the ground and sat down on it. "So? What magic are we up to today, exactly?" he asked.

"Nothing that should concern you," snapped Tamar.

"Says you!" snorted Grandpa. "Anyway, you wouldn't have found this spot without me. I bet you were planning on heading to the lighthouse, weren't you?"

Tamar's shifty expression confirmed it.

"You could have *told* us about this place," she grumbled. "Can't just let the girl train. Always got to *involve* yourself."

"I am involved, whether you like it or not!"

"Involved, you might be. Wanted, you're not."

"Tamar!" said Stella. "*I* want Grandpa here!"

Tamar snorted. "Fine. Just make sure he doesn't get in the way."

"So?" Grandpa asked Stella. "What *are* we doing?"

"Collecting a puffin's growl," confided Stella. She giggled at his look of deep confusion.

"All around here, I reckon," said Tamar. She motioned in a wide semi-circle.

Stella began to pull her reels of magic out of the bag and pile them on the blanket. They'd taken on a soft green hue after being steeped in seaweed.

Tamar picked up two reels and set them down on the ground about a metre apart, near the burrows. "Like this."

Stella jumped up to help. She passed one of the reels to Grandpa.

"Nimbus and I spun that," she said, proudly.

Grandpa raised his eyebrows. "Impressive!" He ran his finger down the reel. "It's wonderfully soft. Alpaca? Cashmere?"

Tamar snorted and Grandpa gave her a swift frown.

"It's magic," said Stella, the wonder of it lighting a little glow in her heart.

Grandpa stared at her. "Magic?" he repeated.

"*Pure* magic," said Tamar. "So I suggest you keep your grimy mitts off it, if you value your fingers."

Grandpa's eyebrows rose so high they seemed to be glued to his hairline. He handed the reel gingerly to Stella, who set it on the ground near the others.

Stella came back and sat down next to him. "She's having you on," she whispered. "It's perfectly safe."

Grandpa huffed in annoyance at Tamar, but his eyes stayed fixed on the reels, as though they might go off like fireworks at any moment.

* * *

Grandpa was pouring tea from the large thermos flask and Tamar was holding the cups steady, so it was Stella who spotted it first. "Look!" she whispered.

A small black and white head, with a brightly striped beak, had appeared out of one of the burrows. Stella's heart thrilled with joy. *A puffin! Right there!*

She brought Grandpa's binoculars up in slow motion, so as not to startle the little bird. As she turned the dial to bring it into focus, the puffin turned side-on, its rainbow beak bright against the blue sky behind. It tilted its head to get a good look at the people camped outside its home, then opened its wings and took off, with a swift purr of wingbeats.

Stella clutched Grandpa's arm in excitement. "That was so cool!" she exclaimed.

Grandpa smiled in satisfaction.

"Didn't growl, though, did it?" said Tamar, in disgust.

Grandpa shrugged. "The longer we're here, the more they'll get used to us. Keep watching." He pointed. Another puffin was fluttering in from the sea, swinging wildly to and fro on the breeze.

It's going to crash! thought Stella, her heart in her mouth. But at the last moment, it spread its wings and landed, with a sudden patter of feet. It strutted briefly up and down, as though to say "Everything's fine. I meant to do that.", but the instant it spotted them, it ducked into its hole and disappeared.

Tamar sighed and slurped her tea.

Stella trained her binoculars on the hole, waiting for it to reappear. Long minutes passed, but it clearly wasn't coming out again.

She sighed. "I wish they'd stay where we can see them." She looked out at the sea and her heart gave a little skip. "Nimbus!" She waved, and the little cloud raced in towards them.

He settled next to Stella on the blanket and she smoothed him. He looked fuller, happier than when he'd left. "I'm glad you're back."

"Yes! We can get some more spinning done tomorrow," said Tamar.

Stella frowned and rubbed her chest. It hurt when he was away. Well, not *hurt*, exactly, but it was uncomfortable. It made her heart feel stretched – an empty ache. She wasn't keen to send him out magic-gathering again so soon.

Especially not until Mum and Dad get back safely . . .

Nimbus rolled a little closer to her.

Oh, I didn't tell you, did I?

Stella silently updated Nimbus on everything that had happened while he was away. When she got to the bit about Heather, he turned a steely grey, floated down to the water's edge and began to patrol the surf.

I don't need you to protect me from her!

Nimbus flickered ominously.

I saw her. You didn't. She's changed.

Nimbus fired a bright fork of lightning into the shallows, throwing up a shower of spray. Grandpa leapt to his feet, spilling his tea.

"Stop it, Nimbus!" *You weren't there. You don't understand.*

Tamar raised her eyebrows. "What are you two talking about?"

"Just about Mum and Dad," lied Stella.

Tamar huffed impatiently. "I've told you. Whatever they've tracked, it's not a Kraken. So stop worrying about it, and stop worrying your cloud too. He's going to scare all the puffins away!"

Several black and white heads had appeared from the surrounding burrows. They had more sense than to come all the way out; they just lurked there, peering out, perturbed by the sudden change in the weather.

Heather asked for help, Nimbus! We have to hear her out, at least.

Find out what she wants.

The little cloud let out a long rumble of disagreement that set all the puffins hopping and fluttering.

One of them let out a low growl, and Tamar's face lit up. "Nimbus!" she hissed. "Do that again!"

"Go on then," muttered Stella. *But no lightning!*

The little cloud rumbled again, and this time all the puffins answered – a crescendo of low groans and growls. One by one, the reels of magic began to glow softly like small lanterns. Grandpa stared at them warily. "Is that meant to happen?"

Stella wasn't sure, but it looked promising. She glanced across. Tamar was grinning in delight. "That's *exactly* what's meant to happen," she confirmed. "Now they're fully charged – ready for weaving!"

* * *

Tamar was in a far better mood on the way home. By the time they reached Grandpa's, she'd just about convinced herself that the thunder had been her idea.

"Thunder sounds just like a puffin's growl. That's why they all joined in. They're very conversational creatures. It's common sense, when you think about it."

Any other time, Stella might have called Tamar out, but right now, she was just glad she wasn't asking *why* Nimbus had started thundering . . .

A plan was starting to form in Stella's mind, but she'd only get away with it if Tamar and Grandpa didn't suspect anything.

Nimbus remained grumbly all evening. Stella wasn't sure if it was because she'd talked to Heather, or because her thoughts kept returning to Mum and Dad, but after the fourth thunderclap, Grandpa insisted he go outside.

"I don't mind him indoors if he's behaving himself, but I'm not risking another lightning bolt in my living room."

Stella glanced at the bare window above the table, and her cheeks heated up with the memory of Nimbus's outburst a few weeks ago. Grandpa had taken down the burnt curtains, but there was still a grey stain where he'd scrubbed the soot off the wall.

She shook her head. "He wouldn't, Grandpa. Not now."

"Still. No thunder indoors. That's the rule."

Stella nodded and sighed. She beckoned Nimbus over to the door and ushered him outside. The little thundercloud floated to the garden wall and stopped. He looked sad and lonely in the narrow strip of front garden; out of place.

"Just for a bit," whispered Stella. "I'll let you in again later – when Grandpa's gone to bed, okay?"

"What are you whispering about?" said Grandpa.

"Nothing," said Stella, closing the door. "I was saying goodnight."

Grandpa grunted in approval. She joined him at the table and pulled the book of monsters towards her. Grandpa put a hand on it. "Uh uh! No, you don't. I'm not sending you to bed with a head full of monsters."

"But I just wanted to check—"

Grandpa shook his head firmly. "We've done what we can. There's no point in stewing on it tonight."

Stella reluctantly let go of the book. Grandpa tucked it under his arm and strode down the corridor. "It's a long journey. Your mum and dad won't even arrive there for another few days. That's plenty of time for the council to check for anything untoward." He disappeared inside his room for a moment and reappeared without the book.

"But what if the council check and there *is* something bad?" asked Stella.

"One, from what Tamar said, that's very unlikely. Two, we'll warn them before they get there." He ruffled Stella's hair. "Come on, bedtime for you, scamp. Let's hope you have dreams filled with puffins tonight."

* * *

As soon as Grandpa had said goodnight and closed her door, Stella quickly pulled on her pyjamas, then knelt on the bed and unlatched the window. Her cloud poured inside.

"No thunder though, alright?" whispered Stella. "If Grandpa hears you thundering in here, we're both toast."

Nimbus settled on the end of the bed, his soft yellow glow casting a warm circle of light on the coverlet.

"Promise not to thunder, no matter what I tell you?"

Nimbus spread himself out a little – the very picture of a relaxed cloud.

Stella nodded. "Okay. Here's the thing. I think Heather wants to come ashore."

Nimbus shot vertically off the bed and Stella clamped a finger to her lips. When she was certain he wasn't going to thunder, she pointed at the coverlet and waited for him to settle again.

"She just wanted to talk. I think she's trying to make friends – she even gave me a present."

She climbed out of bed and lifted her coat off the hook on the back of the door. It swung heavily in her hand.

The conch shell was beautiful – a long spiralling trumpet – bigger than any other shell she'd ever found here. Stella held it out towards Nimbus. "See?"

Nimbus drifted closer. He extended a misty point of cloud and tentatively touched the shell. Stella smiled.

As she turned to hang her coat back on the hook, she became aware of the solid silence. Grandpa was in the corridor, probably checking she was actually going to bed.

He doubtless thought he was being really quiet, but Stella knew all the sounds of the house now – the clink of the iron grate when Grandpa was stoking the fire, the screech of the kitchen tap, the different creaks of all the doors. No sound meant he was out there, listening.

She raised her eyebrows at Nimbus. *I'll tell you everything tomorrow.*

"I don't hear you getting into bed!" called Grandpa.

"I would be if you weren't shouting at me!" called Stella. She sat down heavily so he'd hear the springs creak. At least if she made a pretence of going to bed, he wouldn't come in and pester her.

She nudged Nimbus out of the way and lay down, then held the conch shell to her ear and closed her eyes. The whisper of waves filled her ear, soft and soothing. It was peaceful.

Was this what it was like under the sea?

If so, she could understand why Heather liked it – no noise, no hurry, nobody bothering you – just the distant boom and roll of the waves meeting the cliffs.

Nine

SKY MEETS SEA

*T*HE *Haken's hands were tight around her wrists, pulling her closer to the edge. Dark water churned, stirred by shadowy forms moving hungrily beneath the surface. Stella thrashed wildly, but her feet were slipping—*

She fell out of bed and hit the floor with a thump. Nimbus plunged towards her.

"I'm alright, Nimbus! It's okay." Stella soothed the little cloud and tried to calm her breathing.

The sea-witch nightmare again . . .

She focused on Gran's rag rug, its coarse weave was rough and familiar beneath her hands. *I'm safe – in my room – in Grandpa's house – on dry land.*

"Morning, Stella," called Grandpa. "You up?" The door creaked open and his face appeared in the gap. "What are you doing down there? Are you alright?"

Stella untangled herself from the blankets. "I fell out of bed. That's all."

Grandpa helped her up. "Nightmare?"

Stella nodded. Nimbus settled around her shoulders; a comforting presence.

"I knew I shouldn't have showed you that book of monsters," muttered Grandpa, his eyes filled with concern.

"It's not that! It's just . . ."

I met the sea witch. And I think she's changed. But I can't be sure.

Stella sighed. "Never mind."

Grandpa raised an eyebrow at Nimbus. "I see your cloud found his way in?"

Stella nodded. "He was lonely outside."

Grandpa smiled and shook his head. "Well, as long as he's stopped grumbling, I suppose it's alright."

Stella fished the conch shell out of the gap next to her pillow. Good thing it had rolled down there, or it might have spiked her in the night!

"That's a beauty," said Grandpa. "Where did you find it?" He held out his hand and Stella passed it to him.

"Down on the rocks, near the broch."

Grandpa raised his eyebrows. "It's a wonder it's in one piece! Really unusual. Lovely." He turned it in his hands and smiled. "Hah! This is no ordinary sea shell. I reckon one of the visitors to the broch must have left it behind."

Stella leant forward to look where Grandpa was pointing. There was a smooth polished hole in the pointed tip of the shell.

"Can I?" he asked.

Stella nodded, unsure what he meant.

Grandpa brought the point to his lips and blew. A long low note filled the room, mournful and deep. Goosebumps shivered up Stella's arms. Was this why Heather had left the shell for Stella, so she could call her with it?

"Here, you try," said Grandpa, wiping the hole on his sleeve and handing it back.

Stella blew into the conch, but only succeeded in making a hoarse huffing sound.

"Tight lips," said Grandpa. "Like playing a trumpet." He demonstrated.

Stella tentatively blew a raspberry into the small mouthpiece. The shell amplified it into a loud, rude noise. It didn't sound anything like the note Grandpa had produced.

"Keep practising," said Grandpa with a wink. "You'll get it. Now, let's get some food inside you. I'm guessing you'll be off with Tamar again today, will you?"

"Yeah." Stella nodded and avoided his eyes.

She *was* going to Tamar's today, that much was true, but she had no intention of staying. Tamar might be certain there was no Kraken, but Heather had *met* the Teran – the spirit of winter himself. If anyone could tell her for certain what Mum and Dad were heading towards, it was her.

Today, Stella intended to find the sea witch and get some answers.

* * *

It was surprisingly easy to deceive Tamar. Stella just told her that Nimbus wasn't ready to do more spinning, then offered to gather more seaweed.

Tamar consulted the tide times, then nodded. "Yes. Good idea. We could do with some more. One bucket will probably do. But keep an eye on the tide, this time!"

As Stella trudged along the path towards the broch, she glanced often at Nimbus. She'd given him strict instructions to on what to do, and what *not* to do, if Heather showed up. He didn't look happy about it.

She thought back to the lightning bolt he'd fired into the shallows yesterday and her stomach contracted. If he did that today, Heather might never trust her again.

"I have to talk to her, Nimbus. Heather can't call a Kraken – Tamar said so. But if the Teran has, she'll know!"

Nimbus shaded to purple and Stella pointed a firm finger at him. "Be calm. We need her help. And she needs ours, too!

Besides, we agreed a truce. Do you want to ruin that?"

Nimbus rumbled softly, clearly unconvinced.

"No. Not today." said Stella, hands on hips. "I mean it, Nimbus."

Nimbus rumbled a little louder.

"Right, that's it! Go as high as you can and don't come down unless I call you. From now on, you're on lookout duty."

Nimbus stopped in front of her, right in the middle of the path.

"Please! This is important! It's to keep Mum and Dad safe. I can't have you scaring her off before I've even asked."

Nimbus hesitated a moment longer, then shot straight up.

* * *

The closer Stella got to the beach, the more she wondered if she was making a mistake . . .

She shaded her eyes and scanned the sky. Nimbus had taken her very literally.

There he was! Way up high – a tiny dot in the blue.

She looked along the green ridge of rolling hills towards the broch. She couldn't hear the sanctuary song from here. That's probably why Heather liked this spot.

She ignored the tremble of nerves in her chest and marched on down the path.

It'll be fine, she reassured herself. *We're just going to talk. That's all.*

The little cove was empty, but for a couple of wading birds pecking along in the shallows. There was no sign of the sea witch. Stella puffed in disappointment. Some part of her had been expecting to find Heather right here, waiting for her. But that was stupid – she could be anywhere; anywhere in the whole wide sea.

She cupped her hands to her mouth and called. "Heather?"

Nothing. Not even a curious seal. Stella climbed out along the ridge of rocks, until she had a good view of the sea in all directions.

The tide was still on its way out and the current was strong, making tell-tale drag marks in the water around the point; maybe a riptide. She looked out across the fast-moving water and shivered – not a good day to go swimming ...

About halfway out, she found a wide boulder. She sat down, slipped off her rucksack and pulled out the conch shell.

It was worth a try?

She looked up at Nimbus. *Stay there, okay?*

Stella blew softly into the conch. It let out a wheezy sigh. She licked the salty taste of the shell off her lips, wiped her mouth on her sleeve, and tried again – the conch made a noise like a strangled fart.

She lowered it and shook her head in annoyance. 'Like a trumpet', Grandpa had said. He'd made it look easy.

Stella tightened her lips until there was barely a gap between them and blew into the conch once more. This time, the vibration of it made her lips itch. A long warbling note sounded from the shell, bouncing eerily off the cliff behind her.

She kept it up until she ran out of breath, then lowered the shell and rubbed the buzz of it from her lips.

"You sound like a wounded walrus."

Stella started and whipped round.

Heather had surfaced silently behind her. Her dark hair streamed water down her wetsuit and her face was expressionless – no hint of humour in her eyes.

"I've never used a conch before," Stella replied, a little defensively.

"Clearly."

"That is what it was for, though? To call you."

"I'm here, aren't I?"

Heather wasn't making this easy.

Probably she's not used to being around people, thought Stella, trying hard not to feel annoyed.

Heather slid out of the water with a swift movement and climbed the wet rocks, fast and smooth as an otter.

Stella tensed – her way back to the beach was blocked now. Sea witch ahead of her, rip tide behind. She shifted uncomfortably, working out which way she'd run, if she had to. *Maybe this wasn't a good idea.*

"You wanted to talk to me?" Stella asked.

She hoped that was true. Why else would Heather want her here, on her own?

Heather smiled, her needle teeth making sharp indents in the soft flesh of her lower lip. She slithered forward, closer to Stella.

"Stop there!" Fear made Stella's voice high and tight.

Heather's smile faded. She backed up a little, then slid down into a deep rock pool and wrapped her arms round her knees. The posture made her look younger all of a sudden – more human – and definitely less threatening.

Stella felt bad – she obviously hadn't meant to scare her. But it was hard to read the intention behind that dark-eyed gaze.

Heather picked up a pebble and knocked a limpet off the rock next to her. She scooped the grey flesh out and popped it in her mouth. Her eyes settled on Stella as she chewed. "Want one?"

Stella's throat closed in revulsion. She'd tried a limpet once, with Gran. It was like a rubbery bogey; salty, slimy, hard to swallow. "No. Thanks." She shook her head and tried not to let her disgust show on her face.

Heather looked warily up at Nimbus, floating high overhead. "You brought your cloud today."

Stella looked up at him. "He was gathering magic, before. Normally he's with me all the time."

"It hurts when he's not, doesn't it?"

Stella frowned, uncertain whether that was a threat. "Yes. It does."

"Like you're being stretched until you might tear in half..."

Stella nodded. It wasn't quite that bad, but it was definitely uncomfortable. "Can I ask you something?" she said.

Heather narrowed her eyes and nodded. She knocked another limpet off the rock with a sharp blow. "You can ask. Can't promise I'll answer."

"Do you . . . know anything about a Kraken?"

Heather grinned, revealing rows of teeth.

All the better to eat you with, thought Stella, feeling her skin shrink at the sight.

"Which Kraken?" said Heather. "There are many."

Stella frowned and straightened her shoulders. "In the North Sea, off the coast of Norway. Is it rising?"

Heather leant back on her elbows, the rubber of her wetsuit making a harsh noise on the barnacled rocks. No wonder it looked so tatty. She was still smiling, almost as though she was enjoying Stella's discomfort.

"Tamar said they can only be raised by the Teran," pressed Stella. "I thought, since you're a sea witch, you might know if he had?"

"Sea witch. That's what they call me, is it?"

A doubt crept into Stella's mind. Looking at Heather now, there wasn't much sign of the monster she'd been before.

Stella shrugged, deliberately casual. "Have you . . . stopped, being a sea witch?"

"You tell me, sky witch."

Stella opened her mouth to disagree – *I'm not a witch*! But then she closed it again. Maybe she was? That's what she'd thought Tamar was, when she first met her – some sort of witch. And weather weaving *was* a kind of magic.

Sky witch. She didn't hate the sound of it.

"Witch is just a *name*," said Heather, pushing the words

between her teeth, "given to someone that people fear. Velda's name for me."

Like she called me and Nimbus dangerous. Stella remembered how that had felt at the Gathering – all the other apprentices constantly wary of her, expecting her to do something bad; something violent. It was Velda's secret power; giving you a bad name and making it stick.

Heather narrowed her eyes. "She's clever, Velda. No one listens when they're afraid. Are you afraid?"

Stella shook her head. "No. I'm not afraid of you."

It wasn't entirely true, but it was clearly what Heather needed to hear.

Stella curled her toes inside her boots. It felt risky to keep pushing, but Heather still hadn't answered her question. Not properly.

"So, about the Kraken? The thing is, if there is one coming, I have to know. I need to warn my parents; tell the council!"

Heather's lip curled at the mention of the council. She sucked her teeth, dislodging some limpet. "No. Not a Kraken. A shoal."

Exactly what Grandpa said!

Stella breathed a quiet sigh of relief and glanced up at Nimbus with a smile.

Heather leant forward, fixing Stella with an intent stare, and folded her hands together. "You'll help me now?"

Ten

THE FIRST
STORM CLOUD

"HELP you how?" asked Stella.

Heather gave Stella an appraising look. "Tell me how you won, first. Velda tried to take your cloud too, yes? But you defeated her. How? Did you kill her? Or did you break your cloud free?"

Stella stared at Heather. "Neither! We passed the trials."

A heavy look of disappointment settled on Heather's face. "You didn't defeat Velda?"

"Well, we did," clarified Stella. "We showed the council what she was doing. They didn't know she was trapping clouds."

"Didn't know or didn't want to know?"

"They didn't know!" insisted Stella. "Now they do, Velda's in disgrace and they're going to release all the storm clouds."

"*All* the storm clouds?"

Stella nodded. "Hundreds of them. Velda had them trapped at Winter's Keep all this time, but the council are going to let them out."

"*My* storm cloud, too?" The spark of hope in her eyes hurt Stella's heart.

Tamar was right. Heather didn't know: Fury would never be released. He was gone; destroyed.

Stella swallowed nervously. She did *not* want to be the one to tell her.

It was cruel, though, letting Heather hold on to hope when there wasn't any. Tamar should have told her. But if Tamar wasn't going to, *someone* had to tell her the truth.

She bit her lip and took a deep breath. "Heather, Fury's not coming back," she said, as gently as she could. "Tamar told me – he was destroyed, during the battle."

A stillness came over the sea witch as she absorbed the news. Stella saw it settle inside her, her expression changing rapidly from shock, to despair, to understanding. Heather's head dropped.

Stella's eyes filled with tears. She could imagine all too clearly how painful it would be to lose Nimbus. "I'm so sorry, Heather," she whispered.

Heather raised her head. To Stella's surprise, her expression was determined. No tears. Not even anger. "I always thought Tamar knew." Heather nodded in the direction of the broch. "Follow me," she said, then bounded towards the water and dived.

"Hey! Wait!" Stella scanned the fast-flowing water.

The tide was lower now, but the undertow was still strong – sucking away from the beach. For a moment, her heart tugged with worry, but then she shook her head at her own stupidity. Heather might be getting more human, but she could still breathe underwater.

"Are you coming?" Heather's voice was a distant shout. She'd surfaced a long way away, in the shadow of the big rocks below the broch.

Stella glanced down at the dark water and then back at Heather. No way *she* was getting in – she'd have to take the long way round. She began to pick her way back along the rocks towards the shore.

* * *

The boulders beneath the broch were large – great black slabs shelving out above the deep water. Stella hopped down them until she spotted Heather's sleek head below.

"I always thought Tamar was in on it," said Heather. "Velda must have lied to her too."

Stella knelt down by the edge. "What do you mean?"

"He wasn't destroyed – Fury's here. Trapped. In the broch."

She closed her eyes. "I can feel him, calling me. But against the sanctuary song? I can't get close enough to reach him."

Stella glanced up at the great dark tower and her heart quickened. Was it possible?

"You're sure he's in there?"

"Certain," said Heather. "He was with the Ice Weavers in the beginning. Then I lost him for a while. Velda didn't like me attacking Winter's Keep, so she moved him. Here."

Stella's eyes widened. "And she didn't tell Tamar!" she breathed.

It made so much sense. The broch would be the perfect hiding place for a gem: impenetrable to sea witches, defended by Tamar. And it would be just like Velda to hide the gem here – make it somebody else's problem.

"That's why you kept coming back here?"

Heather nodded. Her eyes shone with hope. "Will you help me?"

* * *

Stella's heart raced as she jogged along the path towards Tamar's. Nimbus scooted ahead. As they arrived, the front door opened and Tamar came outside, carrying a long pole. She had her back to them.

"Tamar!"

She turned towards them and propped the pole against the side of the house. As Stella raced towards her, her expression darkened. "What's happened? Are you alright?"

"Yes, yes, I'm fine, but you've got to listen. We've had it all wrong."

It took a good half an hour for Tamar to stop raging at the fact that not only was the sea witch back, but Stella had *spoken* to her. Now, she was pacing up and down, running her fingers through her hair.

"In the broch?" she growled.

Stella nodded, relieved that Tamar was starting to listen at last.

"We think the gem that's trapped Fury is under the sanctuary stone. Heather could hear him much louder when it broke. That's why she came ashore, even though it hurts her."

Tamar rubbed a hand over her mouth. She looked far from convinced. She rattled her nails on the table. "I still can't believe you've been sneaking off and speaking to her behind my back."

"I didn't mean to. Not the first time, anyway."

Tamar's mouth tightened.

It felt like a thin excuse, even to Stella. "Sorry," she said.

Tamar heaved a deep sigh.

"So? Will you help?" asked Stella tentatively.

Tamar shook her head. "It's not that simple."

"But it is!" protested Stella. "Storm clouds shouldn't be trapped. You promised we'd make sure they were *all* freed. And Fury's been trapped the longest. We've got to let him go!" She glanced at Nimbus, brooding on the low table by the fireplace. He'd shaded to darkest purple, but so far, he'd stayed quiet.

Tamar narrowed her eyes, put her hands on the table and leant forwards. "What *exactly* did the Haken ask you to do?"

"Well . . . let him out."

"How?"

Stella swallowed. That was the bit that had made her hesitate; the reason she'd come running back here.

"She wants us to break the sanctuary stone."

"Mm-hmm." Tamar sat down heavily opposite Stella and raised her eyebrows. "And it didn't occur to you to wonder why?"

Stella remembered when it had been broken before: the howling storm, the putrid water creeping ashore, Tamar and Grandpa trapped inside the broch. Mending the stone was the only thing that had saved them. Heather might be different now, but breaking the sanctuary stone still felt very risky indeed.

"I know it sounds dangerous, but it makes sense. It's got to be there. I didn't break it yet, though – I told her I couldn't do it without your help."

"That's alright, then." Tamar patted her hands on the table as though something had been settled.

"But you *will* help?" said Stella.

Tamar shook her head. "Fury wasn't just the first storm cloud trapped; he was the reason Velda was able to convince everyone that *all* storm clouds should be trapped."

"You knew?!" Stella stared at her.

Tamar shook her head and grimaced. "No! Of course I didn't know. And I'm still not convinced it's true. There's another rather obvious reason that Heather might want that stone broken:

the sanctuary song defends against sea witches."

"We could check though? Just quickly. And if there's no gem there, we mend it again, straight away."

Tamar closed her eyes and shook her head. "Stella, Fury was destroyed."

Stella thumped the table and Nimbus jolted into the air. "That's just Velda's story. Velda's a liar! It's what she does! We have to make sure."

"This isn't just hearsay, Stella, I was there! I saw it – Fury was torn to pieces by the Wind Callers."

Stella didn't want to imagine that. She'd seen Flynn's demonstration of wind calling at the trials and she hadn't liked it then. There was a wrongness to it; and the way he'd smiled while he was doing it . . . like he enjoyed the violence of it. Stella shuddered.

"Did Flynn destroy those clouds at the trials?"

Tamar shook her head impatiently. "No. They will have come back together again. Might have taken a while . . ."

"So what makes you think Fury didn't?"

"Because there's a difference between doing a neat surgical exercise like Flynn did and a team of Wind Callers shredding a cloud!"

Nimbus slid across the floor and curled around Stella's ankles, very small and cold. Stella reached down to smooth him.

"Besides," said Tamar, "you saw how it worked with Tassa's cloud – with his heart trapped, he had to follow the gem. I'm telling you, Fury's not at the broch. We would have seen him."

She scraped her chair back and turned away.

Stella lapsed into thought. Heather was certain, and the more Stella thought about it, the more she believed her. They were missing something.

"*How* does a cloud come back together?" she asked.

Tamar sighed impatiently. "Time and concentration. I'm telling you, if Fury were going to come back together, he would have done it by now."

Stella's eyes lit up. "But that's it! A trapped cloud can't concentrate! That's the whole point of the gems. Clouds can't think for themselves when they're trapped! That's why we haven't seen him. He's probably still in pieces!"

Tamar's brow furrowed. "Hmm . . . If that's true, I'm not certain it would be wise to let him out. It'd be far too dangerous."

Stella gaped at Tamar. "You sound just like the council!" she spat, then scraped her chair back, grabbed her coat and barged outside, Nimbus following closely behind.

They didn't go far. Only as far as the bench by the front door. Where could they go? Not back to Grandpa's. He was always cautious. He'd definitely take Tamar's side. And she couldn't face Heather. What would she say to her? No, we won't help?

Her face ached from scowling. Nimbus snuggled in next to her and she stroked him absently. If she thought too hard about anything, she might cry.

The front door creaked open and Stella looked away in the opposite direction.

"If you're done sulking," said Tamar, "let's go."

Stella looked round in surprise. Tamar had her weather bag on her shoulder and a jar of rainbow rings in her hand. Herbie floated at her side. "'Just like the council!'" she muttered. "I'll show you 'just like the council'!"

"We're going to let him out?"

"Not so fast." Tamar held her hands up. "First, we're going to find out if Fury's there or not. Then, we'll decide what we're going to do about it."

Stella jumped to her feet and followed Tamar as she set off up the path.

"It would be just like Velda," grumbled Tamar. "Hide it here, leave me to deal with the fallout, make me think the attacks were my fault."

"It's typical Velda!" agreed Stella. "She's good at fooling people."

"Yes, *people*, but not *me*!" Tamar snorted and lengthened her stride. "Of course, even if the attacks *were* engineered by Velda, that doesn't mean the Haken isn't still harbouring a grudge."

"But she's not! She just wants her cloud! Don't you see? This is your chance to make things right with her."

Tamar's mouth puckered in a tight moue and she fell silent.

Eleven

FURY

TAMAR'S house cloud, Herbie, was sliding along at ground level with a distinctly stealthy air. Nimbus was shadowing him, but occasionally popping up out of the scrub to check Stella was still following.

"Why aren't we taking the path?" asked Stella.

"The Haken will be watching the path," said Tamar.

Stella frowned. "But that's good? She'll see you're helping!"

Tamar shook her head. "I haven't said I'll help, yet. There are still too many unknowns."

Stella huffed in frustration. "But if we find the gem, we'll tell her?"

Tamar gave a slight shrug. "One step at a time."

Stella scanned the sea ahead of them. She could clearly see the line of current, carving its way round the point; definitely a riptide. Further out, dark patches of wind moved across the surface like an ever-changing map. She couldn't see the shoreline yet, but she imagined Heather must be down there waiting.

She couldn't see why they were sneaking about. The sea witch would be bound to see them when they got to the broch. It was right on the waterfront.

Tamar stopped and spread her arms wide. She began to whisper: "Soft as shadows, white as snow . . ."

Oh . . . Fog.

Stella glanced at Nimbus, a few metres ahead. *Come back,* she thought. *Stay close.* Then she began to whisper along with Tamar.

A minute or so later, fog blanketed the sea, as smooth as milk. Tamar nodded in satisfaction and carried on down the hill.

Stella followed, Nimbus keeping close to her ankles. She was relieved Tamar hadn't called the fog onshore – it might be useful, but she didn't like it. It made everything feel unfamiliar; spooky.

When they reached the broch, Tamar skirted around the slate path and tiptoed across the gritty grass to the entrance. She held a finger to her lips and beckoned.

Stella silently followed.

Once inside the broch, Tamar glanced up at the circle of clear sky overhead. "So far, so good." She pulled the jar of rainbow rings out of her weather bag and undid the lid. Herbie floated obediently next to her, awaiting instructions.

Nimbus wasn't in the mood for waiting about. He spiralled up the huge tower, investigating every nook and cranny in the ancient stone walls.

"Not too high, Nimbus," said Stella, as he approached the top.

Nimbus did one more circuit, then began to sink slowly towards her.

Satisfied that he was on his way down, she picked her way across the uneven ground to the sanctuary stone and crouched next to it.

Originally it had been a single smooth slab, overflowing with songs and stories, but that was before Nimbus had broken it. Now, it looked more like a star – silver lines of magic sealing the fractures that radiated from the lightning strike in the centre.

Was this where Velda had hidden the first gem? The gem that held Fury's heart?

This close, Stella could feel the sanctuary stone's song in her bones: *Be strong, be brave; generations of weather weavers stand with you.* It was fierce and thrilling, filling her heart with determination.

All the storm clouds, she thought. *We're going to rescue ALL the storm clouds, starting with Heather's.*

She looked up at her cloud. "You did a good job of mending it," she said. "But today, we're going to break it again."

Nimbus drifted down and settled on the stone.

"Not yet!" said Tamar. "Let me get set up, first." She nodded at

Herbie. He floated up and began to flatten into a disc. The circle of cloud stretched thinner and wider, reaching down towards the ground in a shimmering dome.

"Why do we need cloud cover?" asked Stella.

"Just a precaution."

Tamar scrabbled in the jar and pulled out a handful of rainbows. She threw them up into the smooth curve of cloud. They stuck, leaving faint circles like popped bubbles and the cloud cover took on a faint rainbow hue. Tamar pursed her lips, then nodded briskly. "Nothing out of the ordinary so far. So, *now* you can set Nimbus to work. But be ready to reverse it in an instant, if I give the word! This smells like a trap."

It's not, thought Stella. All the same, she nodded at her cloud. "You heard her, Nimbus. Time to suck up all that magic. But if anything goes wrong, you drop it again – quick as you can."

Outside, she could still hear the regular slosh of the waves against the rocks, invisible beneath the blanket of fog. If Heather was close, she was staying out of sight.

Stella smiled to herself. *Not much longer, Heather.*

Nimbus settled on the sanctuary stone and immediately there was a fizzing sound. The silver lines of magic began to hiss and boil. The cracks gradually reappeared – sinking deep into the stone – dividing it into fractured shards.

Stella nodded in encouragement. "That's it," she whispered.

The magic rose in a fine sparkling plume and Nimbus inhaled it, growing steadily brighter. The stone's song gradually faded, until Stella could barely hear its reassuring hum. The broch seemed to be holding its breath.

As the cracks deepened, Stella leant forward to peer into the broken centre of the stone. Was there something down there?

Tamar put a cautionary hand on her arm. "Tell Nimbus to slow down." She was staring anxiously up through the cloud cover.

Stella looked up. The circle of blue sky was gone, blotted out by a gathering darkness. In that darkness, four clouds glowed scarlet. Red for violence. Stella's heart quickened – the same clouds that had attacked them before, in the battle!

Heather! What are you doing?!

A deep bass note of thunder shook the air, so low that Stella felt its tremble in her stomach before she heard it.

"Mend it," yelled Tamar. "Now!"

A searing flash lit the broch walls, and a jagged white line cracked across the cloud cover. Tamar stumbled to her knees.

"Hurry, Nimbus!" screamed Stella. "Mend the stone!"

Silver streamed down out of Nimbus.

Herbie's cloud cover rapidly contracted over Tamar.

Stella ducked lower and crawled closer to her. The cloud cover was getting thicker and stronger as it shrank, but her heart lurched to see Nimbus was now outside it, being buffeted by fierce gusts of wind.

"Dump all the magic!" she shouted, flattening herself on the ground and staring up at the bright, dangerous clouds above. The broch boomed with thunder and, as one, the four clouds swooped towards her, their red lights growing brighter as they closed in.

Stella put her hands over her head and scrunched into a ball.

Ping.

A high, pure note sang through the chaos like hope.

She knew that sound.

The last drop of magic falling into place.

A split-second of silence followed, before the sanctuary song blazed into life.

As terror loosened its grip, Stella's senses unfurled. Her side was sodden from lying in the mud and there was a smell of scorched hair in the air. She gingerly patted her head. *Not mine.*

She opened her eyes. The muddy floor was pooled with glittering puddles. Sunlight flooded the broch. Carefully, Stella sat up. Nothing hurt. No injuries.

She could just make out Nimbus on the other side of the cloud cover, a dark smudge beyond the low shimmering dome. High overhead the circle of blue sky was back; no sign of the furious clouds who'd come plunging towards them.

Nimbus had done it. He'd mended the stone – driven the darkness away.

Stella turned to Tamar and shook her leg. "Hey! Are you okay?"

Tamar sat up with a groan and put a hand to her head. A streak of grey ran through the silver of her hair. As she touched it, it disintegrated to ash, leaving her looking even more tufty than usual. She appeared more offended than injured, though.

Stella levered herself off the muddy ground. "Are you alright, Nimbus? Come here."

Nimbus bumped softly against the cloud cover, making a small multicoloured bulge, then moved away again. Stella pushed her way out.

Nimbus had settled on the sanctuary stone. He looked exhausted, his surface mottled with whorls of purple and grey.

Poor Nimbus. Trapped outside the cloud cover. On your own.

"I'm so sorry, Nimbus."

She reached out to smooth him, but he backed away, flickering with static.

"It's alright. They've gone now. You did it!"

Herbie dropped the cloud cover with a soft *pop*, and Tamar got to her feet. She screwed the lid back on the jar of rainbow rings and stuffed it into her weather bag, then turned to Stella with a scowl.

"I told you, didn't I! Did you see them?"

Stella glanced at Tamar and nodded. "Glowing red, like when we battled the Haken before. Those were her attack clouds, weren't they?" She glanced up the broch. There was no sign of them now.

"Clearly tasked with attacking *me*." Tamar shook her head in disgust. "I can't believe I let you talk me into this."

"Are you sure those clouds weren't bits of Fury?"

Tamar let out a growl of frustration. "There *is* no Fury! There *is* no rescue. When are you going to understand! This was a trap! And we walked right into it."

No! Stella's mind raced, trying to come up with some other explanation. Tamar had to be wrong. She hadn't *seen* Heather. She didn't know how much she'd changed.

"Maybe if you talked to Heather, you could—"

"Enough!" barked Tamar. "Trapped clouds don't attack people! Sea-witch-trained attack clouds do. Why won't you believe me? The Haken doesn't want the same things you do! She used you. The only thing she's interested in is revenge!"

Stella swallowed and looked at the ground, feeling horribly unsure all of a sudden.

Could it be true? There is no trapped cloud, it was all just a lie?

She'd wanted so much to believe it: that Heather was turning human; that her cloud was waiting to be rescued; that, maybe, Stella could rescue both of them.

But what if Tamar was right?

Nimbus stuttered with sparks and headed outside.

Tamar frowned. "What's got into him?"

"He faced those storm clouds all on his own," said Stella, scowling at Herbie. "He's a bit shaken up."

Tamar touched her scalp and winced. "He's not the only one."

* * *

They traipsed back to the croft in silence, punctuated only by Tamar's huffing and grumbling. Several times, Stella thought her mentor was about to launch into a rant, but each time she

97

bit back whatever she was about to say and trudged on along the path.

When they were safely indoors, Stella couldn't take it any more. *Better to get it over with.*

"Tamar, I know you think I was stupid. I wanted to believe Heather, but you were right. I should have listened to you."

Tamar snorted and raised her eyebrows. "That would be a first."

"And I didn't mean what I said before. You're nothing like the council."

Tamar nodded. A little of the tension in her face melted away.

Wow! thought Stella. *That was bothering her more than being hit by lightning.* She glanced down at her feet for a moment, then looked up and met Tamar's eyes.

"I'm sorry."

Tamar motioned for Stella to sit down. She pulled out a chair opposite.

To Stella's surprise, Tamar reached across the table and took her hands. "Listen to me. I don't think you're stupid. Not for a second. I think you're brave and kind."

Tamar's voice was unexpectedly gentle. It wasn't what Stella had expected, and it made her want to cry.

"I mean it!" said Tamar. "Your intentions are good and, on the whole, I trust your instincts. But now, I need you to trust mine. Do not – I repeat, do NOT – seek out the sea witch again. In fact, I'd like you to stay as far from the shore as possible."

Stella rapidly blinked her tears away and nodded. She had

no intention of speaking to Heather again. Not after what had happened today.

"From now on, I want your focus on your training. Head down, no distractions. Yes?"

"Yes." But a doubt immediately sprang into her mind. "Can I still come with you when the storm clouds are released?"

Tamar smiled and released Stella's hands. "You'll have a front row seat."

"Thank you." Stella swallowed and glanced up at Nimbus. He was restlessly patrolling the ceiling. *You hear that?* Nimbus didn't respond.

"On the condition you get that sea shawl finished quick-fast. I think we may need it."

Stella nodded seriously.

Tamar wrinkled her nose. "So, I think some clean clothes would be in order. Then maybe a hot bath and a nap."

Stella tilted her head in confusion. *A nap? Now?* It was barely even lunchtime.

"Tonight, we're catching midnight sun," explained Tamar.

Stella glanced up at the cobwebs in the corner and Tamar nodded. "Sid will have your gloves ready this evening."

"I'd better head home and tell Grandpa," said Stella, pushing her chair back and standing up.

"I'll pick you up at eleven tonight. And in the meantime? Stay away from the shore."

Stella nodded and beckoned to her cloud. "We will."

Twelve

GOSSAMER GLOVES

GRANDPA'S eyes widened when he opened the door. "What on earth have you been up to?" He looked Stella up and down, taking in her filthy clothes and dishevelled hair.

"I fell in mud," said Stella.

"Well, I can see that!" said Grandpa. "Right, boots off at the door. And give me that raincoat. I'm going to hose it before it comes indoors."

Stella shrugged off her coat and Grandpa took it between finger and thumb.

"Practising green magic, were you?" he said. "Growing stuff?"

If only. Stella put on an innocent face and kicked off her boots.

"Go on, then. Straight to the bathroom." He frowned suspiciously at Nimbus. "He's not going to start sparking, is he?"

She glanced back at the little cloud. He was still a peculiar colour – marbled with streaks of purple and blue. The experience at the broch had obviously really rattled him.

"No. He's fine, Grandpa."

You are fine, aren't you?

Nimbus didn't bob, but he didn't rumble either. She decided that was good enough.

Inside, the kitchen was a mess of tools. It looked like Grandpa had brought the entire contents of his shed indoors, while they'd been out. The floor around the table was littered with sawdust and wood shavings.

More like a workshop than a kitchen, thought Stella, scuffing her toe through the sawdust. Judging by the mess when she'd first arrived, she was pretty sure Grandpa's house must look like this most of the time, when she wasn't staying here.

Stella led Nimbus into her room and patted the end of her bed. He settled on the coverlet.

"I'm just going to wash, then I'll come back. Okay?"

Nimbus didn't respond. He just sat there, brooding.

Stella frowned in concern. What had happened outside the cloud cover? Had he been hurt somehow, or just badly scared? She resolved to ask Tamar to check him over later.

After she'd got washed and changed, Stella went back to the

kitchen to broach the subject of her night trip with Tamar.

"Um, is it okay if Tamar and I stay out late tonight? It's for something important. Part of my training."

Grandpa was entirely absorbed in sanding a small piece of wood. He didn't even look up. "Sure. I'm guessing you'll need feeding first?"

Stella nodded. Never mind supper, she hadn't even had lunch yet. But the kitchen was buried in woodworking tools. Still, at least it was easier to get Grandpa to agree to stuff when he was distracted.

"Can I get a sandwich?"

"You know where everything is," said Grandpa, waving a hand in the direction of the kitchen cupboards.

"Do you want one?" she asked.

"No, no . . . I'll grab something later."

Stella looked at the short strut of wood he was working on. "What are you making?"

Grandpa looked up and winked. "I'll show you when it's done."

* * *

True to her word, Tamar turned up at eleven o'clock on the dot. She was wearing a grey hat, pulled down low over her ears.

Probably to cover up the patch of missing hair, Stella realised, with a twinge of guilt.

Outside, the horizon glowed orange and pink, as though the

sun had only just dipped beneath the sea. Soft shadows cloaked the hillside and heather flowers shone purple in the bright twilight like tiny lanterns, exhaling a smell of honey and herbs.

Stella followed Tamar along the path to the croft. Nimbus floated on ahead, a soft smudge against the warm sky. Having spent the afternoon mooching cosily on the end of Stella's bed, he seemed better; more himself.

Normally, Tamar would be nattering away by now – explaining stuff, firing questions at Stella. But tonight, though she bustled along at her usual pace, she was uncommonly quiet.

It matched the feeling in the air – a strange sense of stillness.

"I really am sorry," said Stella.

Tamar looked round in surprise. "For what?"

"Everything – sneaking around, not listening to you, believing the sea witch, your hair." She nodded at Tamar's hat.

Tamar harumphed softly. "It'll grow back. I'm just glad you had the sense to come to me before breaking that sanctuary stone."

Stella swallowed and nodded. She almost hadn't.

"We all make mistakes," said Tamar. "The trick is never to make the same mistake twice."

As they reached the slope below the croft, Stella breathed out in wonder. A strange new structure stood outside. A tall pole had been set up a couple of metres from the corner of the house. Between the pole and the wall, the air shimmered with a million fine lines of silver, moving lazily in the soft evening air.

"What's that?" she whispered.

"Sid's loom," replied Tamar. "He prefers weaving outside, under the sky."

Stella squinted at the loom. Now she saw him. A clot of darkness, darting to and fro across the myriad lines. Her feet froze in place.

Tamar tugged her forwards. "Do *not* embarrass me now. Never mind what you think of spiders in general, Sid is a craftsman and he's doing this as a favour."

Stella swallowed hard. *If only he'd stop scuttling about. That would make it easier.* She followed Tamar up the slope.

Thankfully, Sid stopped moving when they got close. Tamar led her around the end of the pole to the far side. Stella glanced up at Nimbus for reassurance. He seemed relaxed – sprawled on the thatched roof of the croft. She gave him a nervous smile, then turned warily back towards the loom.

Behind it, the sea was as smooth as glass, reflecting pink clouds and twilight. It would have been beautiful if there weren't a large spider in front of it. Sid hung motionless, suspended by a slender line near the pole.

"Are you ready for us, Sid?" said Tamar.

The spider extended one long leg towards the centre of the web.

Tamar nodded. "Stella, put your hands up, like this," she held up her hands. "Walk forward and press your palms into the web, here. Then, Sid will fit your gloves for you."

Stella looked at Tamar in dismay. There was no way she was letting Sid actually touch her. "Into the cobwebs? Really?"

There was a flurry of movement by the pole and Stella flinched.

"No, Sid. You *don't* have to accept it," said Tamar. "She just needs to get over it. That's all."

Stella looked from Sid to Tamar and back again.

"He says you should close your eyes while he fits your gloves," huffed Tamar. "He's sadly accustomed to this kind of reaction."

Guilt crept queasily into Stella's stomach and she gnawed her lip.

"I'm sorry," she said, lifting her hands. "I'll try."

I can do this. I'll just hold very still and not think about it.

Tamar glanced at Sid and shook her head. "No. He's insisting – doesn't want you jumping, or snatching your hands away. Then all his hard work would be ruined."

Stella shot Sid an apologetic glance and closed her eyes. She winced as Tamar guided her forward, expecting to feel the stickiness of cobwebs. Instead, a silky softness brushed her palms. She peeped through her eyelashes.

Her hands were completely enmeshed in the silver web. Sid was crawling around her right wrist, cutting threads and gluing others with expert speed. She squeezed her eyes tightly closed again.

* * *

Stella stood there for ages with her hands up in the air, until her shoulders began to ache. Her initial anxiety cooled into impatience and finally boredom. At last, she felt a feathery tap on her wrist.

She opened her eyes.

Her hands were free of the web. All around them, loose ends of silver drifted in the still air. Sid hung next to her wrist. He spread his two front legs towards her and then slid vertically up, away from her hands.

Stella brought her fingers close to her face. She could barely see the silk that covered them. Her skin seemed to sparkle and shine as though it had been dusted with dew, but otherwise, the gloves were practically invisible. Unless you knew they were there, you wouldn't realise she was wearing them.

She looked up at the spider. "Thank you, Sid," she said earnestly. "They're really special."

"You are a maestro, as ever," added Tamar, with a smile.

Sid flourished two of his legs in a complex winding pattern and finished with a low bow.

Tamar nodded. "He says: he's proud to present the young weather weaver – that's you – with the first tools of her trade. And he hopes that you will weave good magic with them."

Stella nodded. "Should I take them off?" she said. "Put them somewhere safe . . ."

"Oh, no. You can't take them off," said Tamar. "They're permanent."

"What?" squeaked Stella. She rubbed her fingers together and plucked at their silver coating. Her hands felt exactly as they did before – like skin.

Tamar swept an arm around Stella, before Sid could see. "Let's leave Sid to pack up, shall we?" She hustled Stella towards the front door of the croft.

Stella glanced back over her shoulder. The spider was already swinging from one side of the web to the other, gathering up loops of silk, scampering, tugging, rolling the fine skein of silver away.

"You didn't tell me they won't come off!" accused Stella, as Tamar closed the door.

"Why would you want to take them off?" said Tamar.

"I don't know. So they don't stick to stuff?" said Stella. "What if I accidentally stick my hands together?"

"You won't. You don't see spiders getting stuck in their own webs, do you? It's the same thing."

It's not, thought Stella. *I'm not a spider.*

She touched her fingertips together. There was a very slight tug as she pulled them apart, but Tamar was right – they didn't stick to each other.

But what about when she wanted to do outdoors stuff, like helping Grandpa in the garden, or climbing rocks, or, well, anything normal?

"I have to be able to take them off," she said. "I don't want to ruin them!"

"You won't," said Tamar. "They may be light, but they're incredibly strong. You could use that silk as parachute cord and you'd be perfectly safe."

"What if I get them grubby?"

"You wash your hands?" said Tamar, frowning at Stella as though she was being deliberately difficult.

"What about when I grow, though!" said Stella. "I grow a lot you know. I had to have two new pairs of shoes last year. They'll get too tight."

She pictured the tight bands Grandpa tied around the tails of the lambs. It didn't hurt them, he said – just got gradually tighter and tighter . . . until their tails fell off.

"I don't want my hands to drop off!"

"Good grief, what a thought!" said Tamar. "Nothing's going to drop off. They're magical gloves. They stretch to fit. They'll protect your hands to some extent, and they'll grow with you. I've had mine on since I was your age." She held up her hands and flexed her fingers.

Stella stared at Tamar's hands, noticing for the first time the faint shimmer of silver on her palms – barely visible.

"What *will* they stick to?" said Stella. "Can I climb up walls?"

"Ha!" Tamar hooted with laughter. "Climb up walls! That's a good one. You don't see me crawling up walls, do you?"

Stella's cheeks heated up. "Well what, then?"

"Midnight sun, for starters," said Tamar, with a smile. She stooped and looked out of the window. "Which is any minute now, so if you're finished with all the questions, we'd best get a move on."

There were hundreds more questions buzzing round Stella's head, but a glance at the window and they faded away. The *simmer dim* twilight glowed outside, full of secrets and promises.

Questions could wait. Midnight beckoned.

Thirteen

SIMMER DIM

TAMAR struck off up the slope behind the house, not taking any of the usual paths.

"Where are we going?" said Stella, struggling to keep up with Tamar's sure stride.

"Not far, just up to the top of the ridge – same spot you caught your gale. There's a nice open space up there. It'll be perfect for this. Careful on the slope though – the grass is wet."

"I'll be fine," said Stella and immediately slipped. Her hand landed right on a thistle.

"Ow!" *Gossamer gloves aren't thistle proof, then.*

Without thinking, she stuck her finger in her mouth to quell the sting, but pulled it out again quickly. Probably not a good idea to put magic in your mouth?

She held her finger close to her face, trying make out whether she'd made a hole in the gossamer. Her skin glistened slightly. She couldn't see any gaps in the silvery sheen.

It was hard to tell though – the night seemed to be getting darker by the moment. She looked up, to see a huge cloud bank sliding across the sky, blotting out the *simmer dim* glow.

"Tamar, it's getting dark!" she called.

"I know."

"Well, isn't that a problem?" Stella persisted. "We want to catch midnight sun. And there isn't going to *be* any in a minute!"

She was panting. The hillside was steep and uneven, with tussocks of grass and lurking boulders. It was a stiff climb during the day, but in the gathering gloom, it was a proper scramble.

"Let's save talking until we're at the top, shall we?" called Tamar. She was quite far ahead now.

"If you call that talking," grumbled Stella quietly. "Me asking questions and you not answering them."

She'd given up trying to protect the gloves now and was scrambling up the hill, using hands and feet to navigate the slope. She couldn't see Tamar any more, but she could still hear her, tromping on ahead. She clambered towards the sound.

At last, the slope stopped rising. She'd reached the top.

"You made it then," said a shadow up ahead.

Stella sighed.

"It's almost pitch-black," she said. "Are we too late?"

"No, not at all," said Tamar. "It's local clouds, that's all – they've come to watch. No pressure, though. There's no need to be nervous."

"Well, I wasn't . . . before," said Stella. "Don't they realise they're getting in the way? We won't be able to do this, if they make it all dark."

"Give them some credit," said Tamar. "They're not just here to watch, they're here to help."

"Very helpful, making it pitch-black," mumbled Stella.

"Just wait," said Tamar, with a smile in her voice.

As she spoke, a faint glow appeared in the darkness overhead and then another.

The clouds were thinning, revealing dappled hints of the sky above. Stella gazed up wide-eyed as the clouds shifted apart. It happened so slowly that it was hard to see them moving – like watching the minute hand of a clock. Gradually, holes began to appear, revealing tiny glimpses of the night sky above. Within minutes, the blanker of cloud was peppered with tiny holes, like one of Gran's shawls. Muted beams of midnight sun began to play over the hillside like searchlights, lighting up the tufty grass and the rocks and the stunted bushes. Nimbus came into view, spotlit for a moment, further up the hill.

"There. You see?" said Tamar. Midnight sunbeams rippled blue and violet over her face and hair.

Stella had the sense that they were deep underwater, looking up at the sky through miles of sea. She shook off the thought with a shudder. They were on top of a hill, far from the shore. The safest place they could be right now.

She watched Nimbus, darting from one glowing beam to the next, and smiled.

"It's beautiful," she said.

"Beautiful, but also helpful," replied Tamar. "You don't want to scoop up a great sheet of it. You're after individual sunbeams. Now, hold out your hands, like this." She held her hands out at arm's length in front of her and strummed her fingers in the air. "To find the right ones, you need to listen – listen with your whole body."

Tamar never was any good at giving clear instructions. Usually, the best thing was to just have a go. Stella held out her hands and wriggled her fingers experimentally.

"Oh! What was that?"

"What was what, exactly?" asked Tamar.

"My chest feels weird," said Stella. "A sort of faraway boom. Like waves against the cliffs."

"Ha!" said Tamar. "Perfect. That's called a Heart Chord. Makes sense – you feel it in your heart. It's the very lowest note and one of the best. So! I want you to clench your fist and then pull, like this," she mimed the action in the air and Stella copied her.

The strange humming in her chest swelled and then stopped as she jerked the sunbeam free. She could still see a soft glow around her hand, but the night was a little darker now.

"Was that right?" she said, hoping she hadn't broken it.

"Exactly right," replied Tamar. "Pop it in the bag, and we'll get another one."

Stella walked across to Tamar, her fist held out stiffly in front of her. Tamar held the weather bag wide open. Stella pushed her hand in and opened her fist.

"It won't fall out when I pull my hand out?"

"When has anything ever fallen out of one of my bags?" said Tamar. "No, it won't fall out. Now, let's try another, shall we?"

Stella moved away and gazed up at the crochet sky.

"Thank you, clouds," she called.

"There's no need to shout," said Tamar. "They can hear you fine. Good that you thanked them, though. After what happened with Sid, I was starting to wonder where your manners had gone."

Stella winced. She'd have to thank him properly later. These gloves were amazing.

She took a deep breath and stretched her arms out in front of her again.

This time, when she stroked her fingers through the air, she could hear it. Shades of hidden song coloured the night air as her fingers brushed past each midnight sunbeam. She moved her hand to the right and the sound changed to a high piping whistle that scampered across her scalp. She reached out to the left and there was a terrible clang. She flinched.

"Not that one," said Tamar quickly. "We'll leave that one where it is. Useful for some purposes, but what we need for this particular project is a bit of harmony."

Stella reached forwards again, to where the sound had been sweetest, and began to strum, and pluck, stuffing midnight sunbeams into the bag hand over fist.

She could have carried on all night, but eventually Tamar began to flag. "Time to get you home," she said, stifling a yawn.

"Just a few more?"

Tamar shook her bag. It jangled gently. "We've got plenty," she said. "More than enough for your shawl." She raised an arm and waved. Immediately, the sky began to clear.

Stella squinted out at the apricot horizon. "It's still sunset!" she said.

"Heading for sun*rise* now," grunted Tamar.

"Never night," murmured Stella, and smiled. She liked the idea. You could just stay up all night if you wanted to. Maybe she'd do it again.

Tamar shook her head. "Not come winter. Then there's barely a glimpse of daylight. The Teran reigns. Night will have its time . . ."

Night will have its time. Why did Tamar have to make it sound so ominous? Anyway, that was all the more reason to stay out and enjoy it now, surely. She glanced at her mentor.

Tamar was gazing out at the midnight sea, her face full of shadows. She looked sad. Why, when everything had gone so well?

"I did alright, didn't I?" said Stella.

Tamar gave a lopsided smile. "More than alright," she said.

"A Heart Chord on your first try!"

"Are you worrying about the sea witch, then?"

Tamar heaved a sigh. "I'm not worrying. I'm pensive. There's a difference. I was just thinking about all those young apprentices missing their storm clouds." She shook her head. "They should never have been separated."

Stella nodded. She and Nimbus loathed the idea of being separated. It had so nearly happened to them. Sure enough, when she glanced across at him, he was frosty with fear.

She beckoned him closer and he settled around her shoulders, chilly against the back of her neck. Stella shivered. "It's alright," she whispered. "I'll never let that happen."

"Still," said Tamar. "Not much longer to wait until they're released."

"Really?" said Stella, in excitement.

Tamar nodded and smiled. "Thanks to you, in part! I meant to tell you earlier. Following your very sensible suggestion, the council are bringing the storm novices to Winter's Keep. Not all of them, of course – there are too many and some of them are far away – but as many as they can. Hopefully they'll be ready to release the first storms within the next week or so." She hitched her bag up on her shoulder and began to pick her way down the slope. "Oh, and Flo's going to bring Tassa along," she added. "She's tasked with teaching the novices about how she called her cloud, when it was first released."

"Yay! Tas! I get to see Tas again!" Stella skipped in delight.

Tamar nodded. "I thought that might please you. Magnus will be there, too, I think."

"You hear that, Nimbus? You get to see Drench again, and Arca, and Briar too!"

Nimbus lifted off her shoulders and turned a swift loop of delight, before racing ahead down the slope.

"The whole gang, back together again! I can't wait."

Fourteen

NO ORDINARY HAMMER

WHEN Stella and Nimbus got home, they found Grandpa snoring in his armchair. His head was tilted back and his mouth was wide open. He sounded a bit like the boat engine – every breath a great growling vibration. Stella giggled silently.

Nimbus floated closer to Grandpa's face to investigate.

"Nimbus! Don't!"

She'd only whispered, but it was enough to disturb Grandpa. He woke abruptly with a loud snort and flapped wildly at the cloud in front of his face. Nimbus rapidly retreated. Grandpa blinked a few times before focusing on Stella.

"You're back. Good. I've been waiting up for you."

Stella bit down on a smile. "With your eyes closed?"

"Just resting my eyelids . . ." huffed Grandpa.

"You were snoring!" said Stella.

"I never snore," declared Grandpa. "What time is it, anyway?"

"I don't know," said Stella. "Late. Past midnight."

"Oof! No wonder I'm struggling to keep my eyes open. So? How was your little jaunt with Tamar? What were you doing, anyway?"

Stella smiled. "Catching midnight sunbeams! It was brilliant. They sound like bells."

"Bells, is it?" Grandpa wiped sleep from his eyes, then pushed himself to his feet with a grunt. "Well, I'm glad it went well. You can tell me all about it in the morning. Right now, it's bedtime!"

"Aren't you going to clear up all . . . this, first?" asked Stella, waving at the gigantic mess in the kitchen.

"You sound like your gran," said Grandpa. "No. I'll clear it up when I've finished. Probably tomorrow. Now, enough of your delaying tactics – off to bed with you. I've already let you stay up way past bedtime, so don't push your luck."

Stella smiled.

Grandpa pushed his feet into his slippers and led the way, shuffling along the corridor to the bathroom. There was the squeak of the tap turning on, then the sound of him brushing his teeth. Stella beckoned Nimbus and they headed to her room.

Grandpa was so different now, compared to when she'd first arrived. Then, he wouldn't even let her go to the beach on her own. It was partly Gran's fault of course – her premonition about 'the storm to end all storms' had made him worried for her.

"Except the storm turned out to be you, didn't it?" she said, nudging Nimbus as he floated past her shoulder. She hung her coat on the hook on the back of the door and sat down on the bed to take her boots off.

"And now he lets us stay out past midnight with Tamar!"

I can't tell him what happened with Heather, she decided. *It would ruin everything.*

Nimbus let out a soft rumble and Grandpa appeared in the doorway as though summoned. "What's that about?"

"Nothing, Grandpa. Sorry. We were just discussing something. That's all."

"No thunder in the house," said Grandpa. "Them's the rules, or he can sleep outside."

Stella nodded and raised her eyebrows at Nimbus. "No more thunder, okay?"

And don't worry. From now on, we're going to stay far away from the broch.

Nimbus let out another low rumble and Grandpa wagged a finger at him.

"I mean it, cloud!"

Nimbus floated sulkily up to the corner of the ceiling and settled there.

Grandpa nodded in satisfaction. "Night night, both of you."

* * *

The following morning, Stella woke from the strangest dream. She'd been swimming deep underwater, trying to find . . . something.

Something important. What was it?

It was no good. The dream slipped away like a fish through her fingers, leaving her with only the faint memory of weightlessness.

She sighed and opened her eyes. Nimbus was prowling in circles around the ceiling. "Nimbus? What's up?"

He didn't respond immediately. Stella sat up and pushed the covers back.

"Nimbus!"

The little cloud started, then dropped abruptly onto the bed next to her. She smoothed him.

"What were you doing? Were you dreaming, too?"

Stella wasn't sure if clouds slept, let alone dreamed – but what else could it be?

"It's okay now, Nimbus."

The little cloud rolled a little closer, until he rested cold against her hip. She gently ruffled him, dispersing the whorls of frost. "You don't have to be scared any more."

Poor Nimbus. Being trapped outside the cloud cover, facing the Haken's attack alone – it had really shaken him up.

"It's alright. I'm here. And they're gone now. The sanctuary stone drove them away, along with the Haken."

Static electricity began to prickle over her skin, crawling up her arm like ants. She lifted her hand away cautiously. "Shh. It's okay."

Nimbus lifted off the bed and drifted to the window sill. He bumped softly against the glass.

"Soon. After breakfast. Just give me a chance to get ready."

Nimbus nudged the window again and Stella shook her head. "Just wait for me, okay? I'd rather we stick together today. I won't be long."

She pulled on her dressing gown and headed for the kitchen. There was a pungent smell in the corridor; not nasty, but quite strong. It reminded her of the weird stir fry oil Mum had tried once – nutty and not very nice. She hoped Grandpa wasn't making something experimental for breakfast.

"Phew! What's that smell, Grandpa?"

"Danish oil," he replied. "I'm nearly finished, look." He moved aside so she could see what he was working on – a rectangular base, topped by two curved wooden prongs.

"What is it?"

"A stand," said Grandpa. "To go on the mantlepiece."

"A stand for what?"

"This." Grandpa picked up a pointy hammer, cradling it in his hands as though it were fragile.

"You made a stand for your hammer?"

Grandpa's eyes twinkled. "It's not just any hammer."

Stella frowned and stepped forward. She'd seen one like it before. Definitely.

"A Trowie hammer?" she breathed, her eyes widening. No ordinary tool, then. Trowie hammers were infused with ancient magic.

Grandpa nodded proudly. "The good folk gifted it to me, as thanks for my work at the Gathering."

"Cool!"

Grandpa's mouth twitched up at the corners and he set it back on the table. "I had a choice – this, or one of their cure-all ointments, but I chose this. Figured it might come in handy if that cloud of yours were ever trapped by a Trowie gem."

Stella wrapped her arms round Grandpa's waist and hugged him hard, her heart swelling with gratitude. He could have chosen something for him – something really special – but instead, he'd chosen something for her. "Thank you, Grandpa!"

Nimbus wrapped himself around the pair of them, glowing sunrise gold.

"That doesn't mean you get to thunder in the house, mind!" said Grandpa.

The little cloud moved away and settled on top of the dresser, not making any promises.

"What's for breakfast?" asked Stella.

"I figured you'd want to get straight back to Tamar's, so I've packed you jam sandwiches and an apple," said Grandpa, nodding at a brown paper bag on the kitchen counter.

Stella looked at the mess still covering the kitchen table. What he meant was: *there's no space to eat breakfast here.*

"I'll have this cleared up by lunchtime," he said.

"Thanks, Grandpa."

* * *

Stella opted for the inland path to Tamar's. She didn't trust the shore. The idea that Heather might still be lurking filled her with a twitchy feeling of unease.

She used you – that's what Tamar had said.

It made everything about their secret meetings feel grubby and itchy; coloured all her hopes foolish.

I can't believe I was stupid enough to trust a sea witch.

Nimbus sped past, dropping an ice-cold shower of rain.

"Nimbus!"

She rubbed her face dry on the edge of her t-shirt and sighed. She should be glad, really. At least that was normal. He'd been really weird since the incident at the broch yesterday – grumbly, sulky, not listening – probably shaken up by the confrontation with Heather's clouds.

Not Heather, she thought. *The Haken. Tamar was right.*

Nimbus let out a long rumble, startling her. "What was that for!"

Maybe he blamed her for what had happened?

She'd wanted so much to rescue one cloud, set one storm cloud free. But it was all a lie. There was no cloud to be rescued.

The Haken had just used her to get to Tamar. She was probably laughing at her right now; at how gullible she'd been.

Nimbus darkened to deepest graphite grey and rumbled again.

Stella huffed and wrapped her arms around herself. "Well? How was I supposed to know?"

She missed Dad right now.

Happy thoughts, little star. That's probably what he'd say. *Focus on what you can do, not what you can't. Find something to look forward to.*

She shoved her hands deep in her pockets and cast around for a happy thought.

We'll still get to see all the other storm clouds released. Tamar promised.

She imagined them streaming out across the sky in all directions, flying back to their weather weavers. That would be wonderful.

"Just think of it, Nimbus! There are hundreds of them. And they're going to be set free, because of us."

Nimbus paled to sunrise yellow.

She let herself feel proud for a moment. If she and Nimbus hadn't passed the trials, that would never have happened; nobody would even know about the trapped clouds!

And we'll see Tas and Magnus again.

She imagined how excited Tas would be, and a smile crept onto her face. Stella gasped as something else occurred to her. *Grandpa's Trowie hammer!* Maybe he could help release the storm clouds?

Nimbus darted ahead in excitement. Stella's heart gave a little lurch of alarm, as she realised he'd taken the turning for the broch.

"Stop!" she yelped.

She jogged to catch up with him. Normally, they only took this path when they were heading for the broch. Perhaps that's why he thought they were going that way? But still!

"Seriously, what is wrong with you this morning?! Have some sense."

Nimbus circled back towards her. He'd turned a mournful lilac blue – he never liked it when Stella was unhappy with him.

"Nimbus, I'm not cross, but this is important. We can't go anywhere near the broch. Not today, maybe not for a while."

She turned towards Tamar's and trudged on up the path. Nimbus trailed along behind.

Fifteen

WARPING SUNBEAMS

TAMAR was in an exuberant mood when they arrived.

"Are you ready to get weaving?"

Stella nodded and smiled. *Actual weaving, at last.*

She glanced back to check on Nimbus. To her relief, he'd paled to a soft grey – much closer to his normal colour.

Tamar was already bustling along the corridor. "This way!"

Stella had never wondered about the other rooms in Tamar's house. The croft was about the same size as Grandpa's, maybe even a bit smaller. In his house, the short corridor just led to the bedrooms and a small bathroom. But Tamar didn't need another bedroom, she realised, as she followed her to the room at the end of the corridor.

Tamar pushed open the door with a flourish. "Welcome to the weaving room!"

The room was slightly smaller than Stella's bedroom at Grandpa's. It was occupied by a large wooden loom, with a low bench in front of it.

Sid was sitting on the top corner of the frame.

I am not scared of spiders. I am NOT scared of spiders.

She swallowed and held her hands up, wiggling her fingers. "I wanted to thank you properly for these gloves, Sid," she said. "They're amazing."

The spider dipped his body in modest acknowledgement and Stella smiled. That wasn't so bad, was it? Maybe she *could* learn to get along with him?

She approached the loom, with a thrill of excitement. This was where Tamar wove magic cloth for never-empty purses, cloaks of invisibility, flying carpets! She ran her fingertips reverently along the polished wood. Possibilities whirled in her mind, bright as wishes.

In the centre of the loom hung hundreds of tiny rods, like a comb. Nimbus drifted through them and appeared on the other side looking distinctly stripy.

"We'll start by sorting those sunbeams you gathered last night," said Tamar. "They're going to be your warp threads."

"Okay."

Sid extended one long leg. A clear invitation to sit down.

127

Stella slid onto the low wooden bench. She rested her feet lightly on the foot pedals and the long comb in the middle jangled, making her heart jump.

"What have I forgotten?" muttered Tamar. "We're missing something." She frowned and drummed her fingers lightly on the side of the loom. It was charred black in places, now that Stella actually focused on it.

"What happened there?" she asked.

Tamar looked at where Stella was pointing. "Oh. Lightning."

"You actually weave lightning!" said Stella.

"Mm. Sometimes," said Tamar. "But you needn't think you're starting with that. I haven't forgotten what you did to my kitchen table!"

Nimbus nosed along the charred wooden strut and Stella stared at the black crackle of burn marks. What would the loom look like, strung with streaks of lightning? How would you hold them? How did the whole thing not catch on fire?

She glanced up at Sid. *He probably knows. He's probably seen Tamar doing it.*

She rubbed her fingertips together, feeling the gentle tug of the gossamer.

"Here," said Tamar, passing Stella her weather bag. "Empty these out and we'll get started." The bag chimed softly as she handed it over.

Stella reached into the bag and pulled out a handful of sunbeams. They cast an eerie glow over the room.

"Ooh, I remember now. Teaspoon!" said Tamar, pulling one out of her pocket and holding it up triumphantly.

"What for?"

"Tuning," said Tamar, with a wink. "Given what happened yesterday, we're going to select tones that are particularly effective against sea-witch storms."

Oh.

Stella swallowed and looked at Nimbus. He'd shaded to dark grey.

It's alright, Nimbus. We're safe here.

Tamar plucked a bright sunbeam from the glowing spaghetti-like bundle in Stella's fist and held it up so that it hung down straight – a single narrow shaft of light. She tapped it lightly with the back of the teaspoon and the room filled with a deep, resonant chime that hummed across Stella's skin.

"Hear the power in that?" asked Tamar with satisfaction.

Nimbus began to dart from side to side, then whirled in a tight circle. For a moment, it looked as though he was dancing. But as the note died away, he began to crackle.

"No, Nimbus! Don't!"

"Out!" yelled Tamar. "Get out, quick!"

Stella scrambled for the door. Nimbus streamed after her, showering the corridor with sparks. She was all set to take him outside, but by the time they reached the kitchen, he'd calmed down completely.

Tamar came stomping down the corridor and scowled at him. She blew out softly. "That was nearly a disaster!"

"Why did he do that?" asked Stella, looking up at her cloud in concern.

Tamar shrugged. "I don't know. But I don't like it. We can't sort sunbeams with him around. I think you'd better spin him and send him out again, before we carry on. We're going to need a few more reels for your shawl. Might as well spin one now."

"Alright," agreed Stella, reluctantly.

She looked at Nimbus and gnawed her lip. She didn't like the idea of sending him out gathering magic on his own right now.

* * *

As soon as they'd finished spinning, Nimbus did that same strange hiccup and bolted outside.

"Stay away from the sea, Nimbus!" she called, running to the door. "And the broch!"

He was already out of sight. She hoped he'd heard.

"Does he seem moody to you?" asked Tamar. She turned the reel of magic in her hands and frowned.

Stella closed the door and nodded. "Since yesterday. He got a real scare, I think."

"But he was definitely calm while you were spinning?"

Stella nodded. "Yes! Calm focus. We haven't forgotten."

"And you're not having some sort of existential crisis?" said Tamar, eyeing her suspiciously.

"I don't know what that is. I'm not cross, if that's what you mean?"

Tamar huffed. "I don't understand it, then." She passed the reel to Stella.

The yarn was full of tiny threads of colour. Stella turned it in the light. It was iridescent. Shards of rainbow glistened within it, like fish scales. Nimbus must have been feeling *all* the feelings while they were spinning.

"At least it's even this time," Stella pointed out. "There are hardly any lumps in it!"

Tamar pursed her lips and nodded. "There is that. I'm not sure we should use it though – there's something not right with it. Put it near the back of your stash."

* * *

The sunbeams were much shorter now – most of their length tightly coiled around the back roller of the loom. Sid had made short work of threading them through the 'heddles' and the 'reed', so they were evenly spaced out – from Heart Chord all the way up to Heavenly Bells.

The warp threads looked a bit like a shining harp. *Sound like one too*, Stella realised, running the teaspoon along them.

"Stop that racket!" said Tamar. She flapped her hand impatiently and Stella handed her the next loose end. Tamar laboriously knotted it on to the front stick. Her tongue poked out of the side of her mouth.

Stella slouched against the wall. Half the loom was strung now, but it was taking ages. She was sure she'd be able to do it faster, if Tamar would only let her have a go. "How many of these have we got to do?"

"Eight sunbeams per inch," said Tamar. "And this frame is about thirty inches wide. You do the maths."

"That's loads!"

"Try using pure spider silk," retorted Tamar. "That's a thousand threads per inch."

Stella groaned. "*Please* can I have a go? I'm meant to be learning, aren't I? And I'm good at fiddly stuff."

Sid suddenly woke into a flurry of leg waving and Stella froze.

Tamar grunted. "Fine!" She motioned impatiently at the loom. "Go on, then."

Whatever he'd said to Tamar had made the difference. Stella gave Sid a swift smile and swapped places with Tamar.

The brightness made it tricky. She couldn't look directly at the sunbeams without squinting. Each knot had to be tied from memory, just by feel. Luckily, Grandpa had made her practise all her knots until she could do them with her eyes closed. On the boat, it was important to be able to tie them fast, even with salt spray flying into your eyes.

A shiver skittered up the back of Stella's neck.

I'm sorry, for what they did to you. She'd been lying on the deck of the boat when she said it – whispering to the water, on the way to the Gathering. *I wish I'd never said that.*

She'd just been talking to herself – figuring out how she felt about Heather; about everything. She hadn't imagined for a second that the sea witch might actually be listening. And now look where they were . . .

Stella glanced at Tamar. She was still wearing the round woolly hat, even though it was warm today – to hide her scorched hair. Guilt pulled at her like an undertow.

It could have been so much worse . . .

She blinked the thought away and held out her hand for another sunbeam.

"I should have let you do the knots this morning," admitted Tamar. "You're faster than me! And I've been doing this for decades."

Sid waved his legs at Tamar and she snorted softly. "Well, that's just rude!"

* * *

It took the whole morning, but at last, Tamar took a step back from the loom, pursed her lips and nodded.

"There. I think we're done! Let's pause for lunch."

Stella smiled and scrambled to her feet.

Strung with midnight sunbeams, the loom glowed, filling the room with a wavering unearthly light. "It's so bright!"

Tamar nodded. "In case you were wondering, the fabric won't glow like that when you're done," she said. "The warp threads are mostly hidden when you weave. Don't want you shining like a lighthouse, do we? We'll leave that to the sun weavers. Bunch of blazing show-offs."

Stella chuckled. "I'll tell Farah you said that."

"Oh, I've called her worse than that."

"Like what?"

Tamar smiled and shook her head. "Never you mind." She patted the loom. "A good morning's work. I reckon you can have this finished in a day or two. Then you can show it off to your friends at Winter's Keep."

Stella grinned and nodded. The thought had crossed her mind . . .

A shadow moved across the room. She looked hopefully out of the window and sighed. Just a gull.

Where are you, Nimbus?

She'd feel better when he was safely back. It wasn't so much the tug of separation that was bothering her, but the thought of the sea witch out there watching; just waiting for another chance to attack.

Stay safe, Nimbus. Please don't do anything stupid.

Sixteen

WEAVING MAGIC

TO Stella's relief, Nimbus returned just as they were finishing their lunch.

Tamar pursed her lips. "Are you going to behave this time? Or should we leave you here in the kitchen?"

Nimbus faded to a warm cream and fluffed himself up.

"I know, I know – like butter wouldn't melt in your mouth," scoffed Tamar. "Alright, but one more spark and you can spend the rest of the day outside. Understood?"

Stella beckoned to Nimbus and he settled on the table next to her. "He seems better, now."

"Let's hope so," said Tamar, pushing her chair back and heading down the corridor.

In the weaving room, Sid was already hard at work, winding Stella's magic yarn on to a tiny reel nestled inside a small oval of wood. Tamar picked it up before he'd finished, leaving him dangling. He lowered himself onto the loom with a slight air of pique.

"This is a shuttle," said Tamar, waving it in the air.

"Looks like a little canoe," Stella observed, with a smile.

"Quite," Tamar nodded. "It's called a *boat* shuttle. Normally, you'd use your cloud to guide the yarn and have it done in half the time." She cast a wary eye at Nimbus. "But I'd like to see what mood he's in before we make a decision on that."

Stella glanced up at him and nodded. *Be good, Nimbus.*

Tamar pressed one of the loom's pedals and the sunbeams separated into top and bottom layers. "The shuttle goes through here," she said, sliding it into the gap between the two layers, "and across to the other side." She pushed the shuttle forward with a smooth motion and it slid all the way to the other side. Stella caught it before it could fall out.

"Then you press the other pedal," said Tamar, nodding for Stella to do it, "and post it back again."

Stella pressed the pedal and the layers of sunbeams switched places, the bottom ones now on the top. She slid the shuttle back.

"Perfect," said Tamar. "Just like that. Away you go!"

* * *

When Tamar came back in to check on her, Stella had only made a strip of fabric about as wide as two fingers; slow progress.

"Getting there!" said Tamar. She bent to look at the narrow strip of green. "Lovely colour. That's the seaweed."

Stella blinked a few times until her vision cleared. Her eyes were watering from staring at the sunbeams. When she closed her eyes, she could still see glowing stripes.

"What does the seaweed actually do?"

"Anchors it to the sea!" exclaimed Tamar. "This sea, specifically. Same with the puffin's growl – this will be a *Shetland* sea shawl. Magic is always more effective when it's anchored to a place. It'll see us safely to Winter's Keep, no matter what."

No matter what. Stella knew exactly what Tamar meant by that. The idea they might have to face the sea witch on the way to Winter's Keep filled her with horror. On land, was one thing. Out on a boat, in deep water? That was another.

Stella looked at the narrow strip of green and swallowed hard. It was the first thing she'd ever woven. What if she hadn't done it right?

"Are you absolutely sure it'll work?" said Stella.

"Certain," said Tamar. She pulled a fine-toothed comb down from the top of the loom and tamped the yarn down hard, making the strip of fabric even narrower. About enough for a ribbon, now.

Stella sighed. "Maybe it'd be safer if we didn't go . . ."

137

"What?!" exclaimed Tamar. "Not a chance. I've never let a sea witch slow me down before and we're not about to start now. Besides, you've been looking forward to it, haven't you?"

Stella nodded, without much enthusiasm. She had. But that was before ...

Tamar patted her shoulder. "You'll see. When this sea shawl is done, the Haken won't be able to touch us."

The crash of thunder made Stella's heart leap. She stared up at Nimbus, coiled furiously in the corner of the ceiling. *What was that for?*

"Out!" said Tamar, hands on hips. "I'm not having that behaviour in here."

"Go on, Nimbus," confirmed Stella.

The little cloud flowed out of the door and she sighed. She'd been hoping to persuade Tamar to let him help. No chance of that now.

* * *

The next three days passed in a flurry of activity. Each day, Stella wove as though her life depended on it, which possibly it did.

The glistening green roll of fabric at the front of the loom grew steadily fatter. With daily reassurance from Tamar, Stella was beginning to believe that the sea shawl would be powerful enough to protect them.

Towards the end of the afternoon on the third day, Tamar

popped her head round the door. "I need to have a word with your grandpa," she said. "Will he be at home now?"

Stella's stomach did a little flip as she remembered where he'd been. "He was heading to Lerwick this morning, to call Mum and Dad, but he should be back by now."

"Good. I've had news from the council."

Stella's heart fluttered with excitement. "They're doing it? Releasing the storm clouds?"

Tamar nodded. "Should be some time in the next few days."

"At last!" Stella glanced out of the window at Nimbus. *We did that!*

But her excitement soon cooled into fright. "The shawl's not finished, though!"

Tamar nodded and narrowed her eyes. "Maybe it's time we get your cloud involved. What do you think?"

Stella looked out at Nimbus and nodded. He'd definitely been quieter these past couple of days. He'd grumbled a few times, but it was almost always when she'd been telling him her worries about the sea witch. As long as they avoided that topic, he should be fine.

"Just, maybe don't mention the H-A-K-E-N," she said.

"Alright, then. We'll get him weaving tomorrow. First things first, though. Let's go and talk to your grandpa."

"Just so we're clear, I'm not getting into a boat until the shawl is finished," asserted Stella.

"Me neither!" said Tamar. "But don't fret. Cloud weaving is far faster. We'll get it finished. No problem."

Grandpa opened the door with a look of mild surprise. "You're back early."

He nodded at Tamar and motioned them inside. Nimbus headed straight for his favourite spot, on top of the dresser.

"So? Did you speak to Mum and Dad?" asked Stella.

Grandpa smiled and nodded. "You can stop worrying. They're in fine form. Still chasing their mythical monster, though it's sounding more and more like a large shoal. The radar's showing a collection of signals now. So – no Kraken!"

"Phew!" Stella let out a huge breath. Even with all his reassurances, she'd still been braced for bad news.

"Told you!" said Tamar.

"Your Dad's a bit glum about it," continued Grandpa. "No ground-breaking discovery, this time. Back to the old sea slugs."

Nudibranchs, thought Stella., but she didn't correct him.

Grandpa's eyes snapped to Tamar, over by the mantlepiece. She was lifting his hammer off its stand. "Hey, hey! Looking, not touching!" he said, hurrying over and taking it out of her hands.

"A Trowie hammer!" she said, staring at it covetously. "I take it they gifted you that, did they? You didn't just walk off with it?"

"Of course not!" said Grandpa, looking scandalised. He set it carefully back on its stand.

"They offered him loads of things," boasted Stella. "Ointments and all sorts, but Grandpa chose that, so he can protect Nimbus."

She glanced up at her cloud. She was still really touched that Grandpa had done that for them. Nimbus shaded gently to gold – it made him happy too.

"You turned down Trowie ointment?!" said Tamar. "You silly fool. Do you know how good that stuff is? It'll cure anything from broken bones to blindness! Would have sorted out all your aches and pains. And mine . . ."

"I don't have aches and pains," asserted Grandpa. "I'm in perfect health." He flexed his arm and patted his bicep.

Tamar snorted in disbelief. "Whatever you say, old man."

"I'm glad Grandpa chose the hammer," said Stella. "It means no one can ever trap Nimbus. It's the best thing he could have got."

Grandpa smiled at her.

Tamar leant to look closely at the hammer. Grandpa gave a warning growl and she straightened up with her hands in the air. "Looking! I'm only looking!"

"Stop it, Tamar!" said Stella, stepping in between them. "Just tell him."

"Tell me what?" said Grandpa, suspiciously.

Tamar rubbed her hands together. "The council are releasing the storm clouds, at last. I want to be there when it happens – to make sure it happens – and I'd like to take Stella along."

Grandpa's expression darkened.

"I haven't promised her anything yet," said Tamar, hurriedly. "I told her we'd have to ask your permission first."

Stella glanced at Tamar. She was starting to get the hang of Grandpa.

Grandpa stiffened his back and straightened his shoulders, preparing to be all head-of-the-household.

"I'm assuming that if she *were* allowed, you'd want to come too?" said Tamar, quickly. "You are her guardian, after all."

Grandpa opened and closed his mouth. A fleeting look of disappointment crossed his face. He'd been all set for an argument.

Stella smiled and tugged his arm. "So?"

"I don't see why not," said Grandpa. "Provided it's not too far."

* * *

It couldn't last. Not ten minutes later, Grandpa was close to losing his rag with Tamar.

"You're telling me it's off the west coast of the mainland?"

"Yes!" exclaimed Tamar. "West of Foula – you must know Foula?"

"Of course I do," snapped Grandpa. "But there's nothing west of Foula! Unless we're heading to America, in which case we'll need a much bigger boat."

Tamar snorted derisively. "It's nowhere near that far."

Grandpa pulled a map out of the dresser drawer. He unfolded it on the kitchen table and roughly smoothed the creases out. "Show me," he said. "Point to where it is, this mythical island of yours."

Tamar poked a finger at the blue space on the far left. "Here."

Grandpa frowned and shook his head. "There's nothing there. You're pointing at sea."

"It's there," said Tamar. "It's just not marked on your map."

Grandpa pursed his lips. "I've sailed those seas plenty of times and I've never come across an uncharted island."

"Well, you wouldn't, would you?" said Tamar, her voice sharp with sarcasm. "It's hidden from normal folk."

Grandpa sighed heavily, marked the spot with a pencil, then folded the map.

As he turned away, he rolled his eyes at Stella and she smiled. Tamar narrowed her eyes at the pair of them.

"I'll need to refuel before we set off," said Grandpa. "I reckon we can make it in a day, with fair weather."

"We can promise you that," said Stella seriously.

Tamar nodded at the Trowie hammer. "Be sure to bring that with you."

"Oh, I see!" huffed Grandpa. "*That's* why you want me along."

"No," said Tamar. "It's for your scintillating company."

Stella nudged Tamar and frowned.

Tamar relented. "Alright. You're invited anyway. But if you want to help, it would be useful. The good folk are still refusing to get involved."

Grandpa nodded. "I'll bring it. But just to be clear, I'm not lending it. If anyone's going to use it, it'll be me. And if it goes walkabout, I know the first place I'll come looking."

Tamar smiled airily. "As though I'd do something like that!"

Seventeen

WRONG TURN

The following morning, Stella strode out along the path to Tamar's with a spring in her step. She was starting to feel properly excited about their trip. If Nimbus helped, Tamar reckoned they could get the shawl finished today. Then they'd be sea-witch-proof! Safe to travel to Winter's Keep.

"We'll get to see our friends again," she told Nimbus. "See all those storm clouds released!" Nimbus veered off the path. "Where are you going? No!"

He was heading for the broch again. Stella sprinted after him. "Stop, Nimbus!"

The little cloud lurched back and forth, grey bulges knuckling up out of his smooth surface, before jolting to a halt and letting out a low rumble.

Stella shook her head. This was not a good start. They were meant to weave together today. She understood why the Haken made him thunder – he was just being protective. But she hadn't even mentioned her, this time.

"What is wrong with you? You know we can't go back to the broch!"

Nimbus hated the idea of clouds being trapped – she knew that – it appalled him. And he must have been so excited by the idea of setting Fury free. Was it possible that he hadn't understood that there *was* no cloud to rescue at the broch? Maybe that's what had been bothering him all this time?

"Nimbus, there's nothing at the broch. Fury's not there. Heather lied to us."

Nimbus let out a clap of thunder that made Stella's heart leap. She snorted in fright and stared at him, her heart racing. She'd never been scared of her cloud before, but he was swirling purple and grey now.

Angry cloud. Angry with me.

Stella took a deep breath for courage, then reached out to him. Eventually, he drifted close enough to rest against her hand. Static electricity prickled softly over her palm.

"Look, I wanted to believe it too, but—"

Nimbus shaded even darker – iron grey, heavy with threat.

He swayed from side to side and squared up to her. Stella withdrew her hand and watched him warily.

Nimbus was never angry with her. It would take something really big.

Like abandoning a trapped cloud . . .

Nimbus abruptly faded to white and drifted close enough to touch. When she didn't reach out, he moved a little closer and wrapped himself around her in a cloud hug.

Stella swallowed. "Fury *is* in the broch?"

The little cloud glowed lemon yellow; tentatively hopeful.

Stella shook her head. She'd always believed Nimbus before. Even over Tamar. But this time she didn't want to. That would mean Heather was still out there waiting, hoping; wondering why Stella hadn't come back.

Bitter guilt curdled in the back of Stella's throat.

The scarlet storm clouds flashed into Stella's mind, plummeting towards her, flashing with lightning. Fury? Pieces of him?

She wrapped her arms around herself and hunched against the memory. Even if Tamar was wrong about Heather, she was right about one thing: Fury was dangerous.

Nimbus began to edge in the direction of the broch again, but Stella shook her head. "We can't! If that's Fury, he's . . . well, you saw!"

Nimbus came to an abrupt halt and rumbled.

"Seriously? Do you *want* me to get struck by lightning?!"

She shook her head at him and stomped back to the path.

"I'm going to Tamar's. If you want to go to the broch, that's your business, but I'm not coming! Not without Tamar."

Stella marched along in silence for a while.

Fury was dangerous. And if they saw Heather again? She wouldn't take no for an answer. Better not to see her at all. Not until they'd figured out what to do.

She glanced back. Nimbus had shaded to a sulky grey, but at least he was following.

* * *

She was scared that Nimbus might start sparking again at Tamar's, but to her relief, he seemed more subdued than angry.

I'll talk to Tamar, she promised him. *Just help me finish the shawl first.*

Right now, she couldn't imagine anything that might persuade Tamar. But at least if they were weaving, she'd have time to think.

Tamar showed Nimbus how to slide between the shining lines of midnight sunbeams, trailing the yarn behind him.

They started really carefully. Nimbus crept from one side to the other, then it was Stella's job to change pedals before he slid back to the other side. Sid took up the role of conductor, raising and lowering one spindly leg in time with the changing of the pedals. Even so, it took a while before they got into a rhythm with it.

Stella kept a close eye on her cloud, to make sure he didn't start sparking.

"Good!" said Tamar. "I'll leave you to it. But if he starts acting up, you stop straight away, yes? I'd rather fix a broken thread than a broken loom."

Stella nodded, feeling a little more confident now.

Thank you, Nimbus.

* * *

With Nimbus's help, the strip of fabric grew rapidly. Tamar came in at intervals, to wind the fabric onto the roller at the front, or swap the reel of yarn. She came in as Nimbus was nearing the end of the last reel. Stella held up a hand to let him know she was pausing on the pedals and turned to Tamar.

"So? What do you think?"

Tamar patted the fat roll of fabric and broke into a broad smile. "I reckon this is enough for a sea shawl!" she said. "I think you're done!"

"Should we finish this reel?"

Tamar shook her head. "Always good to keep a little in reserve."

Sid scampered along the top rail of the loom and cut the yarn.

With his sharp teeth. Stella tried to push the thought out of her brain as Sid scampered around the reel, winding up the loose end and tucking it in.

She ran her hand along the fabric with pride, feeling the tingle of magic in her fingertips. You couldn't see the glow now the sunbeams were woven into the fabric – just the faintest glistening hint beneath the green of the yarn.

"And you're absolutely sure it'll work?"

Tamar nodded. "Definitely. We'll be glad of that, if the Haken puts in another appearance."

Stella's eyes darted to Nimbus. *Heather. Not the Haken.*

Stella was certain now. She'd been silently talking it over with him while they were weaving, trying to figure out what had gone wrong. It was so obvious, when she realised.

"I've been thinking—" said Stella.

"Always dangerous!" said Tamar, with a smile.

"No, please listen. When Tas got her cloud back, she had to shout for it – call it, so it wouldn't make a storm."

Tamar nodded. "That's why we're bringing the novices to Winter's Keep."

"But we didn't do that! Heather wasn't—"

"Stop!" said Tamar, closing her eyes and holding up a finger. "I don't want to hear it." She let out an angry puff, then picked up a long pair of scissors and began to work her way laboriously across the warp lines, cutting the fabric free of the loom.

"But perhaps if—"

"*Perhaps if* you focus on the job in hand, we'll be able to get safely to Winter's Keep without adding another scar to my collection." Tamar pulled her hat off, revealing an angry red stripe across her scalp.

Stella stared at it in shock, then looked down at her hands. There was no arguing with that.

A sharp crackle broke the silence. Nimbus was floating at the side of the loom, looking distinctly off-colour. As she watched, he began to glow an ominous purple.

"Out, Nimbus!"

The little cloud dashed for the door, just as the first blinding spark of lightning ignited inside him.

"That was close!" said Tamar, leaning forward to inspect the side of loom. "Honestly, I don't know what's got into him lately."

Stella knew. Only too well.

"I'm going to go and check he's okay," she said, getting up with a heavy sigh.

Tamar nodded and Stella headed outside.

Nimbus was a little way up the hill, moving to and fro, as though he was still weaving. Stella moved closer, but stopped as he lit up again.

Please don't be angry. I'll talk to her again. I promise.

The little cloud didn't give any indication that he'd heard her. Instead, he began to move steadily up the hill. There was a strange heaviness to his movement – as though he was being dragged.

Stella frowned in concern and followed. "Nimbus?"

Still no response. "Tamar?" she called. "There's something wrong with Nimbus."

Tamar appeared in the doorway, holding an empty reel in her hand. "He's swallowed some yarn," she said, staring up the slope with a distinct air of disapproval.

"No. He wouldn't!"

"He's done it before."

"Only the once!"

"Look at the colour of him," said Tamar.

Stella looked at Nimbus. Purple, whorls of yellow, and yes, a definite tinge of green.

Oh, Nimbus!

"It would explain why he's got a belly-ache," said Tamar.

"Could it hurt him?"

"No. But too much magic makes it harder to control the lightning. Fury was always like this – sparking for no good reason."

Stella looked at her cloud in concern. He was almost at the top of the slope now. "How do I make him better?"

"Take him somewhere quiet and get him to fire a few lightning bolts – that should do the trick. Or you just wait it out. Serves him right, the greedy so-and-so!"

Stella shook her head. Tamar was never big on sympathy, but that was just unkind.

It might not even be his fault! She didn't think Nimbus would have swallowed yarn on purpose. Once, yes, but not now. Maybe he swallowed some by accident while they were weaving? She had pushed him to go faster.

Maybe it's my fault.

Nimbus had stopped at the top of the slope. He was looking really sorry for himself – a dirty smudge above the bright grass, lurching from side to side as though he'd lost his balance.

Stella walked towards him and held out a hand. "Come on, Nimbus," she said, softly.

"Stay away from the beach!" called Tamar. "I've put more cairns up, but I don't want to risk it."

Stella looked back and nodded. She had no desire to run into Heather. Especially not with Nimbus like this.

Eighteen

A SERIOUS
BELLY-ACHE

SHE led Nimbus up to the top of the headland, talking softly to him all the while. "It's not your fault. I know you didn't mean to. We'll just go up here, where you can let it out. You'll feel better then."

When they reached the top of the hill, Nimbus started down the far side. He was still moving really weirdly – caterpillar-fashion – stretching out thin, then edging forward until he was round again.

"Right here is fine. There's nobody around. We'll just fire a few bolts and you'll feel loads better."

She hoped it would be that easy . . .

Nimbus continued determinedly down the slope and she frowned. "Nimbus! Stop!"

Then, she began to run.

Nimbus was having some sort of convulsion – rolling and twisting in the air, violent and fast. As she caught up to him, he stretched, elongating into a figure of eight, then split in two. She stared at the twin clouds.

One of them glowed a murky purple.

The other drifted towards her, gold and peach; obviously pleased with himself.

"What did you do!" she whispered.

Nimbus settled light as a feather around her shoulders.

Together they watched the thundercloud he'd ejected. It fizzed and sparked for a moment, before simmering down to gunmetal grey.

What was it Tamar had said? *Fury was always like this – sparking for no good reason.*

But it couldn't be. If Fury still existed at all, he was trapped in the broch . . . Wasn't he?

The scrap of cloud flashed twice, like a beacon, then began to slide inexorably towards the broch, as though drawn by a magnet.

"Nimbus? Is that a piece of Fury?"

Nimbus glowed smugly and swooped after the scrap of cloud.

He swerved around it, blocking its path, herding it back towards Stella.

"You brought a piece of him with you?"

She watched the scrap of thundercloud warily. It seemed to have settled down now. There was no sign of the wild violence they'd seen inside the broch. If anything, it looked confused – drifting slowly from side to side whenever Nimbus blocked its path.

"What are we going to do, Nimbus?"

Nimbus set off jauntily in the direction of the broch. The other cloud followed, meek as a lamb.

"Nimbus, wait! We've got to think about this."

Nimbus slowed, but he didn't seem interested in waiting.

"We can't go down there. Heather is down there. What if she attacks us again!"

Nimbus let out a clap of thunder and Stella jumped. She put a hand on her racing heart. "What are you saying? She won't? Or that she didn't last time?"

Nimbus paled hopefully and herded the small thundercloud back towards her.

"You feel sorry for Fury? Is that it?"

She did too, if she let herself think about it. *Ripped apart by howling winds.*

It must have hurt.

She frowned. Hurt animals could be vicious, she knew that. What if it were the same with clouds? Maybe Fury was in pain. Maybe that's why he'd lashed out.

But how do you mend an injured cloud?

Tamar probably knew, but there was no way she'd help. She'd made her mind up: Heather was out for revenge. As far as Tamar was concerned, the subject was closed.

Stella's stomach twisted with guilt. She'd promised Heather she would help . . . And if Fury had been hurt by being torn apart, he was probably still hurting now – maybe he had been all this time.

Nimbus set off down the hill again, gently guiding the other cloud along with an occasional nudge.

* * *

"This is a bad idea, Nimbus. This is a very bad idea."

Nimbus had grown tired of shepherding the scrap of thundercloud and rolled him up inside again. She could recognise the difference now – swirls of other colours that didn't belong. No wonder Nimbus had been acting weird these past few days.

They were getting close to the beach. Stella looked at the fringe of grass along the cliff edge and gnawed her lip. Would Heather be waiting? Did she know what had happened? What use was it, bringing only a fragment of her cloud?

Heather will blame me.

When Nimbus reached the edge, he plunged off the cliff, disappearing out of sight, and Stella's heart leapt into her mouth.

"Wait for me!"

When she got to the edge, she knelt and looked over. Nimbus had settled on the beach below. Stella ducked back out of sight, her heart racing.

He wasn't alone.

* * *

Stella scrambled over the rocks, careless of the sharp shells and deep pools. When she reached the hidden cove, she slowed.

Nimbus had settled next to Heather and she was smoothing him. Stella's hands stung as the salt water found its way into scratches. Her blood sang a high-pitched note of fear, but she moved closer. No way she was leaving Nimbus alone with the sea witch.

Heather looked up at Stella, her face cold.

"I thought you weren't coming back."

Stella swallowed; her breath sharp in her throat after the long sprint.

Come away from her, Nimbus.

Heather narrowed her eyes. "You weren't, were you?"

"We tried! We tried to let Fury out, but the lightning . . . Tamar got hurt, and—"

"So, you decided to leave him there."

Heather ran her fingers through Nimbus, leaving little trails of blue.

Stella clenched her fists. "Show her, Nimbus."

Nimbus floated up a little away. Heather's eyes were fixed on him as he unrolled, revealing a small dark heart. The fragment of cloud drifted free, spitting and sparking.

Heather's mouth fell open.

"It's just a piece of him," said Stella, helplessly. "There are lots of pieces."

Heather stood, the water streaming off the slick black skin of her wetsuit. She reached up. The scrap of cloud continued to flicker. It was just like when Tas first saw Arca before he'd been released from the gem's control. There was no recognition; no moment of reunion. Stella watched Heather slide from realisation to despair and her heart ached for her.

Then, Heather closed her mouth in a determined line and turned to Stella.

"We need all of him."

Her dark eyes bored into Stella's and Stella took a nervous step backwards.

"Please!" Heather gestured towards the little cloud. "Look at him! I can't bear it." Her voice was shrill with desperation.

It made Stella want to rush over and put an arm round her, reassure her that they'd help. Of course, they'd help!

But what if Tamar's right? What if she's nothing like me. What if she is out for revenge?

It was confusing.

"I saw the Great Hall," said Stella. "They've mended it to look like a lightning bolt."

"So?"

"Velda used you as the excuse to ban all storm clouds!"

Heather's face hardened and she shrugged. "She didn't need an excuse to take Fury."

"People were hurt, Heather!"

"Then they shouldn't have tried to separate me from my cloud! You wouldn't give your cloud up without a fight. Would you?" She looked pointedly at Nimbus, and Stella beckoned him away. Heather scowled. "You know you wouldn't."

"I wouldn't *hurt* people!"

"You hurt me."

Stella swallowed. That was true. But she'd been protecting everyone; protecting Grandpa and Tamar, Nimbus too.

"I don't want to hurt anyone," said Heather. "I just want to be with my cloud."

Stella sighed. She really wanted to believe that was true.

She looked up at the two small clouds.

I can't tell, Nimbus. What's the right thing to do? Do you trust her?

Nimbus drifted back across the rocks towards Heather. He settled next to her and leant against her leg. Stella's heart pinched with jealousy, but she squashed it down.

That was a definite 'yes'.

Nineteen

RELEASE

"IF I help you, you have to promise not to hurt anyone," said Stella. She was pacing up and down on the sand, her feet as restless as her thoughts.

"Cross my heart," said Heather.

"Not even Velda?"

Heather scowled briefly, but then nodded. "Not even Velda."

Was this a good idea? When she and Tamar had first fought the Haken, the sea witch had brought a whole skyful of clouds – clouds she'd forced to be her army.

Why was Stella making deals with someone who mistreated

clouds? Didn't that make Heather just as bad as Velda?

"You have to release all the clouds you've trapped."

"The ones at Winter's Keep?" said Heather. "I didn't trap them. Velda did."

"No," exclaimed Stella. "The ones in sea caves, under the sea! The army of clouds you used to attack us in the battle. You have to set them all free."

Heather frowned in confusion. "What sea caves? I haven't trapped any clouds!"

"Tamar said—"

But Tamar had been wrong about a lot of things lately.

Stella changed tack. "How did you get them to fight for you, then?"

Heather spread her hands, the sun glinting on her scales. "I asked them!"

"What? And they just agreed? To attack the broch? With all of us inside!"

"No! They agreed to help me release my cloud."

"They threw hail at us, lightning, tried to drown us . . ."

"They were trying to rescue Fury. That's all."

Heather looked up at the little fragment of cloud Nimbus had rescued. He'd calmed down now. Each time he began to move towards the broch again, Nimbus nudged him back to Heather. Right now, he was drifting back and forth, following the motion of the waves. Her eyes softened as she lifted one green-scaled arm, trying to entice him closer.

"You tried to take Nimbus," accused Stella. She couldn't forgive that.

Heather glanced quickly at Nimbus, then out to sea, remembering. "For a moment, he reminded me of Fury." She shrugged. "When I realised he wasn't, I thought maybe I could use him – to bargain with you."

Nimbus backed away from the sea witch. He drifted across to Stella and she curled a protective arm around him. "You don't bargain with someone's cloud."

"I know."

For a moment, Heather's head dropped in shame, but then her jaw clenched and she looked up, her eyes fierce. "Except that's exactly what *you're* doing, isn't it?"

Stella stared at her. "No!"

"My cloud is trapped," said Heather. "Trapped!"

She bared her teeth and looked longingly towards the broch. "It's the worst thing you can do to a cloud. And you're still bargaining about whether to let him go free!"

* * *

It's the right thing to do, Stella told herself, as she walked to Grandpa's. *Isn't it, Nimbus?*

Nimbus bobbed once and she clenched her fists, trying to gather her courage.

"It's not like anyone else is going to help her. And we can't leave Fury trapped in there! It's cruel."

Nimbus swirled with frost at the thought of it.

Stella nodded. She could see now, how Heather might have convinced other clouds to fight for her. The idea of a trapped cloud horrified Nimbus.

She just hoped Grandpa would forgive her for what she was about to do.

They approached the house from the back, slowing down as they got closer. "Go and check," she told Nimbus. "Make sure he's not around."

Nimbus swooped on ahead and did a swift loop of the house, pausing at each window. She waited until he flew back to her, and then carried on.

* * *

Heather was waiting in the deep water, just beyond the shelving rocks below the broch. When she saw Stella approaching, she slithered up onto the edge of the furthest slab.

"Did you get it?" she asked, her eyes shining with hope.

Stella nodded. She felt a bit queasy about what she'd done.

Grandpa would definitely be angry. Not only because she'd taken his hammer, but because she was taking a massive risk.

"You swear you won't hurt anybody?" said Stella.

"I swear on my cloud," said Heather. Stella nodded, satisfied.

She just hoped the sea witch would do her part.

"I'm going to bring the gem out here and you have to call for him. Shout his name. He's going to be angry and confused. You need to let him know you're here. Okay?"

Heather nodded, tensing in discomfort as the sanctuary song swelled again. She had come as close as she could. Stella could see it was paining her. Every time the wind carried the sanctuary song towards them, she flinched slightly, her fingers stiffening and curling. But for their plan to work, Stella needed Heather close. As close as she could bear to be.

As Stella turned to go, Heather reached up and caught her arm. "Thank you."

There was such a weight of emotion in her words that Stella didn't know how to respond. Instead, she hefted the Trowie hammer in her hand and nodded, then headed up the path to the broch, Nimbus following close behind.

* * *

Each deep crack of the sanctuary stone was filled with silver – a shining star in the heart of the great stone tower. Stella crouched next to it, trying to ignore the song that emanated from it; a song of fighting, courage and of banishing sea witches.

She beckoned to Nimbus. "Time to break it again," she said. "But as soon as I've found the gem, you mend it. As fast as you can! Ready?"

If Heather kept her word, and left them alone, Tamar would

never even know the gem was gone. It would be like nothing had ever happened.

She waited for a moment, until she heard Heather calling to Fury, her shout sharp-edged and keening, then she nodded at Nimbus.

The little cloud settled in the centre of the silver star.

Stella looked up the broch as the magic began to melt away. "Don't hurt us, Fury!" she called. "We're here to release you. Go to Heather! She's calling for you. Can you hear her?"

* * *

The broch felt different now – emptier.

Either it was working and Fury was listening, or he wasn't here at all and Heather had lied to her again. Stella wasn't sure which one was scarier.

Without the sanctuary song, the huge stone tower felt hollow and desolate – fear pushed its way inside.

Nimbus lifted off the stone, revealing the shattered pieces, separate once more.

He hovered close by as Stella hurriedly searched for the gem.

Should have brought a torch, she thought, squinting into the dark gap in the centre. But there'd been no time for planning.

She shoved her fingers deep into the cracks and felt about, mud and grit wedging themselves under her nails.

And then she felt it – a sudden round smoothness. She scrabbled at the gem until it came loose, and carefully pulled it out.

Stella wiped it on her jumper, then turned it round in her hand. The gem was larger than the one that had trapped Tas's cloud and it looked older; its surface pitted and scored. When she held it up to the light, it shone; glowing like a milky rainbow. Was it her imagination, or was something moving in the centre of it? A fragment of cloud.

The wind moaned and there was a fluttering high overhead. Stella looked up. Tiny birds were streaking out of the walls of the broch – storm petrels, disturbed from their hidden nests. They circled Nimbus in a whirl of hurried wingbeats, then streamed out of the top of the tower. Wisps of cloud were emerging from the ancient stone wall – some of them weaving to and fro, clearly confused – four of them flickering with threat.

Stella's breath hovered shallow in her chest. "Don't hurt us," she whispered. "Heather's here. She's right outside."

Could they understand her? They hadn't attacked, but that didn't mean they wouldn't.

She gave Nimbus a silent instruction and got cautiously to her feet. Nimbus hovered lower over the stone. A shining drop of magic fell, then another, then a trickling stream, a glowing line of silver cutting through the shadows. After a moment, a whisper of courage crept into Stella's bones. The sanctuary song was returning.

The fragments of cloud circled closer and she watched them warily.

No sudden movements!

She backed cautiously away through the low stone tunnel until she was outside, blinking in the sudden brightness.

"Where are you, Heather?" she whispered. "I've got it!" She held the gem above her head and looked around urgently. Where was she?

There was a loud splosh as Heather pulled herself up onto the furthest slab of rock. She bared her teeth in a grimace and the spines stood out sharp on her knuckles. It was clearly paining her to be this close to the sanctuary stone's song.

Maybe they should have left the stone silent? At least until Fury was released. But it had felt too risky. And was too late now.

"Call your cloud!" instructed Stella.

"Fury! I'm here!" shouted Heather. "Come to me!"

Stella nodded. "Keep doing that." She knelt and put the gem on a rock.

The first blow of the hammer glanced off the gem, striking a spark from the stone beneath and sending the gem bouncing across the ground. She hurried after it, snatched it up and looked around for somewhere secure to wedge it.

Dark cloud was beginning to seep out of the doorway of the broch now, following the gem. It snaked across the ground towards Stella like smoke.

Get it right this time!

She found a narrow gap in one of the large slabs and knelt down to try again. She lined up her swing carefully, practising the motion several times, then brought the hammer down hard.

Clink!

The gem broke and a wisp of cloud flew free.

Stella watched it spiral up into the sky, her heart rising with it. But as it neared the top of the broch, her eyes widened and she scrambled to her feet. The tall curved walls of the broch were leaking cloud, like upwards waterfalls, flowing out of every gap between the stones.

Surely this couldn't all be Heather's cloud?

Stella's coat flapped and she stumbled as a surge of wind came barrelling down the hill and shoved her towards the sea. She glanced back. Heather had retreated into the water, driven back by the sanctuary song. Around her, the waves were whipped white by the biting offshore breeze.

"You've got to keep calling him!"

Heather raised her arms and opened her mouth, but Stella could barely hear her now – her urgent shriek was lost in the howl of the wind.

Stella glanced back at the broch and her breath froze in her throat. It looked as though the stone itself was smouldering – every gap a pouring stream of darkness. Overhead, a mass of thundercloud was pooling and spreading, flickering sickly yellow, each flash brighter than the last.

Fury.

"Nimbus! Get out of there! We've got to go."

The little cloud popped out of the doorway as a crackling arc of lightning sizzled up out of the stone tower. A tremendous boom of thunder shook the air, the sheer volume of it making Nimbus shudder as he sped towards her.

Far away up the hillside, someone was running towards them, a flash of frenzied purple against the green.

Tamar, realised Stella, with a rush of dread.

Twenty

THE STORM TO END ALL STORMS

STELLA felt her hair begin to rise, floating away from her head, suddenly weightless, then Nimbus was diving towards her.

He made it just in time, arcing over her head in a protective bubble as the lightning crashed down.

Stella wrapped her arms around herself and scanned the sea anxiously.

Where was Heather?

Had Tamar scared her away? Or had she changed her mind,

and decided to let Fury take his own revenge?

The bubble of cloud cover trembled around her as the rain began to fall, hard and unforgiving; hammering out the frustration of years of imprisonment. Lightning flashed again and thunder roared; a monster unleashed.

What have we done?

Tamar hurried inside the broch to check the sanctuary stone, then reappeared again a few moments later, her mouth taut with condemnation.

She took Stella's arm and dragged her roughly towards the path.

"Ow!" protested Stella, pulling her arm free. "Where are we going?"

"Where do you think?" snapped Tamar. "Away from here! This is going to be the storm to end all storms. We need to get to higher ground." She looked up through the cloud cover, her brow creased with worry, then strode on up the path.

Stella hurried after her.

* * *

Stella was puffing now, struggling to keep up with Tamar's punishing pace. "It'll get better," she said, trying to reassure herself as much as Tamar. "It did with Tas's cloud. She just needed to call him – get him under control."

Tamar whirled to face her. "What makes you think this cloud will ever be 'under control'?"

"Be-, because she—" stammered Stella.

"Because she said so?" Tamar's tone was sarcastic, her face dark with disappointment.

"Well, yes . . ."

"It won't," said Tamar, her voice full of cold certainty. "It's only going to get worse. Lightning? Rain? This is only the start."

"But when he calms down—"

"You think a cloud called Fury is going to CALM DOWN?!" yelled Tamar. "I can't believe you'd do something this stupid!"

Stella stumbled backwards, tears starting in her eyes, but Tamar wasn't finished.

"That bottled hurricane you used? Who do you think conjured it?"

Stella shook her head.

"Heather! It was the first wind she ever called."

"I didn't—"

"Sahara Sunshine? Why do think I always keep that?"

"For—"

"For protection against blizzards! Oh yes, she likes a good white-out, does Heather!"

"She won't—"

"Won't what? Drown us all? Blast us with lightning? Batter us with hail? No! Not if I've got anything to do with it."

"But she's not just a sea witch any more!" protested Stella, hoping desperately that was true. "She's back to herself again!"

"That's exactly what I'm afraid of," retorted Tamar.

By the time they reached Grandpa's, the wind had picked up into a steady gale. The rain hammered down relentlessly and the sky boomed with thunder.

They'd had to take down the cloud cover, for fear of losing their clouds. Nimbus was edging determinedly through the grass ahead of them, but Stella's heart skipped every time the wind picked up, fearful he'd be plucked from the ground and blown far away.

She leant forward into the wind, shielding her face with her arm, shivering as the wind drove rain inside her hood; it ran in cold rivulets down her back, sticking her clothes to her skin.

Grandpa was out the back, his oil slicker flapping wildly. He was hammering tent pegs into the ground, anchoring ropes over the chicken coop. The shed door banged wildly.

"Go and help him," shouted Tamar, over the wind. "Then both of you get indoors."

"What are you going to do?" said Stella.

"Nothing that concerns you," said Tamar, then turned her back on Stella and marched away.

"Go inside, Nimbus. Stay safe," said Stella. She hurried over to put an extra rock on top of the bin lid before it took flight. Grandpa turned as the bin lid clanged. He stood up, his face grim.

"Where is it?" he growled. "My hammer. Has Tamar got it?"

Stella's heart sank even further.

"No, it was me. I took it," she confessed. She shrugged off her rucksack, pulled the Trowie hammer out and held it out to him.

Grandpa took it and slotted it into a loop on his tool belt.

"I take it this is your doing, then?" he said, wincing as the rain lashed down.

Stella nodded.

"Here, help me with this," he said, throwing her a loop of rope. Stella caught it and ran round to the other side of the chicken coop – the side that wasn't yet anchored. There was no sign of the chickens. She hoped they were in the nesting box.

Stella looped the rope over the hook on the side and Grandpa hammered another tent peg into the ground. "Storm shutters next," he said, disappearing into the shed and reappearing with a big board. He turned it edge-on, so that the wind wouldn't tear it out of his hands and struggled across to the nearest window. Stella helped him lift it into place and turned the catches that held it there.

* * *

It was dark inside the house with the storm shutters up. Outside, thunder ranted and raged, and the wind was a constant howl. When he'd realised how drenched she was, Grandpa had run a hot bath for her, before heading into his room to peel off his own wet clothes.

The water was beginning to cool now, but Stella didn't want to get out. She wasn't under any illusion that the conversation was over. Grandpa was going to want to know everything. And he wasn't going to like it.

There was a tap at the door. "You going to be much longer? You'll turn into a prune if you don't get out soon."

Stella sighed and hauled herself upright, setting the water sloshing. "I'm getting out now."

When she came out, dressed in dry clothes and a thick jumper, there was a mug of hot chocolate waiting for her on the table. She pulled out a chair and sat down.

"So?" said Grandpa. "What have you been up to this time?"

"I released a storm."

Grandpa rolled his eyes. "I can tell that. I mean *exactly* what have you been up to? Why did you steal my Trowie hammer?"

"I didn't steal it. I only borrowed it. I was bringing it back."

"You didn't ask first," said Grandpa. "That's stealing in my book."

Stella looked down at the steam rising from her mug.

"Sorry," she said, in a small voice.

"What did you do with it?" said Grandpa. His voice was level; not nearly as angry as Tamar. But only because he didn't know what she'd done.

Stella sighed. "I found another trapped storm cloud. Here. In the broch. I had to let it go."

Grandpa shook his head. "I take it that's this storm, is it?" he said, gesturing at the front door, rattling in its frame. Stella nodded.

"And it's none too happy?"

"No." Stella bit her lips together. *My fault. This is all my fault.*

Nimbus drifted silently down from the top of the dresser and

175

settled on the table next to her, as though to remind her that they'd both done it. They were in this together.

Thunder crashed outside and rumbled all around, making her jump.

"It'll blow over," Grandpa reassured her. "All storms do. I've weathered worse. I'd guess this is what Broonie warned us about when he let Tassa's cloud go? You remember? She had to call her cloud. Then it calmed right down."

Stella nodded. She did remember. That's exactly what she'd hoped would happen.

"But . . . I don't know if this one is going to calm down," she admitted.

"Why not? Surely when it finds its weather weaver again . . ." He smiled hopefully.

Stella swallowed. "Its weather weaver is the sea witch, Grandpa."

All the colour drained from Grandpa's face. He pushed his chair back, stood up and began to pace up and down. "And you released it?"

Stella nodded.

"But why?!"

"Because it was trapped."

"Did you not think it might have been trapped for good reason?" said Grandpa, incredulously. "It didn't cross your mind that this might happen?"

"She promised it wouldn't."

"She . . . You *spoke* to her?!"

* * *

The following morning, the storm still hadn't calmed; neither had Grandpa. After his initial apoplectic reaction, he'd settled into a furious grumpy silence. If anything, it was worse.

Nothing Stella said could convince him that Heather was a girl first, and a sea witch second. And as the storm raged on, Stella was beginning to doubt it herself.

After Grandpa had growled and grumbled all through breakfast, Stella had retreated to her room. She was hoping to find some nugget of reassurance in the reference books she'd borrowed from Tamar but, so far, there was nothing. Every book was equally damning: sea witches cared nothing for the land, or the people on it. Their loyalty was only to the Teran.

Not one of them described sea witches as trustworthy, or peaceable, or even just different. They were inhuman. They were to be feared.

Most of the books were devoted to methods for driving sea witches away. None of them gave any suggestions about why a sea witch would want to attack in the first place. Stella wondered whether any of the writers had ever actually spoken to a sea witch – asked them.

She closed her eyes.

Please, Fury. Leave us alone. Go and find Heather. Go somewhere far from here.

If the storm outside could hear her, it gave no sign.

Twenty-One

PUSH BACK
THE TIDE

STELLA had moved to the front room. She was huddled in Gran's chair, under a blanket. The howling wind had sucked all the heat from the house. Right by the fire was the only place that was warm.

It didn't help that Grandpa had been constantly going in and out of the front door, checking on the chickens, piling extra rocks on the bins, checking the storm shutters. He didn't seem to feel the cold like she did. Either that, or he was doing it on purpose, to remind her quite how horrible the weather was outside. Currently, he was down at the jetty, checking that the boat hadn't broken its moorings.

He'd been gone for a while now and she was starting to feel nervous. If anything bad had happened to *Curlew*, he'd definitely blame her . . .

There was a loud hammering at the door and Stella leapt up to open it. Grandpa had said to bolt it after him – he didn't want it blown off its hinges – but he wouldn't be happy if she left him standing outside.

It wasn't Grandpa. It was Tamar.

Tamar glanced at Stella then pushed her way inside. Stella closed the door behind her. It bucked against her. She had to lean hard against it to slide the bolt back into place.

"Where's your grandpa?" said Tamar, taking off her coat and shaking water out of her hair.

"He's gone to check on the boat."

Tamar nodded. "Wise."

She pulled a large package out of her weather bag and dumped it on the table. "That's yours," she said. "We're going to need it."

Stella went over and unwrapped the brown paper parcel. Shimmering green spilled out across the table. Her sea shawl. The first thing she'd ever woven. She ran her fingers over the silky fabric. She wanted to feel happy about it, but she couldn't.

"Turned out alright, didn't it?" said Tamar, briskly. "Sid did a little tailoring for you, but you'll definitely want a brooch or something to hold it on. Don't want it blowing away."

Stella's eyes widened. Surely, Tamar couldn't mean—

There was a sharp knock at the door and she hurried across to open it for Grandpa. He came inside and wiped rain out of his eyes. "Tamar," he said. "Proper storm you two have cooked up this time!"

"Oh, it's nothing to do with me," said Tamar, glaring at Stella. "I think you'll find this is all your granddaughter's doing."

"Humph." Grandpa stripped off his coat and hung it on the peg. "So? What can we do for you?" he said, gruffly.

"Is your boat still afloat?" Tamar raised her eyebrows.

Grandpa nodded and cast a look at Stella that meant 'no thanks to you'.

"Good," said Tamar. "We need to get to Winter's Keep."

"In this!" exclaimed Grandpa. "You must be joking."

Tamar shook her head. "The storm is heading west, towards Winter's Keep," she said. "We need get there before it arrives."

Stella's eyes widened. *No! Heather promised!* She glanced up at Nimbus and he slid out of sight behind Gran's cookery books. There was only one reason the storm would be heading for Winter's Keep. Fury was going after Velda.

"*Curlew* is a sturdy little boat, but I'm not taking her out in this. We'll be swamped."

"No," said Tamar, with a smug smile. "We won't." She turned to Stella. "Because *you're* going to make sure of it." She patted the fabric on the table, meaningfully.

Stella shook her head, fear rising sour in the back of her throat. "I can't. I've never done it before! What if we sink?"

"The seas are too high," agreed Grandpa, putting a hand on Stella's shoulder.

"All the better to practise on," said Tamar, with a determined glint.

* * *

Grandpa refused to take them anywhere unless Stella could demonstrate that the sea shawl was as powerful as Tamar claimed, so they all traipsed down to the jetty, the wind and rain making every step a battle.

Stella was half-tempted to not even try. If she did it wrong on purpose, Grandpa would refuse to take them out and that would be the end of it. But there was another part of her curious to see if it would work.

She clutched the sea shawl tightly around her neck, the back of it flapping wildly.

"Reach out with one hand and command the water!" said Tamar, confidently. "Just like you would with your cloud."

In Stella's experience, asking nicely worked a lot better with her cloud, but she didn't argue. Under Grandpa's watchful eye, she joined Tamar, halfway along the jetty.

The wooden walkway juddered under her feet as another wave slammed into it, sending trembles up into her knees. *It's too strong. It won't listen.*

"Find your inner sea witch," said Tamar. "Shouldn't be too hard, given that you're *friends* with one now." Stella scowled, but Tamar was unrepentant. "You made this mess," she said. "Now fix it. We've got places to be."

Stella closed her eyes and frowned. It was hard to concentrate, with the jetty bucking under her feet and the wind whipping the shawl around. She gripped it tightly and held her other hand out in front of her.

Calm! she thought. *Be calm!*

"You have to say it out loud," said Tamar, impatiently.

Why didn't you just say that? thought Stella.

"Unless you're in the water, of course," added Tamar, "but I wouldn't recommend that. Not unless you *are* interested in turning sea witch?"

Stella wished Tamar would just get it over with and shout at her. It would be better than this poisonous mix of practical advice and cutting comments. It wasn't like Tamar to be spiteful. Not to Stella, anyway.

Stella glanced up at Grandpa, watching anxiously from the steps. She looked out at the churning waves beyond her fingertips and shouted. "Calm!"

The shout seemed to spread like a ripple, flattening every wave in its path. It spread out beyond *Curlew*, creating a pond of smooth water. Stella gaped at it, then glanced at Grandpa. His eyes were wide with amazement. He nodded at Stella, then turned to look again at the smooth water and shook his head in wonder.

"Calm enough for you?" said Tamar to Grandpa, with a wide smile.

Anxiety sprang back into Stella's chest. Would it work like that every time? How long could she keep it going? What if her shawl blew away when they were far from land? What if the boat sank?

"Impressive," said Grandpa. "Can you push back the tide, too?"

Tamar raised an eyebrow. "Best not run before she can walk, hey?"

Grandpa looked a bit flummoxed at that, and nodded. "Quite right."

"Can I?" asked Stella. "Push back the tide?"

Tamar turned towards Stella, her expression cooling. "Not today. You're on essential duties only, until I know I can trust you again. Now get packing. We leave in the morning."

Twenty-Two

KILT PINS

GRANDPA had lent her three kilt pins to keep the shawl in place. One probably would have been fine, but he'd been a bit alarmed when Stella explained what would happen if the shawl blew overboard during the crossing.

"Pin them through your jumper, too," he said, with an anxious frown.

"I have, Grandpa. Look." She tugged at the shawl. It wasn't going anywhere.

Not unless it takes me with it.

It wasn't a comforting thought. If a strong gust caught the

shawl, it might lift her right out of the boat. Nimbus settled around her shoulders and Stella shook her head at him. "You've got to get in the bag, Nimbus!"

The little cloud didn't move. He'd only been inside a weather bag once before and he didn't like it. But the wind hadn't calmed at all since yesterday – it was definitely too strong. He might be blown away. Last time that happened, it had taken ages for him to find his way back. She didn't want to risk it.

"Please. It's not safe. I don't want to lose you!"

Nimbus grumbled softly, but then slid down her arm and into her weather bag. "I'll let you out in the cabin, when we're onboard," she reassured him, before rolling the top closed.

* * *

Onboard *Curlew*, Grandpa refused to be hurried, despite Tamar's impatience to get going. He bent to check Stella's harness one more time. He was wearing one too – a strappy waistcoat of neon webbing straps. At the back was a long leash that clipped onto the boat. Stella didn't like it – it was uncomfortable and she kept getting the leash tangled. But Grandpa said it was non-negotiable.

Satisfied that she was clipped on properly, Grandpa moved on to checking the fuel gauge and making sure all the hatches were securely closed.

"All set, now?" said Tamar, drumming her fingers on the seat. She cocked her head for a moment, as though listening. "The sentinels say there's a gap opening up in the storm front, but we'll have to be fast to catch it."

Tamar had refused to wear a harness. She claimed it might interfere with her weather conjuring, but Stella knew the real reason: it might crush Sid. She'd spotted him clinging to the front Tamar's cardigan, silent and unmoving. With his silver legs and body, he looked like a large brooch.

Stella glanced at Grandpa – he obviously hadn't noticed. She gave the large spider a surreptitious wave. Sid raised one long elegant leg in a silent salute, then settled back into position.

At last, Grandpa was satisfied that everything was in order. He started the boat engine and undid the ropes connecting them to the jetty, then pushed the lever, putting the boat into gear. They moved slowly forward into the bay.

The calm water stayed with them. Stella twisted to look. It was weird. The water of the bay was choppy and confused – chunky green waves, topped with white caps. But around the boat was a circle of calm, like a pond. As the boat moved, the water flattened ahead of them, as though an invisible hand was ironing it flat.

At her side, the weather bag rumbled and Stella's eyes widened. "Nimbus! I forgot to let him out!" She got to her feet.

"I'll do it," said Tamar, standing up.

"Sit down, both of you!" said Grandpa.

"I'll only be a moment!" Stella stepped through the cabin hatch, but as she clambered down the steep steps into the cabin, the boat heaved suddenly, sending her tumbling to the bottom. "Ow!"

"Drop that bag and get back up here!" barked Tamar.

Stella tried, but the floor tipped. She grabbed the handle by the steps and clung on. Tamar reached down and hauled her up. Stella lurched out of the hatch and her insides turned to water. The waves were coming at them from all angles, tipping the small boat this way and that like a toy. Her stomach flipped.

Tamar grabbed Stella by the wrist and held her arm out. "Give it some orders!"

"Calm," yelped Stella. The movement of the boat settled a little.

"Calm!" she called, louder this time. A ripple of smoothness spread like ice over the sea.

"In case you'd failed to notice," said Tamar, "we need you up here, or we're in for a very rough crossing indeed. I'm just glad it happened in the bay."

Grandpa stared at Stella, his knuckles white on the tiller. He nodded in agreement with Tamar. "Definitely," he said. "Keep it up, whatever you're doing."

"I'll go and deal with Nimbus," said Tamar, making for the hatch. "You stay put."

Stella sat down heavily on the bench at the side of the cockpit, her stomach churning, and clutched the edge of her shawl in her free hand. It was going to be a long journey. She just hoped the sea kept listening.

* * *

After a couple of hours, all of them had relaxed a little. Even Grandpa felt confident enough to let Tamar take a turn at the tiller, while he brought the fenders in.

Tamar leant towards Stella. "Calm isn't the only command you can use," she said, quietly. "Useful, for right now, but it would be worth spending some time practising when we arrive. Build up a bit of a repertoire."

"Can't I practise now?" said Stella.

Tamar scoffed. "No!"

"Why not?"

Tamar rolled her eyes. "Freeze, rise up, whirlpool . . . You want to try those while we're afloat, do you?" She shook her head impatiently and leant back with a scowl.

Stella looked away towards Grandpa up on the foredeck and sighed. Tamar was still being cold and snappy – every instruction paired with a criticism. How long would it take for Tamar to stop being angry with her?

It wasn't *all* her fault. How was she supposed to know that Fury was nothing like Tas's cloud?

Not once had she pictured a storm that would last for days, never mind the gale-force winds! She'd imagined there might be a bit of thunder and lightning at first, but then . . . happiness. Surely Fury and Heather would be happy, being reunited after all this time?

She looked up at the narrow gap of blue sky, shining like a sliver of hope, between the looming black towers of cloud. "The weather's a *bit* better today," she pointed out. "Maybe Fury is starting to calm down?"

Tamar snorted. "Don't kid yourself," she said. "That cloud can rage for days. We're just lucky the sentinels spotted a gap."

* * *

"Are we nearly there yet?" said Stella.

She'd resisted asking for ages, but the sun was getting low in the sky now, and she did *not* like the idea of sailing through the night.

"Not long now," said Grandpa, with a smile. "Maybe another hour, if Tamar's directions are to be trusted."

Tamar didn't react to his jibe. She was staring off into the distance again.

Probably talking to her clouds, thought Stella, with a slight twinge of envy. *Wonder when I'll be able to do that?*

"Are you hungry?" asked Grandpa.

Stella nodded.

Grandpa dragged a cool bag from under his seat and produced three waxed paper packages of sandwiches and a flask of tea. "You want one?" he said to Tamar, giving her a nudge to get her attention.

"What?" said Tamar. She blinked rapidly, as though waking from a daydream.

"Sandwich," said Grandpa.

"Oh, yes!" said Tamar, taking it from him. "Just so you know, the weather's worsening up ahead, particularly around Winter's Keep. Nasty seas building up, too." She pursed her lips and levelled an accusing look at Stella.

Stella sighed.

"Please tell me there are some good anchorages?" said Grandpa.

Tamar nodded. "There's a harbour on the south side of the island." She tore a scrap of ham from the side of her sandwich and passed it to Sid. Stella's eyes widened and she glanced at Grandpa, but he still hadn't noticed. He was busy unwrapping his own sandwich.

"Now's probably the moment to tell you," said Tamar, "that you're not just here for your sandwich-making skills."

Grandpa narrowed his eyes. "What do you mean?"

"We've got a bit of a situation with the Trows," said Tamar. "I'm hoping you can talk some sense into them. Since they found out Velda broke the Cloud Covenant, they've been, er, hostile, shall we say?"

Grandpa shook his head and carried on shaking it. "No. No, no, no. No! Don't you try and get me involved in any of your weather-weaving politics. I'm just the boatman."

Normally, Stella would have stuck up for him. But this was too important.

"Grandpa, we need their help to let the storm clouds go."

Grandpa growled unhappily. "What makes you think they'll listen to me? The good folk are a law unto themselves. You don't *negotiate* with them!"

"A little catch-up," said Tamar. "An evening of banter. That's all I'm asking. Remind them we're not all like Velda."

Grandpa crossed his heart with a soft mutter.

"And whatever you do, don't do that!" said Tamar.

* * *

The seas were much heavier on the far side of the mainland. Great steep ridges, fringed with white. Stella could smooth the water, but she couldn't flatten the waves – they were too big. Her stomach rolled as the boat nosed higher and then dipped down another long blue hill of water. She swallowed hard and gripped the edge of the bench.

"North Atlantic rollers," said Grandpa, looking at her in sympathy. "You'd need an iron stomach not to be bothered by these."

"I don't understand why the shawl's not working?" said Stella.

Tamar chuckled. "There's an ocean of power behind these. It'd take a lot more than one sea shawl to slow them down."

Ahead of them, a heavy mass of storm cloud loomed, stained scarlet by the setting sun. Beneath the storm, a grey smear of rain blurred the sky into the sea and the island flickered in and out of sight, like a mirage – a jagged fortress of dark sea stacks, gaping caves, and towering cliffs.

Winter's Keep, thought Stella. *Looks about as friendly as Velda.*

"Is that the entrance, there?" said Grandpa, pointing to a dark gap in the towering cliffs ahead of them.

Tamar nodded. "Keep to the right."

Grandpa nodded and turned the boat. Stella closed her eyes and breathed through her nose, wishing she'd turned down the sandwich.

The motion of the boat changed as they entered the harbour. Stella opened her eyes to see huge black cliffs sliding past them on either side. On the left of the narrow channel, the water licked around sharp rocks. Grandpa was giving them a wide berth.

The weather had calmed too – the rain stopping abruptly at the harbour entrance. From inside, it looked like a waterfall. Barely more than a whisper of breeze moved within the high cliffs that encircled them.

"Can Nimbus come up now?" she asked Tamar.

Tamar nodded. "Sure. The weather is pretty constant here – at least when the council are in residence."

Stella slid open the hatch to the cabin. "Nimbus? We're here."

The little cloud popped out of the hatch and flew vertically upwards.

"Not too high!" called Stella. She wasn't sure how far the council's influence extended.

The channel widened into a stone walled harbour, packed with boats. The quayside bustled with people, despite the late hour. The seafront was lined with colourful stands that looked much like the stalls she'd seen at the weather market.

Excitement tiptoed into Stella's chest. Not long now until

she'd see her friends again – Tas, Magnus too. She smiled at Grandpa and smoothed out the sea shawl where it had rucked up under her harness.

We made it!

Twenty-Three

REUNION

"STELLAAAAAAHH!"

Grandpa had barely turned off the engine before Tas was bowling down the jetty towards them, arms waving, hair flying, screaming at the top of her lungs. Stella leapt to her feet and climbed up on the side of the boat, only to be yanked back by her harness.

"Hold your horses!" said Grandpa. "Let me get you unhooked, unless you want to end up dangling over the side?"

Stella wriggled impatiently as Grandpa helped untangle her from the webbing straps. The instant she was free, she bounded over the side of the boat and into Tas's arms.

"YAAAY! Storm sisters! Together again!" yelled Tas, jumping up and down. The jetty juddered and bounced beneath their feet, setting all the boats gently rocking. "We're going to have so much fun."

Stella laughed and hugged her tight. "I've missed you."

"Not as much as I've missed you. Aw, look at the three of them!" Tas pointed up. Nimbus, Arca and Drench were spinning around one another in a series of high-speed loop-the-loops. All three clouds glowed like golden puffs of pure joy in the deepening twilight.

"So happy!" said Stella, smiling up at them. She hadn't seen Nimbus look this cheery since the Gathering.

One of the little clouds set off towards the harbour at high speed, swiftly pursued by the other two. "Wait for us, Arca!" called Tas. "We're coming!"

Stella glanced back at Tamar and Grandpa, to check that was alright.

Tamar nodded. "Go on, then. I've got a few things to sort out. But I want you back here in an hour. You needn't think I'm carrying your bags for you."

Grandpa looked up from tying the ropes and smiled. "Good to see you again, Tassa."

"You too, Stella's Grandpa. We'll see you in a bit," said Tas, already towing Stella away down the jetty towards the quayside. "That's where I'm staying, with the storm novices." She pointed. "I'll introduce you later – you'll like them. Oh no, hold on!"

Ahead of them, Arca had swooped into a narrow alleyway, swiftly followed by Drench and Nimbus. Tas dodged between the row of stalls on the quayside and hurried after them. "Arca! Don't you get me in trouble again!"

There was no sign of the three clouds when Stella got to the alley. *Come back, Nimbus! Don't leave us behind.*

Nimbus reappeared around a corner, looking slightly sheepish. The other two clouds followed him, Drench darting cheerfully towards Tas. Arca followed reluctantly.

Tas put her hands on her hips. "Seriously, Arca?" The little cloud trailed after Nimbus and Drench, sparkling with frost.

"Has something scared him?" asked Stella, in concern.

Tas shook her head. "No. He's a blizzard cloud. He does that when he's thinking of icing someone."

Stella stared at him in alarm and Nimbus darted to her side.

Tas shook her head. "Not today, Arca."

The little cloud slunk towards them, dropping a trail of sleet as he came. He floated sulkily to the mouth of the alleyway where Drench waited.

"Good," nodded Tas. "You and Drench wait here. We won't be long." She gave Arca a firm look. He slid from side to side, clearly in a combative mood. "I mean it!" said Tas, levelling a finger at him. "Come on, we'd better be quick," she said to Stella.

"Where are we going?" asked Stella as Tas tugged her forward.

"To see Magnus."

"He's here?" said Stella, with an excited smile.

"Yeah. I haven't spoken to him yet, but I've seen him. We'll have to be sneaky about it, though. He's staying with his mum."

Stella stopped abruptly. "Velda's here?" A shiver scampered up her neck.

"Yup."

"I thought she'd be in prison, or something?"

Tas snorted. "Pfft! No. Weather weavers don't do prison. She's in disgrace. Lost her place on the council. But she's refused to step down as head of the Ice Weavers. Officially, she has to, now she's off the council, but . . ." She shrugged. "It's Velda. She was never going to go quietly. She's blocking the release of the storm clouds."

It was so wrong!

Velda had lied to everyone; trapped who knew *how* many clouds; broken the Cloud Covenant . . . How did she still get to have a say?!

"But the council promised they'd be released!" exclaimed Stella. "I thought it was all agreed? Why do they need Velda at all? They should just let them out."

Tas rolled her eyes. "You make it sound easy," she said. "But nobody gets into Winter's Keep without an invitation. Not even the council."

Stella stomped along in silence. *Stupid Velda. Stupid council. Stupid everyone.*

It didn't need to be like this. It should be simple!

"Here we are." Tas pointed up at a two-storey stone building.

It looked older and grander than the adjacent buildings, set back from the street, behind a tall stone wall. Along the top of the wall, a frieze of weather symbols was carved into the stone – suns, snowflakes, rainclouds, sheaves of wheat, swirls of wind, and lightning bolts.

"*This* is Winter's Keep?" said Stella, unimpressed. It didn't look that hard to get into.

Tas laughed and shook her head. "No. This is the back of the council building. Winter's Keep is up the hill. You'll see. It's a proper fortress." She reached up and put her hands on the top of the wall. "Give me a leg up."

Stella glanced up. The wall was taller than head height, but not impossibly high. She laced her fingers together and hoisted Tas up.

Tas scrambled onto the top and straddled it. "Perfect. Thought so. No guards on this side." She grinned.

"Guards?" said Stella, looking up at Tas suspiciously. This wouldn't be the first time Tas had led her into trouble.

"Don't sweat it. They're not to keep people out. Their main job, right now, is to make sure Velda stays put. Up you come." She held out her hands. Stella grasped them and climbed up, her toes finding purchase on the rough stone.

The top of the wall was wide and flat. On the other side, the courtyard was a pool of shadow. Stella peered across it and smiled. "Magnus is definitely here."

The building on the far side of the courtyard was smothered

in climbing roses, their perfume filling the cool evening air with a heady sweetness.

Nimbus floated over the wall and across the courtyard.

"Nimbus, wait!" she hissed.

The little cloud ignored her, nosing along the green wall. He seemed to be searching for something. He stopped at one of the second-floor windows, gave a soft rumble, and bumped against the glass determinedly.

"Nimbus! We're meant to be being sneaky!"

The window opened and a mass of cloud poured out, briefly enveloping Nimbus. A riot of rosebuds burst into bloom as the big cloud tumbled down the wall. Stella grinned.

Briar – it couldn't be anyone else.

A curious face leant out of the window and peered down at the two clouds frolicking below. Magnus broke into a smile. "Nimbus? Is that you?"

Stella waved to catch his attention and Magnus's smile widened. "Stella! What are you doing up there?"

Stella shrugged. "Looking for you. Can we come down?"

Magnus glanced behind him and shook his head. "Better not. Stay there. I'll come round." He disappeared inside and closed the window.

Stella and Tas slid back down into the alleyway. Soon there was a crunch of hurried footsteps on gravel and Magnus jogged round the corner. He frowned briefly at Tas. "Where's Arca? You didn't bring him?"

"No. Left him down at the harbour." Tas gestured over her shoulder with her thumb.

Magnus nodded and turned to Stella with a smile. "Hello, Sparky! It's good to see you." His gaze settled on her green shawl and his eyes widened. "Don't tell me I've turned you into a Verdure Weaver?"

Stella laughed and shook her head. "No danger of that. The best I've managed is helping Grandpa water his veg patch."

"So? What's with the green?" he said, reaching out to touch the fabric of the shawl.

"It's my first weaving project," said Stella. "A sea shawl." She looked down at it, suddenly embarrassed about the line of kilt pins and the crumpled fabric. "I didn't have time to finish it properly."

"It looks awesome!" said Tas, firmly. "A masterpiece of weaving!"

Stella's cheeks heated up slightly. "I don't know about that . . ."

"What does it do?" asked Magnus, peering at it curiously.

"Calms the sea," said Stella. "I mean, other stuff too, but I haven't really had a chance to practise yet."

"Nice!" said Tas. "Check you out – master of the seas – weather weaving like a pro."

Magnus shook his head and laughed softly. "Mum's got completely the wrong end of the stick as usual," he said.

Stella frowned. "About what?"

"She told me you'd turned sea witch, like Tamar's last apprentice. I mean, I didn't believe her, but it *is* good to see you're still you."

200

"Hah!" Tas guffawed with laughter. "Stella turning into a sea witch. Good one!"

"That's just one of her theories. She's convinced everyone's out to get her – you two, the Haken, the council, the Trows . . . you name it." Magnus looked at the ground and there was an awkward moment of silence.

Tas glanced at Stella and raised her eyebrows: *Change the subject!*

"Have *you* done any weaving yet?" Stella asked Magnus.

He looked up and shook his head. "Silvan was going to start me on camouflage, but then we got called here." His lips twitched. "Mum's insisting I stay with her, but she's done nothing but complain about Briar since we arrived."

"Why?" asked Tas. "He's such a sweetie!"

Magnus shrugged. "You saw the courtyard. There's not much space. They've had to cut it back twice. And whenever they chop it down, Briar rains indoors in protest."

Tas chuckled and Stella smiled sympathetically. "Couldn't you ask to stay with Silvan? I'm guessing he must be somewhere with green space?"

Magnus nodded. "Yep. The Verdure Weavers are camped up on the hillside. Silvan's mostly been stuck in council meetings, though. Anyway, it's hard to say no to Mum."

Stella nodded. She could imagine. Hardly anyone could say no to Velda. It must be even harder if she was your mum.

"You can hang out with us tomorrow, if you like?" said Tas.

"You might not be a Storm Weaver, but if you got Stella through the quest, you can't be all bad."

"Er, thanks, I think?" said Magnus.

"Magnus!" The shrill shout came from one of the highest windows. "Get in here!"

All three of them looked up.

Velda stared down, her eyes sharp with icy rage.

Magnus pulled a face. "Gotta go," he whispered. "Sorry. I'll catch you later." He jogged back the way he'd come.

Stella stared up at Velda, her heart boiling with resentment. There she was! The woman who'd threatened to separate her and Nimbus; who'd trapped so many other storm clouds. Nimbus let out a menacing rumble and flickered purple. He hadn't forgotten either.

"Both of you," Velda levelled an accusatory finger at them, "stay away from my son!" She disappeared back inside and slammed the window shut.

"Who does she think she is?" exclaimed Stella.

"Queen of blooming everything, clearly," shrugged Tas.

Twenty-Four

A FLASH OF PURPLE

BY the time they got back to the harbour, sunset had melted into twilight. Grandpa was unloading the last of the bags onto a trailer on the jetty. "There you are!" he said. "I was starting to worry."

Tamar appeared out of the cabin hatch. "Tas. You know the way to the Gate House?"

Tas nodded. "Yep."

"Then you and Stella can transport our bags," said Tamar.

"It's not close," said Tas, shifting from one foot to the other. "And it's up a big hill."

"Hence the trailer," said Tamar, with no trace of sympathy.

"Can't Grandpa help?" said Stella, looking hopefully at him.

"Leave them there," said Grandpa, with a smile. "I can deal with them when I'm back."

"Nonsense!" said Tamar firmly. "They're two fine strong girls with nothing better to do." Her eyes darted to the quayside. "They're coming. Are you ready?"

Grandpa slotted his Trowie hammer into his belt loop and nodded. "Now I am."

"Girls? Time to make yourselves scarce," instructed Tamar.

Stella turned to look and her heart skipped with nerves.

The Trows were hard to see – just a suspicion of movement in the gloom – yet the crowd melted away in front of them, some with a swift shudder or a fleeting look of confusion, as though some unseen force had nudged them aside.

They're from the ancient times of magic. Always treat them with respect.

Knowing how Velda had angered them, Grandpa's advice felt even more vital,

"Go now!" said Tamar.

It wasn't worth arguing. Stella picked up the handle of the trailer and began to tow it along the jetty. She felt the moment the Trows passed by – a sudden coldness that raised goosebumps up her neck.

Be safe, Grandpa.

"Is Tamar in a mood?" said Tas, as soon as they were safely out of earshot.

Stella nodded. "Been like that for days."

"Probably annoyed with the council?"

"Mm."

"Nervous about the good folk?"

"Maybe."

Neither of those were the reason for Tamar's mood. But she didn't want to tell Tas about the sea witch. Not yet. Not until she could explain properly. A busy quayside didn't feel like the place to do it.

"I hope I get to speak to the good folk at some point," said Tas.

Stella glanced at her sideways. "Why?"

"To say thank you," said Tas. "I wouldn't have got Arca back if they hadn't agreed to help."

"Let's hope they'll do the same for the rest of the storm clouds."

"Dunno," said Tas with a sigh. "Doesn't sound like it."

"It'll be alright," said Stella, nudging her. "Grandpa's going to talk to them. Besides, I'm not leaving until we see all the storm clouds released."

"That's my Stella." Tas grinned. "You know I'll be getting a front row seat?"

"How come?"

"I'm the only apprentice whose cloud has been released so far," said Tas. "So, I'm in charge of showing the novices how to do it."

"Cool!"

"That was your idea, wasn't it? Bringing them here?"

Stella nodded.

"Well, the council took your advice – transported a little crowd of them here. They'll be the first ones to get their clouds back."

"They're going to be so happy!"

Tas grinned. "I know. I can't wait. Look! There's some of them over there. Let me introduce you."

As Tas darted on ahead, Stella hung back a little, feeling shy. She wasn't sure why, but she'd pictured the novices as little children. These weren't children. All of them were older than her and Tas; some of them were practically grown-ups.

The novices were clustered in front of one of the food stalls.

Even though they didn't have clouds, most of them wore flashes of purple in their clothing, proudly marking themselves out as Storm Weavers – it was probably the first time they'd safely been able to do that.

Storm clouds might not be outlawed any more, but the presence of the storm novices had still created a bit of a stir. There was a definite gap around them, noticeable on the packed seafront – people were avoiding them.

They're afraid of us.

Velda's lies still lingered.

Stella had thought it would be over when she and Nimbus passed the trials. But convincing the council wasn't the same as winning over the entire weather-weaving community.

Tas waved Stella over. "Storm weavers? I'd like you to meet my very good friend *Stella*."

"Stella?"

"What, *the* Stella?"

Stella was suddenly surrounded; everyone patting her on the back, touching her shawl, jostling forward to shake her hand. Most of them were a good head taller than her and it rapidly began to feel claustrophobic. She gave Tas a wide-eyed glance.

"Alright, alright! Give her some air!" called Tas, but none of them paid any attention. "Some food, then? She's only just got here!"

Someone pressed a carton of street food into her hand. "Here. Have mine. I'll get another." And just like that, she was one of the group.

"Thanks!" Stella looked around at them, took a deep breath and smiled.

A black man with a square jaw and an easy smile stepped away from the group. He raised his arm and pointed. "Is that Nimbus?" he asked.

Stella looked up and her heart did a little flip. Nimbus was weaving rapidly towards them between the masts of the boats, shading gradually darker.

Hey! Stop that! I'm fine.

"Yep, that's Nimbus."

"You going to show us some lightning?" said a red-haired woman, watching the little thundercloud eagerly. "There's space. He could do it over the water."

Pretty sure that wouldn't go down well here, thought Stella, glancing along the crowded quay. She shook her head. "No. It's, er, only for special occasions."

Nimbus swooped down to float at her shoulder and let out a low rumble. Several faces turned towards them. Fingers pointed and people leant their heads together to whisper.

"I think I'd better take him somewhere less crowded," she said, backing away from the group. "But it was great to meet you. Thanks for the food!"

Tas grabbed the handle of the trailer and followed her. "Short and sweet," she called to the group. "I'll be back in a bit, alright?"

Stella tucked into the carton of food as they walked. It was bubble and squeak – a stodgy, comforting mash of sausage, leek and potato. *The sort of thing Gran used to make,* she thought with a smile.

She kept a close eye on Nimbus as they moved through the crowd, but to her relief he didn't rumble again. Maybe he'd just been reacting to her nervousness on meeting the novices. *Calm, from now on, okay?* she thought. *Like when we were at the Gathering.*

Towards the end of the quay, Tas turned into a quiet street. Stella dropped the empty carton in a bin by one of the stalls and followed.

As soon as they moved away from the crowded quayside, Nimbus relaxed. Before long, he'd goaded Arca and Drench into a high-speed game of rooftop tag.

Tas manoeuvred the trailer of bags through a maze of narrow cut-throughs until they reached a wide cobbled street. The houses on either side were crowded, huddled in a long higgledy-piggledy row, each propping up the next. With their small windows and sharp slate roofs, they looked braced for harsh winters.

"This way," said Tas. She nodded up the hill.

"You know your way around, then?" asked Stella.

Tas nodded. "Spent quite a lot of time here when I was first training with Flo. This is the fastest route out of town. After that, we take the coast path."

"Here, my turn," said Stella, taking the trailer handle from Tas.

She glanced up the street and let out a puff. "The novices are a bit intense."

"Storm Weavers – what do you expect?" Tas grinned. "But, hey! They all think you're a bit of a hero."

"I'm not," said Stella.

Tas shrugged. "You're the reason they're getting their clouds back."

"I thought they'd be our age – younger, even."

Tas shook her head. "The youngest one is two years older than me. The oldest?" she shrugged again. "I haven't asked. They've been waiting a long time for this. Some of them have had two or three storm clouds taken. That's probably why the council picked them."

"Two or three clouds?!"

Tas nodded. "Storm Weavers don't give up easy."

"But that must have been heart-breaking!" exclaimed Stella. "Hoping to catch a different kind of cloud each time, only to have it taken again?!"

Tas sucked her teeth and nodded. "Velda's got a lot to answer for."

And yet she's still in power, thought Stella, with a shiver. *Leader of the Ice Weavers.*

* * *

The coast path was long and steep, but at least it was wide and fairly flat – easier than the cobbled streets. Stella and Tas took turns hauling the trailer behind them. Outside town, the path was deserted, so Stella quickly filled Tas in on everything that had happened since the Gathering.

"—three days of thunder and lightning. Full-on gales, too. She *promised* she wasn't out for revenge, but then Tamar found out the storm was heading here."

"You think she's coming after Velda?"

"I hope not . . . Pretty sure Magnus would never forgive me."

Stella looked out to sea. The storm had moved away during the evening, revealing the lilac *simmer dim* sky, but a dark smudge of cloud marred the horizon. As she watched, it flickered ominously.

Tas followed Stella's gaze and her eyes widened. "What, you reckon *that's* the Haken's storm cloud?"

"Fury." Stella nodded. "Tamar thinks so. That's why she's mad at me."

"Wow!" said Tas, with a hint of admiration. "You've got a serious talent for trouble."

Stella pursed her lips. "I don't think that's a good thing, Tas."

As they crested the hill, Stella gasped.

"*That's* Winter's Keep!" Tas told her.

Ahead of them, the island seemed to have split, as though part of it had thought about falling into the sea, then changed its mind at the last moment.

Clinging to the top of the stony outcrop was a castle, its walls rising precipitously out of the rock. It looked like it had grown there. Narrow windows, like arrow slits, peered suspiciously down the hill. The walls were topped with spikes of ice.

"That does *not* look friendly."

"Told you it was a fortress," said Tas.

Between the main island and the castle was a deep chasm, bridged by a narrow arch of rock. Stella moved a little closer and peered over. The cliffs between were tall and craggy, dotted with nesting fulmars. Far below, waves surged and crashed in the narrow channel.

At the near end of the bridge was a wide building with a heavy pair of gates in the centre of it. "The Gate House," said Tas, nodding at it. "That's where you're staying."

Twenty-Five

THE GATE HOUSE

THE door was unlocked and Tas made short work of exploring the whole house. "First here, so you get to pick your bedroom," she called. Stella grabbed her bag and trotted up the stairs. The ceilings were low upstairs – attic space. Tas was standing in the doorway of the bedroom at the far end. "Ta dah!"

Stella looked in. It was a spacious room, with a double bed and windows on three sides. The craggy towers of Winter's Keep loomed large outside. She twitched her nose and shook her head.

"Oh, come on!" said Tas. "It's high class! Practically a flat all on its own!"

"With a massive view of the Castle of Doom!" retorted Stella.

She headed back down the corridor. Nimbus was exploring the room at the far end. There was a single bed and one narrow window that looked out over the sea. She smiled at the little cloud. "This one?"

Nimbus tucked himself onto the deep windowsill.

"That's settled then." Stella dumped her bag on the end of the bed.

Tas leant on the doorframe and looked around the small room with a disparaging expression. "This one? You sure?"

"Yeah. It's cosy. And Nimbus likes it."

She glanced across at Winter's Keep, over to the left. At least from here, it didn't feel like it was looking in at them.

Stella smoothed Nimbus and gazed out at the storm flickering over the sea. Tas joined her and gave her shoulder a friendly nudge. "You know that might *not* be Fury. There's been all sorts of weird weather since I got here."

Stella frowned. "I thought the council control the weather here?"

Tas chuckled. "So did they. But we had frost every day last week!"

Last week? That couldn't have been Fury.

"Everybody knows who's behind it," said Tas, shaking her head.

"Velda?"

Tas nodded and rolled her eyes.

"But if everyone knows it's her, why do it?"

"Flexing her wintery muscles? Embarrassing the council? I mean, it's not a good look, if you've got the whole council here, and you can't keep it sunny in the middle of summer! There's loads of talk around town about omens and portents – *unseasonal* weather."

"She's spreading fear," said Stella, with a sigh.

Tas nodded. "The council aren't buying it, though. Flo told me." She sat down on the narrow bed, bouncing to test it.

Stella sat down next to her. "I thought the council were ready to release the storm clouds! Tamar made it sound like it was going to happen any day, now."

"Don't stress. They will. Especially if your grandpa can talk the Trows round. That's the missing piece of the puzzle. And if they take too long about it? We'll set Tamar on them."

Tas pulled a monstrous face and Stella giggled.

Tamar didn't arrive until much later. Stella and Tas came trotting downstairs when they heard the door open. Tamar looked even grumpier than she had at the dock.

"Where's Grandpa?" asked Stella. "Is he on his way?"

Tamar shook her head. "He's out partying. Said not to wait up."

Stella stared at her.

Tamar shrugged. "Trows! What do you expect?"

"Can I meet them at some point?" said Tas.

"You?! Why?"

Tas glanced up at her two clouds. "I wanted to thank them again; show them how Arca's getting on."

Tamar nodded. "If Stella's grandpa does his bit, they'll be joining the rescue mission. You'll see them then."

Rescue mission. Stella hadn't really thought of it like that, but it was. She looked at the dark shadow of Winter's Keep and a shiver scampered up her neck. How many storm clouds were imprisoned in there?

* * *

Stella was woken by a crash of thunder, swiftly echoed by another inside her room.

"Nimbus!"

Nimbus settled on the window sill, still simmering purple and blue. Stella climbed out of bed to join him. The sky flickered yellow, throwing Winter's Keep into sharp silhouette. In the distance, a fork of lightning cracked down, a flash of brightness spearing the rough sea.

Tas was wrong. No matter what weather weirdness they'd had here over the last week, that wasn't any Ice Weaver's cloud. That was a thunderstorm. A massive, furious, thunderstorm. Stella rested her chin on her hands and nudged Nimbus with her shoulder. "No joining in," she murmured.

Was Tamar right? Was Heather somewhere out there, too?

"Go away!" whispered Stella. "Forget about Velda. Go and be happy together!"

She promised she wouldn't do this. Promised! On her cloud!

But maybe Heather wasn't in control? Perhaps Fury hadn't heard her calling?

"Would you want revenge, if you'd been trapped all that time?" she asked Nimbus.

He nestled closer to her, the prickle of static making the hairs on her arm stand on end. It wasn't a clear answer.

* * *

The following morning, Grandpa was very late down to breakfast. Stella was washing her plate in the deep double sink, when he appeared in the kitchen.

"Morning, Grandpa! How did it go with the good folk?"

Grandpa winced and put a hand over his eyes. "Remind me never to go to another party."

"Did they agree to help?"

Grandpa shook his head and sat down gingerly at the table. "No. Not yet. Broonie's up for it, but he's in a minority." He rested his head in his hands.

"Do you want a cup of tea?" asked Stella, looking at him in concern.

"Coffee," said Grandpa. "Black. Three sugars." He rubbed the sleep from his eyes and gave her a smile. "Thank you, love."

Tamar appeared in the doorway, her hair sticking out in all directions and her face sour. Stella poured her a coffee, too, hoping it might soften her mood.

Tamar took a sip and shuddered. "How much coffee did you put in that pot! This is practically paint stripper!"

"It's how Grandpa likes it."

"I might have known. Revolting." Tamar stuck out her tongue in disgust and pushed the mug away from her.

Grandpa chuckled softly and smiled at Stella.

"So?" said Tamar to Grandpa. "What news? Are they going to help us break those clouds out?"

Grandpa shrugged. "Broonie's up for it. Karl, too. The others are more interested in restitution – they want to reclaim some special gem. It was part of the hoard given to the weather weavers way-back-when, apparently."

"Special gem?" said Tamar, shaking her head. "Care to be more specific?"

"The master gem, they called it," said Grandpa, rubbing a hand over his eyes. "Some ancient Trowie treasure. They reckon the council have it."

"I've no idea," said Tamar. "But once they're inside Winter's Keep, they can take whatever they like, as far as I'm concerned."

"That's what I told Broonie," said Grandpa, getting up and putting his mug by the sink. "I'm hoping he can talk the others round. We'll see."

"He'd better," said Tamar, impatiently.

"They also want a full and public apology from the Ice Weavers."

"Velda? Apologise? Pigs might fly," she scoffed. "Right now, we'll be lucky to be granted entrance to Winter's Keep, never mind an apology."

"I thought it was all agreed!" said Stella. "You said the council had come to a decision?"

"The council? Yes. The Ice Weavers? No. And *they* control access to Winter's Keep."

Stella groaned.

Grandpa pinched the bridge of his nose, clearly not in the mood for dealing with either weather-weaving politics, or Tamar's brusqueness. "I'm going to head down and check on the boat," he said. "You fancy a stroll, Stella?"

Tamar shook her head. "I need Stella here. You go on."

Grandpa raised his eyebrows at Stella, checking she was okay with that.

Stella nodded. "I'll see you later Grandpa."

* * *

As soon as Grandpa had left, Tamar's expression darkened. She pointed out of the window at the distant thunderstorm. "So? What are we going to do about *that*?"

Stella peered out at it. "It's not getting any closer . . . Maybe it'll go away?"

"Pfft! You wish!" said Tamar. "I'm going to have to warn the council. Do you have any idea how embarrassing that's going to be?"

Stella crossed her arms and hunched her shoulders. "Do you

have to tell them? I mean, we're safe here, on the island. They protect it?"

"They protect it from passing weather! Not from a vengeful thundercloud set on getting in." Tamar sucked her teeth, making a concertina of wrinkles across her top lip.

Stella shifted awkwardly. She turned away from Tamar's accusing stare and busied herself rinsing out Grandpa's mug. "Tas said it was frosty here all last week . . ."

"Quite! Things were already delicate with the Ice Weavers," grumbled Tamar. "Velda might not be on the council any more, but until they elect a new one, she's still their leader. How's it going to look if I've brought along a cloud intent on attacking her? Honestly! You don't make my life easy."

Stella heaved a sigh. It wasn't like she'd meant this to happen. She hadn't planned it!

"Heather promised she'd just take Fury and go!"

"The promise of a sea witch." Tamar snorted. She looked out of the window again and shook her head. "I can't tell them today," she said. "We're right on the verge of a breakthrough. But I want you *here*, keeping an eye on him! If he gets any closer, or you see any sign of the sea witch, you come and find me. Understand?"

Stella bit her lips together and nodded. That was fair. She and Nimbus could be lookouts. And maybe, just maybe, Fury would give up and go away . . .

Twenty-Six

MAGNUS

AFTER Tamar had headed into town, Stella took up a position outside, on a stone bench facing Winter's Keep. Nimbus entertained himself chasing seagulls as they swooped up from the ledges on the cliffs below.

Stella took it seriously – watching the distant cloud for any change – holding her fingers up on either side to try and work out if it was moving.

It wasn't. The storm cloud just lurked; not moving away, but not coming closer either.

Like it's waiting for something.

Maybe for the other storm clouds to be released?

She'd told Heather it was happening. Maybe they just wanted to see it?

"Stella!"

Stella glanced down the hill and broke into a smile. "Magnus! You got away!"

"Not for long. I've got to be back for lunch. But Mum was called before the council again, so I brought Briar up for a dose of green space. Where's Nimbus?"

At the sound of his name, Nimbus popped up over the cliff edge and went bowling down the path to greet Briar.

"Here, I brought this back," said Magnus, reaching inside his coat.

"My sunshine scarf!" exclaimed Stella, taking it. The fine fabric was warm in her hands, glowing steadily.

"I'm sorry I walked off with it, after the Gathering. I felt really bad about it."

"It's fine," said Stella. "I forgot to ask for it back."

"You've got it glowing now, look!" observed Magnus. "You a bit happier than when we were stuck in those tunnels?"

Stella smiled. "Happy to see you!"

Magnus gave a brief smile, then turned away to look at Briar and Nimbus. They were painting trails of flowers across the grassy slope. "So? What do you reckon to Winter's Keep?" he said, nodding at its towering walls.

Stella pulled a face. "Pretty scary looking place. I wouldn't want to be trapped in there!"

"You know it's where I grew up, right?" said Magnus.

Stella stared at him in embarrassment. "Oh. N-no. I didn't know. Sorry," she stammered. "I mean . . . it's probably much nicer on the inside?"

Magnus laughed. "It's not."

Stella frowned up at the dark castle. Even now, its towers were rimed with frost, despite the morning sunshine. *Cold on the inside,* she thought. *Just like Velda.*

She couldn't imagine Magnus living there.

"To be honest, since I got Briar, I've spent most of my time out here," said Magnus, nodding at the sloping hillside. "And after Silvan started mentoring me, I went to stay with him and the other Verdure Weavers."

"What's it like to be back?" asked Stella.

Magnus shrugged. "I haven't been inside, yet. Mostly I've been stuck down in town with Mum. I reckon she'll agree to let the council in, though. She hates being locked up down there. She can't wait to get back to Winter's Keep."

"Will you go with her, when she does?"

Magnus nodded. "It'll be to release the storm clouds. So, yeah. I want to see that."

Stella nodded. "Me too."

Magnus gave a sad smile. "I'm sorry about everything – the Storm Laws, her trapping all those clouds."

"It's not your fault," said Stella.

"No, but it'll be good when they're released. It'll feel like a new start. A chance to put all this behind us."

"You're not going to stay here afterwards, are you?"

Magnus shook his head. "No! Just right now. She needs me. Afterwards . . . hopefully, I can get back to training with Silvan."

Stella nodded. "That'll be good." She frowned briefly. "I don't understand why the Ice Weavers won't let the council into Winter's Keep? Why not just get it over with?"

"It's not them, it's Mum." Magnus looked at his feet. "She's convinced that when the storm clouds are released, they'll want revenge for having been trapped."

Stella glanced guiltily at the dark smudge out on the horizon.

"Arca didn't," she pointed out.

"Oh! Tas didn't tell you?" said Magnus, raising his eyebrows.

Stella shook her head.

"Right after Tas got here, Arca had a good go at freezing Mum solid."

"Yikes!"

"Yeah. He's not allowed near the council buildings, now. It totally stalled the talks. Mum's demanding council protection, but they don't want to make her any promises because it'll wind the Trows up even more than they are already."

"Will she *ever* be ready to let the storm clouds go?"

Magnus nodded. "She knows she's got to. She's just scared. That's what the talks are about: safeguards, planning. It was your idea bringing the novices here, wasn't it?"

Stella nodded.

Magnus smiled. "That was a good shout."

* * *

Stella had forgotten how easy it was to spend time with Magnus. The morning passed quickly. Briar and Nimbus were happy as lambs, bouncing around the green slope behind the Gate House. By the time Magnus said he had to leave, the meadow was a constellation of flowers.

"You can't tell me you two are no good at Verdure Weaving!" said Magnus, watching as Nimbus embellished Briar's trail of sea pinks with tiny splashes of yellow and white.

"He's only doing it because he's with Briar."

"Means that he can," Magnus pointed out. "Listen, I'd better get back. I'll come back in the afternoon, if I can get away."

Stella waved until he was out of sight, then called Nimbus back. She pulled her coat closed and sat down on the bench again. Despite the blue skies overhead, the wind was cold and steady. It carried the grey scent of storm.

She held up her fingers on either side of the heavy grey smudge on the horizon and gnawed her lip.

Either it had got bigger, or it was getting closer . . .

* * *

Stella was still watching the distant storm when Tamar and

Grandpa arrived back for lunch. She heard them before she could see them. They were arguing.

She stood up to greet them, but Tamar stomped straight past her into the Gate House.

"What's going on?" Stella asked Grandpa.

He shook his head. "Just Tamar being bone-headed," he said.

Stella shook her head, wanting more explanation.

"I went to check on the boat," said Grandpa. He looked sideways at her.

"And?"

"And I thought I'd just check in on your parents. They've a tracker on their boat. All big boats do – so you can see where they are."

"Where are they?"

Grandpa shrugged. "Close. About a day north of here and heading in this direction."

"Do they know we're here?"

Grandpa shook his head. "No. There wasn't time to let them know, before we left."

"So, what's Tamar cross about?"

"I suggested I radio them our coordinates, in case they fancied swinging by," said Grandpa. "Tamar got in a right flap about it: 'top secret', 'tricky negotiations', 'council rules'. The long and the short of it is: she doesn't want them turning up here uninvited."

"I don't know if they'd even be able to find it. It's hidden."

"Sure," said Grandpa. "But Tamar's still in a stew about it."

"Lunch!" bellowed Tamar from inside the house.

"Why would they be coming here? I thought they were up near Norway? Do you think they're still tracking something?"

"I've no idea," said Grandpa. "But don't you worry about it. I'll check on them again, later this evening." He patted her shoulder. "If there's any real problem, of course we'll bring them here. And in the meantime, no catastrophising! Deal?"

Stella nodded. "Deal."

Twenty-Seven

TROUBLE ON THE HORIZON

Stella was clearing the plates off the table when she heard a chatter of voices outside.

"Winter's Keep!"

"That's where they're holding them . . ."

"I don't see why we can't just storm in there?"

"I'm in."

"No! Definitely not! Please!" Tas sounded uncharacteristically stressed.

Stella opened the door to see Tas standing in front of a milling group of novices. She was a good head shorter than most of them and she was thoroughly outnumbered.

"Trouble?" said Stella, with a smile.

"Thought I'd bring them up here to get the lay of the land," said Tas. "But now I'm thinking that wasn't a great idea. Hey! No. We're stopping here." She dodged sideways with her arms out, barring their way to the bridge.

Stella had thought the small group at the quay was all of them. But no. It looked like the council had rounded up at least thirty novices. *Maybe more,* she realised, as novices continued to appear through the gates.

"We're not going in," shouted Tas, over the growing jabber of conversation. "I just wanted to show you where we'll gather when the clouds are released. We'll line up along the cliff here, okay? Everybody got it?"

Tamar stuck her head round the door jamb. "You lot? Get!" she growled, pointing back down the path. "You're not needed yet."

A red-haired woman that Stella recognised from the quayside stepped forward with a combative air. "We're Storm Weavers! It's about time they realise what that means," he said, nodding in the direction of the castle.

"You're storm *novices*, Morag," said Tamar, unimpressed. "And you're not going to help anyone by making a scene."

"Come on," said Tas, patting her elbow. "Let's head back to town."

"And do what? Wait some more?"

"Look, I *know* how hard it is to be patient," said Tas sympathetically, "but soon—"

"They've been saying *soon* ever since the Gathering," exclaimed Morag, her voice rising. "I want my cloud back, *now*! Who's with me?"

She was greeted by a noisy ripple of agreement from the crowd.

"Enough!!!" bawled Tamar, finally gaining the attention of the whole group. They all turned towards her, their expressions ranging from startled, to flat-out rebellious.

"I will *get* you your clouds back. I swear it!" declared Tamar. "But if you start stirring up trouble, you'll jeopardise that – not just for yourselves, but for all the novices who *can't* be here!"

The mood abruptly shifted. Some of the younger novices drifted apart from the others, looking a bit shame-faced and shifty.

"Right! Time to go, gang!" said Tas, her voice full of forced jollity. She waved an arm in the air, indicating that the group should follow, then set off down the path. Stella was relieved to see the novices turning to follow her.

Tamar stood with her hands on her hips until the last stragglers had meandered away. "Bunch of hot heads," she muttered. "See what I have to deal with?"

"Shall I go and help Tas?" asked Stella. "I could talk to them, maybe? Help calm them down."

"You! Calm *them* down? That's rich," scoffed Tamar. "No. Go and get your sea shawl. I want you practising."

"So, I don't need to watch the storm any more?" said Stella. She glanced at the horizon and hope flickered in her chest – the cloud had receded since she'd last checked. Maybe it wasn't Fury, after all? It would be just like Tamar to discover that and not tell her.

"Don't be ridiculous!" snapped Tamar. "You're surely capable of doing more than one thing at once? There's a beach just beyond Winter's Keep. You can practise there and keep a lookout at the same time."

* * *

Stella looked doubtfully down at the beach. The way down was a precipitous staircase of stone steps, carved out of the rock face. A rusted chain, bolted into the rock, served as a rudimentary handrail. At the bottom was a meagre strip of seaweed-strewn sand, hemmed in by rolling waves. Submerged rocks reared up now and again, tearing the water to shreds.

Nimbus plummeted down the cliff, making her flinch at the speed of the fall.

Yeah, easy to get down there if you're a cloud . . .

Stella followed cautiously, picking her way carefully down the steep steps. Nimbus skimmed out over the waves, dodging the white spray of the breakers.

When she reached the bottom, she walked the short distance to the water's edge. The waves rolled in steadily, heaving themselves over the rocks, then cascading across the beach in a churning mess of foam. The rhythm of them was steady, predictable.

Stella watched for a few minutes, making sure she could judge what counted as a 'normal' wave. She moved up above the high-tide line to make sure she had space, then planted her feet in the sand and pulled her shawl tighter around her shoulders.

"Alright. Let's give this a go."

Hands out, fingers spread – that's how Tamar had said to do it. "Rise up!"

The water surged up the beach towards her; over the wet sand, past the high tide line, towards her feet. Stella skipped swiftly backwards, then scampered up the first few steps. The water sloshed over the bottom step. It was still rising.

"Go back, go back!" she yelped.

This was going to take a bit of practice.

* * *

The stacked boulders on the far side of the beach were a better spot to stand, she discovered; out of reach of even the biggest waves, and with a better view of the water. She was starting to feel a bit more confident now.

"Whirlpool!" she commanded.

The water began to circle; slowly at first, then faster and faster, as though disappearing down a drain. Stella climbed a little higher on the rocks and leant forward, peering down the deep sucking tube of water as it reached for the sea bed.

"Not bad," said a voice from behind her.

Stella started and her foot slipped. She windmilled her arms to keep her balance.

"Calm! Flat calm," she shouted, teetering on the edge.

The whirlpool filled rapidly and the water settled into unnatural stillness. Stella turned, her hand on her racing heart. "Tas, you nearly—"

But it wasn't Tas. Heather was half out of the water, her scaly arms hooked over a half-submerged rock.

"Getting in touch with your inner sea witch?" she said.

"You!" exclaimed Stella. "What are you doing here? We had a deal! You promised you wouldn't come here."

"No, I didn't." Heather shook her head.

"You promised you wouldn't take revenge!"

Heather gave a dark smile. "Trust me, if I were in a vengeful mood, you'd know it."

"Three days of gales and lightning?!" snapped Stella, staring at Heather with a mixture of fright and anger.

Heather shifted, looking uncomfortable. "It took a while to get Fury under control. But he's listening now. He's calmer."

"We had to sail through that storm. We nearly sank!"

"No, you didn't!" retorted Heather. "I was watching out for you – I made a gap."

Stella scowled. Okay, it was a massive exaggeration – they hadn't come close to sinking – but it *had* been scary. Especially the last bit. Ocean rollers were Stella's idea of hell, she'd decided.

And why else would Heather be here, except for revenge?

"You're after Velda. Don't tell me you're not!"

Heather shook her head. "I'm not."

Stella shifted to find more secure footing. "What do you want, Heather?"

"To warn you," said Heather. "I owe you that much." She pulled herself up out of the water and onto the rock in one smooth motion.

"The Teran is coming."

* * *

Stella sat cross legged on the rocks, clutching her sea shawl around her. She rocked back and forth, shaking her head. The spirit of winter was coming here? To this island?

She didn't want to believe it. She couldn't even imagine what the Teran would look like. Like a monster? Like a person? Like a huge storm?

Like frost on a summer morning . . .

"But why?!" she said.

"Because he knows time is short. The council intend to release all the storm clouds," said Heather.

"So? What does that matter to the Teran?"

Heather's eyes slid away from Stella's. "As long as they're trapped, they're an army, there for the taking."

"What?!"

"He can use them to win. Defeat the Sea Mither."

"What does that mean?"

"No more seasons. He gets what he's always wanted. Endless winter."

Stella's mouth dropped open.

Heather picked a piece of seaweed from the rock and flicked it into the water. "Look, if I'd known you were going to help, I never would have told him . . ."

"You?! You told him!" Stella gaped at her. "Why would you do that?!"

"Because you didn't come back!"

The statement landed with a brief stab of guilt, but it didn't excuse what Heather had done. "You bargained with all the other storm clouds."

Heather winced and her head dipped. "It was the only way I could think of, to get Fury back. The Teran doesn't do anything for free. I know that better than anyone."

"Can we stop him?"

Heather's shoulders hunched and she shook her head.

"Then how do we fight him?"

Heather stared up at Stella. "You can't *fight* the Teran."

"I don't mean you and me, I mean, like, the whole council?"

"He's the spirit of winter, Stella! He has more power than all of them combined. If it comes to a fight, they'll lose. Look."

Heather pulled her hair aside, revealing the gills that scarred her slender neck. She bared her needle teeth in a horrifying grimace.

Stella shrank back.

"The Teran did this," said Heather. "Transformed me, with barely a thought. For fun. You think you can fight that?"

"Then what are we meant to *do*?!" said Stella.

A tiny part of her hoped that this was all just a twisted joke; a lie, intended to frighten her.

"Your only chance is to let the storm clouds go," said the sea witch. "All of them. Before he gets here."

Heather's gaze flicked to the steps behind Stella and her eyes widened. She launched herself back into the dark water, disappearing in a lick of foam.

"Who was that, Stella?"

Stella twisted and looked up.

Magnus stood near the top of the steps, his face pale, his fingers tight around the chain handrail.

"Mum was right, wasn't she?! That was the sea witch!"

"Magnus, it's not what it looks like . . ."

Magnus turned and began to hurry back up the steps.

"Magnus, wait!"

By the time she reached top of the steps, there was no sign of him.

I've got to find Tamar. She'd be at the council buildings, at the meeting.

At least, she hoped so.

Twenty-Eight

COUNCIL MEETING

ENDLESS winter! Stella hammered at the door of the council building, her mind whirling with needle teeth, scaled skin and threat. She'd expected to be able to run inside, but the big doors were locked.

"Tamar! I need to see Tamar! Let me in!"

There was a heavy clunk as the doors were unbolted top and bottom, then the handle turned. The door was opened by a grizzled-looking council guard. His watchful eyes scanned the sky and the street before settling on Stella.

"I've got to speak to Tamar. It's urgent."

"Stay there." The door began to close, but Stella wasn't up for waiting. She darted through the gap and dodged his grasping hand. A shout went up behind her as she sprinted across the wide hallway towards the grandest doors she could see.

She burst through them, Nimbus following close behind. All faces turned towards her. On the podium, the council members sat frozen, interrupted mid-discussion.

Ilana got to her feet. She pointed at Nimbus. "Remove that cloud. No clouds in the council chamber." A guard carrying a cloud net approached.

Stella urgently motioned to the door. "Go, Nimbus! I'll be alright." The little cloud dodged the net and darted out of the doors, right into the face of the following guard.

The air inside the chamber was stuffy and stale, musty with the stink of too many bodies. Stella turned and rapidly scanned the crowd, hunting for Tamar, but the first face she recognised was Velda's. She was seated on the far side of the room, surrounded by a crowd of Ice Weavers and a cohort of council guards.

Stella's heart sank. *I'm too late . . .*

Magnus straightened up from whispering in his mother's ear. He shot Stella a look of cold contempt that cut her to the core.

Tamar pushed her way through the throng and grabbed Stella by the shoulder. She leant in close, her expression furious. "What do you think you're doing?" she whispered.

"It's—"

"The Haken has returned." Velda's voice cut across the babble of noise in the room. "We are no longer safe here." She stood, the Ice Weavers closing around her in a tight circle. The council guards closed ranks around the group before they could move.

"The whole *point* of you keeping lookout was that I'd be the first to know!" hissed Tamar in Stella's ear.

Stella glanced at Tamar in silent apology, then waved at Ilana to get her attention. No more secrets. They all needed to hear this. "I came to tell you—"

Ilana held up a finger to pause Stella. "Sit down, please, Velda." The instruction was calm, but it carried a hard note of authority. "I can assure you that you are perfectly safe here. You are under the council's protection, until these negotiations are concluded."

"Protection?!" Velda's voice was laced with sarcasm. "Let's call it what it is: house arrest."

"Call it what you will," said Ilana, "but sit down."

Velda adjusted her robes and sat down, with deliberate ceremony. "*That* young Storm Weaver was seen colluding with a sea witch. I told you. They're out to get me." For a moment, Stella glimpsed the fear in her eyes, but she rapidly composed herself. "As I've been telling you for some time now, releasing those clouds is nowhere near as straightforward as you'd like to make out – vengeful Storm Weavers are a danger to us all."

Stella clenched her fists and glared at Velda.

She was still pushing the same old message? Even after everything? Stella glanced along the row of council members and saw with dismay that Velda's words had landed.

Velda grasped Magnus's hand in hers and glared spitefully at Stella.

Stella shook her head, feeling horribly outnumbered.

How can this be happening again?

"Stella?" Ilana was looking at her, awaiting an explanation.

"Heather's not out to get her! Neither am I!"

"So, you admit to knowing this sea witch?"

A cold sweat broke beaded Stella's top lip. She wiped it away. "Um . . . yes?"

"You know that this same sea witch was behind a series of vicious attacks on Winter's Keep last year?"

"She was only trying to get her cloud back. But she's got him now. Nimbus and I set him free. So, she came to—"

"How much more evidence do you need?" screeched Velda, over the hubbub of noise that greeted Stella's revelation. "Collusion and open threats!" She raised her arms towards the open doors at the back of the council chamber. An explosion of cloud poured into the room, filling the air with whirling white.

"Oh, sleet!" muttered Tamar. "That's torn it."

There was a clatter and crash as people leapt to their feet, overturning their chairs. Tamar put an arm around Stella and drew her back towards the wall. Through the raging blizzard, Stella glimpsed the Ice Weavers rushing past, Velda hidden in their midst.

It took a while for the snow to settle and the air to clear. When it did, Stella was surprised to see that not all the Ice Weavers had left with Velda. She nudged Tamar and surreptitiously pointed. Tamar glared at her, tight lipped and Stella suddenly realised – she didn't know yet!

"Tamar, Heather's not here for revenge, she came to—"

Tamar shushed her impatiently and Stella bit down in frustration.

Why would nobody just listen?!

"The Teran is coming!"

Tamar's head whipped round. "What did you say?"

"I said the Teran is coming. Here! To Winter's Keep. Heather came to *warn* us."

Tamar's eyes widened. "Stay there," she said, then pushed her way forward to the very edge of the stage, where the council guards were righting overturned chairs and attempting to restore order.

Moments later, Stella stood at the very front, facing the council. She could feel the critical eyes of the crowd on her back, making her neck crawl.

How many of them still believed Velda's lies?

It didn't matter. As long as the council were willing to listen.

Ilana held up a hand for silence. "You came here to deliver a warning?"

Stella nodded. "We have to release the storm clouds. Now. Today."

One of the elderly Verdure Weavers cleared his throat. "We were *all* working towards that end," he said, with a curl of his lip, "until you disrupted proceedings."

"I know that!" said Stella. "But you're taking too long."

The old Verdure Weaver shook his head, making the wattle under his chin wobble. "Typical Storm Weaver. No *patience*," he muttered. He turned to the other council members. "If, and I say *if*, Velda is willing to talk to us, we'll have to restart the whole—"

"The Teran is coming!" shouted Stella, finally losing her temper, "and you're just sitting here talking!"

The council chamber burst into loud conversation. Ilana held up a hand and waited for the noise to die down.

The old Verdure Weaver leant forward, his face full of contempt. "Perhaps you didn't study weather lore, during your *brief* training?" he said, casting a scathing look at Tamar. "The Teran is the spirit of *winter*. He is confined during the spring and summer months."

"He's not *confined*. He's coming *here*," insisted Stella, "for the trapped storm clouds! If you don't let them go, he'll take them; make it winter all the time!"

Stella looked along the row of council members. They looked more outraged than scared. Probably they weren't used to being shouted at.

Ilana was looking at her curiously, her head cocked to one side. "How do you know this, Stella?"

Stella swallowed. But she'd come too far to back down.

"The sea witch told me. She came to warn us. She said she owed me."

The council chamber filled with noise again.

No wonder they never get anything done.

Ilana banged her stick heavily on the ground for silence and the guards stepped forward to make their presence felt in the rowdier sections of the crowd.

Tamar glanced around at the unfolding mayhem and shook her head. "Right. You've said your piece. Time for you to go," she said.

"But they have to listen!" protested Stella.

"Leave it to me," said Tamar, hustling Stella out of the hall. "I'll *make* them listen. They have to."

At a gesture from Tamar, the guard opened the front door. Immediately, a sharp breeze whirled inside, punchy and cold, speckling the floor with fine flakes of snow. Tamar pursed her lips anxiously and gave Stella a gentle shove. "Go on, now. I'll meet you back at the Gate House."

As Stella exited the council building, Nimbus flung himself at her and settled around her shoulders, filling her hair with static. Behind her, the bolts slammed back into place.

"I tried, Nimbus!" she told him. "I just hope they'll listen."

Twenty-Nine

A CHOICE

SHE'D probably only been at the Gate House for half an hour, but it felt like far longer. Stella stared out of the window at the craggy walls of Winter's Keep. The waiting was making her itch.

Hurry up, Tamar.

Heather's warning still skittered around the edges of her brain. *He's coming. How soon? How will I know?*

She wished she'd had a chance to ask her. She would have done if Magnus hadn't interrupted them.

Magnus! The shock on his face ... If only I could explain.

But he was gone. Into Winter's Keep with Velda. Out of reach.

I've got to warn him!

Winter's Keep was a fortress, though. No way she was getting in. No way anyone was getting in. Stella stared up at the towering walls.

You're not safe there, Magnus.

Nimbus bounced off the windowsill and disappeared into the kitchen. *At last!* Stella followed him into the other room, just as the door opened and Tamar marched inside. She dumped her weather bag on the table and filled a glass of water from the tap. Her expression didn't inspire much hope.

"So?" asked Stella.

Tamar downed the glass of water, wiped her mouth on her sleeve and shook her head. "They're not going to help. Not fast enough, anyway. They're still debating. I told them! 'As long as those storm clouds are still trapped, they're an army there for the taking.' The trouble is, right now, they're an army under Velda's control. The council can't just march in there. It would be a declaration of war between the weathers."

Stella gaped at her. "But we can't let the Teran have them!"

"No. That would be infinitely worse," agreed Tamar.

"So, what do we do?"

"We're taking matters into our own hands," said Tamar, with a determined look in her eye. "A quiet infiltration, rather than a head-on confrontation. Your Grandpa's on his way here now. But first things first: I want to talk to Heather. We need details."

Stella swallowed. *Tamar, talk to Heather?*

"I don't know if . . ."

Sid danced to life on Tamar's chest, but she just flapped at him. "I will!" she said impatiently. "I'll start with that."

"Will what?" asked Stella.

"Apologise," said Tamar, chewing uncomfortably on the word. "I misjudged her," she muttered. "Sid's been saying so for years."

Sid raised four of his legs. Tamar glanced down at him and raised her eyebrows at Stella. "In case you were wondering, this means 'I told you so!'"

Stella gave Sid a brief smile. All the same, she wasn't certain it was a good idea for Tamar to meet Heather. So far, Heather had kept her word about not taking revenge, but Fury might have other ideas.

"How about *I* talk to her?" she said.

"Yes! That would work," said Tamar, in relief.

Stella turned and ran upstairs to her room, hoping against hope that Grandpa hadn't decided to repack her bag like Mum would have done.

No. Thank goodness! Beneath her hastily packed clothes, her fingers closed around the hard curve of the conch shell. She hadn't intended to bring it; she'd just forgotten to take it out. She pulled the shell out and turned it over in her hands.

Over by the window, Nimbus rumbled.

"Who are you worried about? Fury? Or Heather?"

Nimbus was silent.

"Neither?"

She moved over to join him at the window and frowned. The glass was speckled with snow. Outside, the storm front had moved closer. It seemed larger, too – stretching the full length of the horizon.

That's not Fury, she realised with a shiver.

* * *

Stella pushed the hood of her raincoat back and glanced anxiously at the sky. Grey clouds blotted out the sun and a cold wind whisked spray off the choppy waves.

Storms offshore were one thing, but on the island? The council dictated the weather. This wasn't meant to happen. Time was running out.

She pulled her hair back into a ponytail, to stop it whipping round her face. "Alright, let's do this."

The conch shell tasted salty. Stella tightened her lips and blew. A long low note; it echoed off the towering cliffs like a warning.

She climbed carefully down a few more steps. She couldn't go all the way to the bottom. The tide was high and the waves were tearing between the rocks, tumbling all the way to the cliff, covering the bottom steps in a churning mass of foam.

Come back, Heather. Please.

She lifted the shell and blew again. Nimbus floated out a little way over the waves. Beneath him, a pale face broke the surface and ducked under again. Nimbus swung round and flew back towards

Stella, arriving just as the sea witch emerged in the shallows. She wiped her arms, flicking sea foam from her fingers, then slithered up the steps towards Stella.

Her movements were fluid and fast, but there was a distinct slurp each time she lifted her foot, as though her feet had suckers on their soles.

Heather sat down a couple of steps below Stella, her head bowed.

Stella clutched the conch shell nervously and scanned Heather's back. There was something different about her. Stella didn't remember the fine webbed fins. Or maybe it was the colour of her scales that had changed – deep blues and greens, darker than before.

"They are ssstill imprisssoned!"

The sibilant hiss of accusation in her voice sent a shiver up Stella's spine.

She's changing back. Stella clutched the conch shell and looked at Heather warily. "We've been trying. It's complicated."

"Too ssslow!" said Heather. "You don't have time for thisss,"

"How long?"

Heather flexed her fingers. Fine spines moved like fishbones under the skin of her hands. Stella stared at them, remembering their sharp sting.

Sea-witch venom.

"Ssssoon," said Heather. "He's close. Ever closer. I hear him calling."

"Calling?"

"Calling all of usss; all his creaturesss." Heather turned and looked up at Stella. Her eyes weren't human any more – just two dark orbs in her pale face. There was a glazed hunger in their inky depths.

Stella recoiled slightly and Heather nodded as though that's what she'd expected. Nimbus moved closer and wrapped himself around Stella's shoulders.

Heather's gaze settled on him and a flicker of emotion crossed her face. "None so loyal as a storm cloud . . ."

"Where is Fury?" said Stella.

Heather frowned and closed her eyes, silently listening.

"Singing a storm, out over the sea."

"But we freed him so you could be together?!"

Heather bared her teeth. "We freed him so he could be free!" She looked down at herself and spread her webbed hands. "I belong to the deep. No place for a cloud . . ."

"You don't have to listen to the Teran."

Heather's lips closed in a thin line. She looked at the churning water and shook her head. "That's the price. He calls, we answer. He's coming – for the storm clouds. You should leave, while you can."

Stella shook her head in frustration. "I can't leave! My friends are here. One of them's inside Winter's Keep!"

She doesn't care, Stella realised. *Why should she? She doesn't even know them.*

Stella changed tack. "You know the Teran's not going to let

those storm clouds go, right?! He's going to keep them trapped! Forever! Make it winter all the time. Is that what you want? Really?"

Heather glanced up at Winter's Keep, then down at the churning water. Her narrow fingers curled around the edge of the stone step. The muscles in her forearms twitched like wires beneath her scaled skin, fighting some internal battle.

She's trapped, realised Stella.

"Heather, come ashore!" she blurted, on impulse.

Heather stood abruptly and for a moment, Stella thought she was going to dive. But she didn't. She just stood there, swaying gently, as though the waves were pulling at her.

"The Teran needs me."

There was a note of uncertainty in her voice and Stella leapt on it.

"But you've got Fury now. He needs you. We need you! The storm clouds need you."

Heather wrapped her arms around herself, her hands rasping over the scales on her arms. "You talk like there's a choice . . ."

"There *is* a choice!" insisted Stella. "Please. Stay!"

The sea witch stared out at the water, seeking answers in the pattern of the waves. After a long moment, she turned her gaze up to the sky. Her shoulders straightened and a shiver rippled down her back. She nodded.

"So be it. Until they are *all* free."

Thirty

COCOON

STELLA glanced anxiously up at Winter's Keep as they approached the Gate House.

Don't look now, Magnus.

Tamar opened the door as they got close and ran forward a few steps. Heather stiffened and bared her teeth with a hiss.

"Stop there!" said Stella.

Tamar stopped. She clasped her hands in front of her chest and rocked slightly. Her eyes filled with tears. "My poor, poor girl. Look at you."

Heather's mouth tightened and she flexed her neck, making

the scales ripple. Stella cautiously reached out and took her hand. It was icy cold. Heather looked down at it, as though unsure how she felt about the contact. She didn't let go, though. Instead, she looked at Stella with a fierce plea in her eyes.

"Tamar," said Stella, "you need to give us some space. Heather's not herself right now."

Tamar nodded and moved away from the door, making room for Stella to lead Heather inside.

Stella didn't have a plan. How do you help a sea witch?

Heather winced as she walked across the kitchen, her feet adhering to the smooth flagstone floor. Every now and then, she gave a slight shiver, sending oily reflections shimmering across her scales.

Get her warm. That'd be a start.

Stella led Heather to her room, flapping covertly at Grandpa as he opened his bedroom door.

He gave a wide-eyed nod and stepped back, as Stella led Heather past.

In her room, she pulled a towel off the radiator and handed it to Heather, then dragged a random selection of clothes out of her bag and put them on the end of the bed.

"They might be a bit small. You're taller than me. But they'll be warm."

Heather wrapped the towel around her shoulders. "Understand this: I'm not here for Tamar, just for the storm clouds."

Stella nodded. "I'll leave you to get changed," she said.

"And I'll get Grandpa to make hot chocolate. He makes the best hot chocolate."

The hint of a smile crept onto Heather's face. "Hot chocolate . . ."

As Stella closed the door behind her, she let out a massive breath. *That could have gone worse!*

* * *

"She says the Teran's calling all its creatures. I had to get her out," said Stella.

Tamar nodded. "You did the right thing, bringing her here."

Grandpa stirred the hot chocolate. He hadn't said much yet.

"Back on land, at last," said Tamar, thoughtfully. "I didn't think she'd ever choose that over the sea."

Stella frowned and shook her head. "She's only here to help rescue the storm clouds. I don't think she's planning on staying."

Tamar pursed her lips. "Trust me – she's made a choice. The Teran gave her those powers. He can take them just as easily. She's turned her back on the sea's call. That's not likely to be forgiven – not by the Teran, nor his creatures."

Stella glanced towards the stairs. She hadn't realised how much she was asking when she brought Heather ashore. She just hoped Heather understood the choice she'd made.

Tamar pulled a scroll of paper out of her bag and unrolled it on the table. She weighted down the corners with the salt and pepper pots. It was a map.

A map of Winter's Keep! realised Stella, recognising the narrow bridge that led to the entrance. "Where did you get this?"

Tamar raised her eyebrows, looking momentarily pleased with herself. "Some of the Ice Weavers are starting to see sense. It's their home under threat, after all. We'll have some help tonight."

"Tonight? Tamar, I don't know if we have that long!"

Grandpa poured the hot milk into the mugs, his hand trembling slightly.

"We do," said Tamar, her voice certain. "Winter loves the darkness. The Teran will wait until the darkest hour. Besides, we need the Trows and they don't emerge until dusk. It'll be tight, I admit. But if we let the clouds go, there'll be no reason for the Teran to attack."

Stella looked out of the window. Winter's Keep loomed over them, heavy with shadowy threat. *And somewhere inside there is Magnus.*

* * *

When Stella went back upstairs, she was confronted by a horrifying sight. Heather lay asleep on her bed, but only her face was visible. The rest of her body was encased in a dense mat of spider silk. Loose ends drifted in the light breeze as she opened the door. Sid scampered up the soft bulge of silk that hid Heather's shoulder and raised himself up on four legs. Stella backed out of the room, her heart racing.

"Tamar!" she whispered urgently. "Come here!"

Tamar peeked in through the door and smiled. "Oh, good thinking, Sid. Well done."

"Well done?" whispered Stella. "He's turned her into a cocoon!"

"Did you not see how much pain it caused her, coming ashore? Sid will take care of her. Spider silk has wonderful healing properties." Tamar nodded in satisfaction.

Stella looked at Sid doubtfully. He'd settled on the pillow next to Heather's head.

"Do you not remember the cure for sea-witch venom?" asked Tamar

Stella pulled a face. She remembered. Tamar had insisted on packing the wound in her shoulder with spider silk.

"Leave her the hot chocolate," said Tamar. "She can have it when she wakes up." She turned and made her way back to the kitchen.

Stella tiptoed in and set the mug down on the bedside table.

"Take good care of her, Sid," she whispered.

The spider lifted one spindly leg in salute and settled back into position.

* * *

When Stella got back, Grandpa was poring over the map with Tamar.

"What kind of creatures are we talking about?" said Stella.

"What?" said Tamar, without looking up.

"Heather said the Teran is calling all his *creatures*?"

Tamar glanced up and shrugged. "Who knows? There's all sorts lurking at midnight depth, most of them under the Teran's sway. Sea witches, brigdi, marool, maybe a Kraken if we're unlucky."

Grandpa straightened up. His eyes grew wider as the list went on.

Tamar glanced at him and rolled her eyes. "Hopefully we won't encounter any of them, if we can release the storm clouds fast enough."

Stella crossed to the window. The sea looked cold and hard under the heavy grey sky – like shifting shards of slate.

She bit her lip. She didn't want to ask the question, but she had to. "Do you think that's what Mum and Dad have been tracking? The Teran's shoal of *creatures*?"

Tamar looked at her, but she didn't say anything. It was answer enough.

"Oh, Lord! We've got to warn them!" said Grandpa.

"No!" exclaimed Tamar. "That is *not* our priority! We have to get into Winter's Keep! Release those clouds! If the Teran retreats, they don't even need to know."

"*If?*" Grandpa shook his head angrily. "And if it doesn't?" He pulled his cap on, swiped his coat off the back of the chair and strode out of the door.

Stella ran after him.

"Be back by dusk," Tamar called after them. "And Stella? Tell Tas to be ready."

* * *

Stella couldn't keep up. Grandpa had long legs. "Grandpa, wait for me!"

His jaw was set, his face hard as granite, but when he glanced back at Stella, he softened. "Don't you worry," he said. "I'll make sure they're safe."

Stella trotted to catch up with him, took his hand, and they carried on down the hill, with Nimbus close behind.

The wind was whistling up Main Street and as they reached the harbour end, they were greeted by a smattering of sleet. Grandpa pulled his cap a little lower and led the way between the brightly coloured stalls, making purposefully for the jetty.

Most of the stalls had packed up, Stella noticed; their counters empty, their awnings flapping forlornly in the breeze. Word must have got out. The locals were taking the sea witch's warning seriously, even if the council weren't.

When they got to the boat, Grandpa slid open the cabin hatch and disappeared below with practised ease. Stella clambered down the steps behind him.

Grandpa sat down at the small navigation table. He turned all the instruments on and frowned at the readings glowing onscreen. He pointed to a little triangle on the screen. "This is them, here,"

"*Arctic Star*," read Stella.

Grandpa nodded. "And this is us," he said. He slid his finger across to the right. "They're definitely heading in our direction, though they're a few hours out, yet."

"Are they okay?"

Grandpa nodded. "I'd say so. But I think we should radio them and check."

"We can do that?" said Stella.

"We can try on the emergency channel," said Grandpa. "I just hope they're listening in."

Thirty-One

GRANDPA CHECKS IN

GRANDPA selected the right channel, then unhooked the black microphone from its stand, stretching the long curly cord to hold it close to his mouth.

"This is *Curlew*, *Curlew*, calling *Arctic Star*, *Arctic Star*. Do you read me? Over."

Stella watched Grandpa anxiously, as he waited for an answer. Static hissed out of the speaker. Grandpa raised the microphone again.

"*Curlew*, *Curlew*, calling *Arctic Star*, *Arctic Star*. Do you read me? Over."

Nothing; just a gritty drift of white noise, like waves over gravel. It set Stella's teeth on edge. Grandpa sighed and hung the microphone back on its hook. He stood up and began to put away the maps and pencils that he'd left out on the chart table.

"Try again!" insisted Stella.

Grandpa looked at her and nodded. "I'll keep trying. In the meantime, let's get everything properly stowed. I'd like to have everything ship shape, just in case."

Stella narrowed her eyes at him. What was he planning?

Grandpa caught her look. "It's just good seamanship," he said. "Look lively!"

Stella made sure the cupboards were properly closed, and wedged Grandpa's Thermos flask safely on a shelf. Beyond that, there wasn't much to tidy. It was a very tiny space.

Grandpa kept repeating the same call, then waiting. The waiting seemed to get longer each time. It didn't make sense. It was a big vessel, with a whole crew on board, that's what Dad had said. Surely, you'd have someone listening in?

Stella narrowed her eyes. "Did you tell them where we were, after Tamar said not to?"

Grandpa gave a slight shrug. "I gave them coordinates," he said, "but only so they'd know where we are. They weren't planning a visit."

"They're coming here," said Stella, with absolute conviction.

The radio crackled to life. "*Curlew, Curlew*, this is *Arctic Star*, over." There was a crashing sound and then the message repeated.

"*Curlew, Curlew*, this is *Arctic Star*, please come in, over." The voice sounded tinny through the radio's speaker, but there was no mistaking it.

"That's Mum!" exclaimed Stella.

* * *

"Right, off you get," said Grandpa. "I'm going out to fetch them."

"Let me come with you!" said Stella.

Grandpa shook his head. "No. Go and find Tamar. Let her know what's going on. I'm not sure if *Arctic Star* will make it into this harbour – it's a large vessel. If I can, I'll guide them in. If not, they can anchor off and I'll ferry the crew ashore."

As soon as she was on the jetty, Stella undid the kilt pins at her shoulder. She balled up the sea shawl and thrust it at Grandpa. "Take this."

Grandpa shook his head. "That's kind of you, but hang onto it. I'm afraid there's nothing magic about me."

"You don't have to be!" insisted Stella. "The magic is in the shawl."

Grandpa frowned briefly, but took it from Stella. He wound it round his neck and pinned it to his jumper. He patted it briefly and gave her a worried smile.

"I made it for you," said Stella. "You saw how I used it on the way here? Just do that. It might help."

"Thank you, love. I'll take good care of it."

"Take good care of *you*!" said Stella. "And Mum and Dad."

Grandpa nodded.

Stella backed out of the way as he undid the mooring ropes. "What if you can't find your way back?"

"I've got it marked on the chart," said Grandpa. "And I've done it once."

"It's hidden by magic, Grandpa!"

"Then ask Tamar to help. I'm sure she'll think of something." With that, Grandpa put the engine into gear and manoeuvred carefully away from the jetty.

* * *

Stella ran along the quay towards the low building Tas had pointed out to her. The storm novices' quarters.

"Stella!" Tas opened the door with a grin, but her smile faltered as she clocked her friend's expression. She hooked her arm through Stella's, drawing her inside, and closed the door.

Tas led Stella into a large room with sofas and comfy seats ranged around the place. Most of them were occupied by storm novices. At the far end, there was a long dining table, where a noisy card game was taking place.

Stella recognised Aaron, he was the one who'd first spotted Nimbus. He looked up as they came in, and nodded.

Tas pointed to two unoccupied seats over by the window. They sat down and she leant in close. "So? Tell me everything."

Stella took a deep shuddering breath.

"That bad, huh?"

A moment later Aaron approached and put a cup of tea in Stella's hands. "Two sugars," he said. You look like you need it."

Stella nodded gratefully.

"Spill the beans then," said Tas.

"We're going to release the storm clouds tonight. And we're going to need your help."

"Yes! Finally!" Aaron whooped, pumping his fist in the air.

"Shh!" hissed Stella.

But it was too late. Every other novice in the room was moving towards them.

Stuff it. They deserve to know. It affects all of them.

Stella heaved a deep sigh and looked around at them. "Look, I'll tell you what's going on, but you have to swear that you're not going to go storming off anywhere. Tamar's got a plan."

It didn't take long to tell them the whole story. When she'd finished, most of the novices looked shaken. Aaron paced up and down, clenching and unclenching his fists as though yearning for something to fight. In contrast, the red-haired woman, Morag, had become increasingly still, her expression bleak.

"So, we get them back tonight, or never?"

Stella nodded.

Tas took her hand and squeezed it. "Storm sisters," she said quietly, like a prayer.

Stella stood up. She looked around at their worried faces. "Meet me at the Gate House at sunset, not before. Trust your clouds. And listen to Tas. She's done it before."

Aaron punched his hand with his fist and exchanged nods of encouragement with some of the others. "We'll be there. You can count on it."

* * *

Tamar was still poring over the map of Winter's Keep when Stella got back. Stella swiftly updated her on Grandpa.

"He's gone where?!"

"To guide them in. There's heavy seas and they can't steer properly. Mum said the rudder is jammed."

"Ugh!" Tamar looked at the ceiling. "Infuriating man. I need him here! Not off playing the hero."

"Tamar! That's my mum and dad on that boat!"

Tamar closed her eyes and shook her head briefly. "Fine. We'll have to go in without him. We can't wait."

"Will the Trows still help?"

"We'd better hope so," said Tamar. "He picked a fine time to go wandering off!"

"You need to make sure he can find his way in, when he gets back," remembered Stella.

"Seriously?" Tamar banged the table in frustration and the map rolled itself up. "I'd have to talk to Ilana! There's no time!"

"You'd better hurry, then," said Stella.

She didn't care whether Tamar was happy about it or not,

as long as Mum and Dad and Grandpa got ashore safely.

She opened the door. "Let's go."

Tamar hooked her bag over her shoulder and shook her head. "You stay put," she growled. "Someone needs to be here, in case Heather wakes up."

Thirty-Two

THE GOOD FOLK

AFTER Tamar had gone, Stella tiptoed into the bedroom to check on Heather. The sea witch was still sleeping, her chest rising and falling slowly under the gauzy mat of cobwebs. She definitely looked better than before, though. A hint of colour had returned to her cheeks. Sid waved one leg towards the door and Stella backed quietly out again.

She'd just sat down to study the map of Winter's Keep, when there was a soft tap at the door.

Stella hastily rolled up the map and stuffed it into one of the kitchen drawers. She wasn't sure how Tamar had got hold of it, but knowing her, they probably weren't meant to have it. She opened the door a crack.

"Magnus!" Stella threw the door wide open. "I'm so glad to see you. I wanted to explain!"

Magnus gave a cautious nod. "I heard. When the others got back from the meeting. Is it true. . . about the Teran?"

Stella nodded and motioned him inside. Magnus came in, but hovered close to the door, clearly uncertain whether he should be here.

"Heather's trying to help. She's not here to hurt your mum. She came to warn us."

"Heather?"

"The sea witch," clarified Stella. "That's her name. Or it was."

Magnus tugged on his fringe. "One of the Ice Weavers who was at the meeting tried to take control of the gems from Mum," he said. "She totally lost the plot. She's locked herself inside the final retreat. She's not listening to anyone now. Not even me." He sat down, leant his elbows on the table and put his head in his hands. "I don't know what to do."

"Oh, Magnus, I'm sorry."

Stella pulled out a chair and sat down opposite him. Magnus didn't look up.

She wanted to tell him the whole plan, reassure him that it was going to be okay. But what if he went back to Winter's Keep and told them? It might ruin everything.

"The master gem controls all the others. Mum told me about

it before," said Magnus, quietly. "We could use it to free all the clouds at once."

Stella leant forward, her heart quickening with excitement. "Magnus, that's brilliant. We've got to get it! If we can let them *all* go, Winter's Keep will be safe!"

Magnus shook his head. "That's the point – we can't. She's taken it in there with her. To 'protect it', she said." He looked deflated. "There's no way in. I tried to talk to her. So did the elders. She thinks she's keeping us safe by hiding in there, and the more anyone tries to convince her otherwise, the more she thinks everyone's against her."

Stella scrunched up her face in frustration. "But it's the opposite – she's putting everyone in danger!"

"You don't need to tell *me* that."

Stella reached out and took his hand. "We can still do it," she reassured him. "With or without this master gem. We'll break every gem if we have to."

Magnus sucked his teeth, looking doubtful. "There are lots. I've seen them."

"As many as we can, then," said Stella.

She glanced out of the window. With the clouds so low, it was hard to tell if the sun had set yet, but it was definitely getting darker. She looked at Magnus, his face drawn with worry, and came to a decision.

"At sunset, the Trows are coming," she told him. "We're going to break into Winter's Keep. Will you help?"

Magnus looked at her. His mouth was pinched with worry, but he nodded. "I don't think you'll have to break in," he said. "Mum's not in charge any more. The Ice Weavers are in a flat panic, fortifying everything. But I'll come with you; talk to them. They know me."

There was a soft shuffle of movement in the corridor and Stella's eyes widened.

Magnus turned as the door swung open, he leapt to his feet. He and Heather stared at one another for a long moment.

"You're up!" said Stella, for want of something to say.

"Looks like it," said Heather dryly. She looked far more human than she had before. The whites of her eyes were no longer dark and she was dressed in Stella's clothes, though they did nothing to hide the scales on her neck and wrists.

Magnus was still frozen, halfway to his feet.

"Magnus? This is Heather," said Stella. "The, er—"

"Sea witch," supplied Heather.

She smiled widely, revealing a mouth bristling with teeth, and Magnus took a sharp step backwards, knocking into the sideboard. Immediately the air in the room felt charged.

Stella moved a little closer to Magnus, and Nimbus gave a soft rumble of warning.

Heather gave them a scathing look. "I don't bite. Not generally, anyway. Speaking of which, is there any food? I'm starving."

* * *

By the time Tamar came clattering in through the door, Heather was devouring a sandwich and Magnus was looking, if not relaxed, at least not about to run away. Nimbus had settled up in the corner of the ceiling, where he could keep an eye on things.

"Magnus!" exclaimed Tamar. "I'm so glad you're here. Has Stella told you our plan?"

Magnus gave a tense nod.

"And Heather! You're looking much more yourself!"

"That's good, is it?" said Heather, with a deadpan stare.

Tamar paused awkwardly, then flapped at Stella. "The good folk are going to be here any minute. Go and find your grandpa's hammer. Hurry!"

"Bossy as ever, then?" said Heather, glancing at Stella.

Stella gave her a swift smile then dashed upstairs to Grandpa's room. Nimbus followed her. He settled on Grandpa's bed as she searched for the Trowie hammer.

It didn't take her long to find it – carefully wrapped in a soft cloth, in the bottom of his bag. It made her heart hurt a little, seeing all his clothes neatly folded.

Come back safely, Grandpa.

* * *

It was full twilight when four Trows appeared, accompanied by Tas and the novices. Tamar ushered them all inside. Tas took one look at Heather and rapidly herded the novices through to the sitting room, before any of them could start asking questions.

She raised her eyebrows at Stella as she closed the door: *I hope you know what you're doing.*

Broonie gave Tamar a curt nod. "Are we ready?"

"Where are the others?" said Tamar, looking at the door behind him, as though more Trows might appear at any moment.

Broonie shrugged. "Not coming. But you've got us."

"Do they not understand what's at stake?!"

Broonie stiffened slightly and drew himself up tall. He still only reached Tamar's shoulder, but his dark eyes smouldered with indignation. Karl tapped Broonie's arm and nodded towards the door. *Let's go.*

Stella stepped forward. "Thank you for coming to help," she said. "We're really grateful."

"We just want our gems back," said Karl, unsmiling.

Tamar nodded. "All the gems that don't contain clouds – agreed? The rest, you'll help us break?"

"I told you, didn't I?" muttered Karl, to the other Trows. "Those gems should never should have left our hands. Hoarding clouds! And now they demand our help to break them? Where's the respect? Where's the apology?"

Broonie clapped a hand on Karl's shoulder. "We break those that contain clouds. All the remaining gems will be returned to us." He nodded at Tamar. "This Storm Weaver has given her word."

Karl said something hard and sharp that sounded like a curse.

On Tamar's shoulder, Sid danced to life.

"A master gem?" repeated Tamar.

Karl scowled at her, surprised to be understood. "It's ours. It should never have been relinquished. Not for any foolish covenant."

"It controls all the other gems," Stella told her.

Karl narrowed his eyes and nodded. "The council still have it," he said. "We *told* them. If they'd handed it over to us, this could all have been done by now."

"Actually, the council don't have it," said Stella. "It's in Winter's Keep."

Karl burst out laughing. It was an uncomfortable sound – raucous and grating – loud in the small kitchen. "That's like keeping matches in with your dynamite!" he said, his tone mocking.

"We know where it is," said Stella, glancing at Magnus.

Thirty-Three

A SIMPLE PLAN

OUTSIDE, the wind had picked up, moaning and whistling around the turrets of the Ice Weavers' fortress. Stella had put on an extra jumper, her sunshine scarf, and her coat. The temperature had dropped considerably since sunset.

Not that Winter's Keep is ever warm, she thought, looking up at its ice-spiked outer walls.

They had only a rough plan, but Tamar insisted it was good enough.

"There's no need to overcomplicate things. Simple plans are the best. We've all got our tasks. And the first one is to get inside."

Stella looked across the narrow bridge of rock that spanned the deep chasm between the island and the castle. Far below, the crash of the waves was loud – a booming rumble as they hit the rocks at the base of Winter's Keep, followed by a long sloshing splash as the water forced its way through the channel below, and gurgled its way out again.

Magnus jogged the length of the bridge without looking down once, and Stella was suddenly reminded that this was his home. At the far end, he rapped at the huge gates. A small grating opened, bright as a candle in the gloom.

She couldn't hear what he said, over the crashing of the waves, but a moment later the gates opened and Magnus beckoned. Tamar and the Trows went first, then Tas and the novices. Stella tightened the straps of her rucksack one last time, then followed with Heather.

The sea witch had become more subdued on hearing Tamar's plan. Coming ashore was one thing. Going to the heart of Winter's Keep, it seemed, was another.

Stella had lent her one of Grandpa's jumpers. The long sleeves hung down over her hands, covering the scales. A scarf and hat completed her disguise. But she was still edgy about coming face to face with the Ice Weavers.

"You alright?" asked Stella.

"Stop worrying about me," said Heather, "and watch where you're walking."

Stella glanced down and saw a froth of foam far below. She

gasped and stepped back quickly. She'd strayed too close to the edge. She moved back to the centre of the walkway. Nimbus swooped down and floated along directly in front of her, leading the way.

I know, I know. Keep to the middle.

At the far end of the bridge, a small door had been opened in the heavy gates. The light from inside shone like a beacon.

A tall Ice Weaver hurried them inside, his eyes constantly darting between the sea outside and the large group of novices. Heather slipped past him and stood in the shadows close to the wall, her head dipped to hide her face. With a final glance to check no one else was coming, the Ice Weaver swung the door closed. He bolted it top and bottom and slid a heavy wooden bar across it, then turned to face Broonie and bowed deeply.

"My name is Nevis. I am deeply honoured to welcome you to Winter's Keep."

Broonie was unimpressed. "What happened to honour when you decided to use those gems of ours?"

Nevis shook his head briefly and swallowed. His Adam's apple bobbed rapidly in his throat. "On behalf of all the Ice Weavers, I'd like to deeply apologise, for our *previous* leader's actions," he said. "And I'd like to reassure you that she is no longer in charge."

"Where *is* Velda?" interrupted Tamar.

Nevis glanced along the stark hallway. "She's . . . indisposed."

His voice was neutral, but a small muscle by his eye twitched. Stella couldn't tell if he was embarrassed or angry.

"You have our master gem?" asked Broonie, bluntly.

"Velda's got it," piped up Stella.

"Where is she?" asked Broonie.

Nevis opened his mouth and closed it like a fish. Two bright circles of colour flushed high on his cheekbones. *Embarrassed. Definitely.*

"We can't reach her. She's in the final retreat. It can only be opened from inside."

"I think you'll find we've got a key for that," said Broonie, hefting his hammer in his hand.

"Er, the thing is," said Nevis, looking increasingly nervous, "it's . . . iron-bound."

Karl spat on the floor as though Nevis had delivered the grossest insult. "You made it Trow-proof?!" he snarled.

"Well, then – plan A it is," said Tamar briskly. "We'll free the clouds one by one."

Magnus tugged on Stella's sleeve. "I'll go and talk to her again," he said quietly. "She might open up for me . . ."

Stella nodded. "Good luck."

"Right, what are we standing about for?" said Tamar. She flapped imperiously at the gangly Ice Weaver. "Take us to the gems. No time to waste."

* * *

The dark stone walls echoed with their hurried footsteps. Cellar stairs, steep and gloomy, stretched down into the rock beneath the castle. The stairwell smelled of wet stone and old, cold air.

As she stepped through the archway at the bottom, Stella's eyes widened. They were in a huge vaulted space beneath the castle. Metal racks stretched away down the cavern, as far as she could see. All of them contained trays of gems.

How many were there?

"Here's the list," said Tas, pushing her way to the front. "These ones first." She glanced at the novices and smiled.

Nevis took the list and disappeared into the depths of the cavern. The Trows commandeered a long stone-topped workbench and began to lay out their tools.

Tas gathered the novices in a wide circle. "You all know what to do," she said. "It's likely to get a bit hectic in here, but just focus on *your* clouds. Call them in, calm them down. They might not recognise you at first, but don't take it personally. Arca and Drench are going to provide cloud cover so that nobody gets accidentally zapped."

Stella looked at Tas in surprise and smiled. Surrounded by storm novices, all of them older than her, she was calling the shots. And all of them were listening.

Maybe this would actually work.

"Make sure they know you're here," continued Tas. "Once you've got them under control, we need them providing cloud cover to the Trows and leading other clouds outside. Look, here comes Nevis. Who's first?"

Nevis glanced down at the label on the tray as he set it down in front of the Trows. "Aaron."

Aaron stepped forward and rubbed his hands together nervously.

"You want us to break them one by one?" Broonie asked Tamar.

She shook her head. "We don't have time for that. All four are his."

Broonie looked up. "Be ready, then." Aaron nodded. Four hammers came down and the cavern filled with darkness.

"Fizzboom! Terror! Night's Breath! Sparks!" Aaron's voice was powerful and clear. It echoed around the vaulted chambers of the crypt. Stella peered up through the cloud cover at the boiling ceiling of storm.

He shouted the names again, and again. The darkness gradually resolved into four distinct clouds, cannonballing between the stone arches, flickering like broken bulbs. One of them plunged towards Aaron. Stella's breath stopped in her throat.

The ominous patch of darkness wrapped itself around him.

A cloud hug.

The novice's eyes filled with happy tears. He looked up and shouted again. "It's me, Aaron! I'm here. I've missed you so much." He let out a yelp of laughter as the remaining three clouds dived towards him. For a moment, he was lost from view, shrouded in darkness, then the clouds gradually lifted and began to circle him. "I told you!" he said. "I told them I'd get you back!"

Stella took Heather's hand. *This is why we're here.*

Tas came over to Aaron, rubbed his arm and smiled. "Fizzboom?!"

Aaron shrugged and gave her a half smile. "Hey, I was five when I caught him." He looked up, his face glowing with joy. "Anyhow, it suits him."

"Who's next?" said Broonie.

"Leela," replied Nevis, reading the next label.

* * *

Four of the novices had got their clouds back when Heather began to get antsy. Not all the reunions had gone as smoothly as Aaron's. The high arched ceiling bore snail trails of ice and several scorch marks, where storms had exploded to life the instant they were released.

"This isss taking too long," whispered Heather. For the past few minutes, she'd been pacing. Now she stood still, vibrating with nervous energy, her fists clenched.

Stella glanced anxiously at her. "Can you feel the Teran? Is he here?"

"He's clossse." Heather hissed through her teeth.

All the hairs on the back of Stella's neck stood on end. "I'll tell Tamar they need to go faster," she reassured her.

The main body of the crypt was fogged with whirling clouds now. Stella followed the sound – a steady clink of metal against stone. The Trows stood in a row, their hammers coming down with swift precision, the floor around them littered with sparkling shards of crystal.

Tamar was working alongside them, enthusiastically wielding Grandpa's hammer. As Stella approached, she brought it down hard. A cloud screamed out of the broken gem like a lit firework. Stella dodged.

"Watch yourself!" said Tamar. "You shouldn't be this close without cloud cover."

Stella glanced up and was relieved to see Nimbus nudging the frantic cloud away in the direction of the novices.

"Heather says we're going too slowly. The Teran is nearly here."

Tamar glanced at the long line of Ice Weavers, carrying tray after tray of gems to be broken, and her mouth tightened. They were nowhere near finished.

Tamar put her hammer down and clapped Broonie on the shoulder. "Fast as you can."

"You think we're not?" he growled, as he pulled the next tray towards him. "Bring us that master gem."

Tamar hurried over to Heather. One look told her all she needed to know. She scooped Sid up and sat him on Heather's shoulder, then she collared a passing Ice Weaver and took the tray of gems he was carrying.

"You! Take these two up to the lookout tower. This one knows what to watch for," she said, nodding at Heather, "and the other is handy with lightning."

The Ice Weaver's eyes widened as he took in Heather's scaled skin and needle teeth.

"Quickly, now!" chided Tamar.

He turned and led them through the swirling haze back to the stairway.

"We'll keep going as long as we can," Tamar called after them, "but you must do everything you can to buy us time . . ."

Thirty-Four

RISING TIDE

THE Ice Weaver led them through a series of passages and winding staircases, until they emerged on an outside walkway. The sky overhead was dark and the air whirled with sharp flecks of ice. He pointed to a doorway ahead of them.

"Through there," he said, his eyes fixed on Heather's teeth, then he turned and scurried back the way he'd come.

Heather bristled and Stella put a hand on her shoulder. "Ignore him. Let's go."

A long spiral staircase led them dizzyingly up. The door at the very top opened onto an octagonal stone platform. There were low walls on every side and a pointed roof overhead. Stella moved to the edge and looked out.

It wasn't the highest turret of Winter's Keep, but it was close. The castle made more sense from above; not just a towering collection of jagged rocks, after all. The walls were arranged in concentric circles; the tallest in the centre.

Far below, she could see Ice Weavers patrolling the outermost wall like little blue ants. Beyond the sharp grey rooftops, she could see the Gate House. The narrow shard of the bridge looked impossibly fragile from up here.

"You're looking in the wrong direction," said Heather.

She was standing on the far side of the tower. The wind had blown her hat off and her dark hair whipped around her pale face.

"What are we looking for?" asked Stella.

The flicker of a smile moved across Heather's face. "Anything unusual . . ." she said. "Anything untoward."

It was strange hearing Tamar's phrase on Heather's lips. But of course, she'd been Tamar's apprentice too.

Stella moved across to join Heather and looked out at the huge expanse of sea. The long ridges of waves rolled relentlessly past, capped with white foam that glowed in the twilight. She pulled her binoculars out of her rucksack and hung them round her neck, then tucked her bag into the shadow of the wall, out of the way.

As she stood up again, she snuck a sideways glance at Heather.

Her skin looked blue in the twilight, her scales shimmering in the *simmer dim*. She definitely seemed more at ease on land since

Sid had worked his magic, but she was still far from human.

I just hope she'll still be on our side when the Teran gets here.

* * *

They'd been watching for almost an hour now, and Stella was beginning to feel like an icicle. Nowhere in the turret was protected from the freezing wind.

Her hands had gone from cold to completely numb, and when she tucked them under her armpits they seemed to suck the heat from her body, rather than gaining any warmth.

"There," said Heather, pointing.

Stella leant forwards. She squinted into the distance, beyond the headland. Was there a patch of darkness there? A gap in the regular pattern of the waves?

She brought her binoculars up and swallowed. All around the headland the water fizzed with silver. A whole shoal of fish twisted and flipped on the surface: jumping, falling, jumping again. Normally that meant dolphins or whales, hunting beneath the surface. Tonight? Who knew? She trained the binoculars on the dark sea around the panicked shoal and wished she could see through water.

"It's starting," said Heather. "Any second now."

Nimbus was floating a little way outside the turret. Stella leant forward on the wall and nodded at him. *You ready?*

The little cloud flickered and sparked.

Immediately, the heavy clouds above him lit up blinding white. A bone-trembling rumble of thunder shook the air.

Stella ducked back under the edge of the roof; her heart hammering double-time. "Is that the Teran's storm?"

"No," said Heather, with a sly smile. "That? Is Fury."

Stella gave a nervous laugh. "I'm glad he's on our side."

Heather gave a slight shrug. "Can't promise that," she said. "He's never been big on taking orders. Even less so since being locked up. Still, he seems to have taken a shine to Nimbus."

Stella smiled at her little cloud, patrolling valiantly beneath the far larger one. A flash of orange off in the distance caught her attention. She brought the binoculars up again and gasped. A boat; a big boat, the neon orange of a life raft box bright on the foredeck.

Its prow jutted past the headland, close to where the water frothed with fish. It was listing heavily to one side and far too close to the rocks.

Her heart clenched in horror. Mum! Dad!

Were they still on board? And where was Grandpa?

"Get back," snapped Heather, pulling Stella back from the edge.

There was a huge crash and the tower trembled under their feet. Stella gaped in horror as a wide section of the outermost castle wall tottered and fell, scattering huge blocks of stone across the courtyard below. A solid green river of water poured through the gap.

At least, that's what it looked like, until it turned. The suckers underneath were as large as tractor tyres, flexing like gaping mouths as they reached for the next wall.

"Kraken," said Heather grimly.

"Nimbus! Lightning! Get it!"

The little cloud swooped low and a bolt cracked down, striking with a hot sizzle. The tentacle shrank back, but was soon questing forward in another direction.

"Again, Nimbus!"

Heather raised both her arms. The castle was lit by a raging blast of lightning. One bolt after another, crashingly loud, blasting wet chunks of fishy flesh high into the air.

Fury! realised Stella, in awe.

The huge tentacle contracted, muscular and fat, then disappeared back over the wall.

But it was too late. The damage was done.

Beneath them, Ice Weavers swarmed along the walls to defend the breach. Blue ice began to grow from the broken walls, as their clouds set to work.

Stella looked beyond them, searching for any new threat. Her eyes widened. The rock bridge was almost submerged. The sea was rising, each huge wave bringing it higher; an endless tide, climbing the walls of Winter's Keep.

Moments later, a raging torrent of water flowed through the gap, shattering newly formed shards of ice and surging into the castle.

"More, Nimbus! Don't stop!"

Nimbus darted to and fro, throwing bright bolts into the turbulent water.

Heather began to direct Fury with wild stabs and slashes of her arms. The sky flashed and boomed. Huge arcing forks of power snapped down, throwing up geysers of steam.

But what use was lightning against the rising sea?

The water was filling the courtyards below, streaming onwards through archways and doors.

The crypt will flood! It's the lowest point . . . The realisation flowed like ice water through Stella's veins. She grabbed Heather's arm. "Can you stop the water?"

Heather pulled her arm free with a rough tug. "Only as a sea witch."

"But Tas, Tamar, everybody; they're all down in the crypt. They'll drown!"

Heather shook her head. "I can barely control Fury as it is."

"Nimbus can help."

Heather let out a strangled groan. "Weather weaver, or sea witch?" she said. "I can't be both." Sid danced to life on her shoulder, a staccato stream of protest.

For once, Stella was glad she couldn't understand him.

"Sea witch."

Guilt churned in her chest as she said it. Heather had only just come ashore; given up being a sea witch. And now she was asking her to turn back.

Heather looked at Stella for a long moment, then nodded.

"I can't hold it back forever," she said. "You need to release the storm clouds. All of them."

Stella nodded. "I'll try."

Heather scooped Sid up and gently put him on Stella's shoulder. The spider scrunched himself into a tight knuckled ball and clung there, looking defeated.

Heather closed her eyes and shuddered. She ran her fingertips down her neck. Gills opened like bloodless wounds, gaping in the freezing air.

Stella reflexively put a hand to her own throat. It looked so painful; so unnatural.

Green rippled across Heather's skin, like the shadow of a cloud across the sea. When she opened her eyes, they were as black as a shark's and just as hungry. "Sssstand back," she hissed, through bristling teeth.

Stella took a sharp step backwards.

The sea witch opened her mouth and screamed; a strange two-tone shriek that went on and on. The sound seemed to coil around itself, full of sharp harmonics and warbling discords.

Stella clapped her hands over her ears.

Beneath the breach in the castle wall, the rising wave gradually dipped, as though someone had pressed a glass bowl into the water.

The Haken paused to draw breath and the dip in the water grew a little shallower. Angular fins and winding tentacles broke the surface. The wave pushed higher.

Stella turned and sprinted for the stairs.

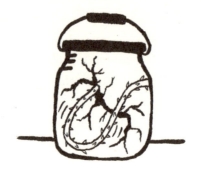

Thirty-Five

ALL OR NOTHING

HER first thought had been to warn Tamar, but when she reached the inner wall, the novices were already piling out of the door, their trousers clinging wetly to their legs, staring around in horror at the devastation outside.

Tas pushed past them. "The crypt's flooded."

"Where's Tamar?"

"Still down there with the Trows. They'll keep going as long as they can. Every storm they release is one less for the Teran. She said to find Magnus. That master gem's our only hope to stop this, now."

"Did she say *where* to find him?"

Tas shook her head. "The final retreat, is all I know."

High overhead, Heather let out another long howling shriek. The novices all looked up, their faces pale and their eyes wide.

"She's gone sea witch, hasn't she?" said Tas in horror, staring up at the turret.

"She's still on our side," insisted Stella. "She's trying to hold back the tide." She glanced towards the breach to see if it was working and her heart skipped. *Briar!*

A tangled network of brambles stretched across the gap, creating a hurried scaffold of reinforcement for the ice.

"Look! Magnus! It's got to be!"

As she watched, another detachment of Ice Weavers ran towards him, adding their clouds to the effort. "I've got to get down there," she said.

"No way," said Tas, shaking her head vehemently. "If he wants to be a hero, that's his business. Doesn't mean you have to—"

But Stella was already jogging away from her. "See if you can get that lot weather weaving," she called over her shoulder, pointing at the novices. "And watch the water."

As she said it, a tentacle snaked up out of the courtyard. *They're inside, already!*

"Nimbus!" she yelled.

The little cloud swooped down and fired three swift sizzling forks at the tentacle's tip, making it curl and writhe. Stella sprinted for the outer wall.

* * *

The ramparts near the breach were a hive of activity, jostling with blue uniformed Ice Weavers, their attention focused on the swirling blizzard of clouds working to fill the gap. They didn't even notice her. Stella slipped through the crowd like an eel, ducking under raised arms, sliding between the packed bodies. Where was he?

The noise as she approached the breach was overwhelming. A constant thundering rush of water, riven by the sharp creak and crackle of growing ice.

"Magnus! Magnus!!" She cupped her hands around her mouth, trying to make herself heard over the din. At last, she caught a glimpse of green amongst the blue and darted forward. "Magnus."

His face was tight with concentration, encouraging Briar to expand the growing lattice of green. She tugged on his sleeve. "Magnus!"

He glanced at her, then back at Briar. "Bit busy here."

"We have to get the master gem!"

"I tried." The words were ground out between his teeth.

"Then try again! It's our only chance."

Magnus shook his head in frustration, his concentration broken. "Stick at it, Briar!" he called, before turning towards her. "The final retreat isn't something you break into. That's the point of it. And she's iced herself in," he said. "Trust me, I tried, but I don't think she could even hear me. I'm better out here, protecting the castle."

"If we don't do something now, there's not going to *be* a castle!"

Magnus paled slightly at that, then looked up at the network of vines, which were rapidly icing over. As he watched, another surge of water pushed its way through, tearing the newest growth up by its roots. He set his jaw. "Follow me."

He quickly led the way back towards the inner keep. Stella followed, her gaze darting between Magnus's back and the water below. The outer courtyard was awash, the dark water seething with nightmares. A blue flame surfaced, revealing a bulging hump of scaly head, covered in staring fish eyes. Stella stifled a whimper.

Marool. Knowing its name didn't help. Why didn't any of the books explain how to fight them?

Because you can't, whispered a cruel fear at the back of her mind.

As they neared the inner walls, Magnus faltered and slowed. He turned to Stella with a look of horror on his face and pointed. The way ahead was blocked by a fallen tower – a tumbled rubble of stone, littered with massive chunks of ice. "It's buried," he said, weakly. "Under that lot."

Stella stared at it in dismay. "There's got to be another way in?!"

Magnus swallowed and pointed back towards the most dangerous section of the wall. "Yeah," he said. "Down there."

A long flight of stone steps led down to a doorway. The steps were littered with blocks of ice, blasted from the defences above. The doorway itself was almost directly beneath the breach and perilously close to the rising water. The net of briars above looked immensely fragile. Even if they made it down there, would they be able to make it out?

* * *

Stella and Magnus looked over the edge. A sloping scree of ice stretched from the top of the wall all the way down to the inky pool in the courtyard. The stone steps that had led to the doorway were partly buried in ice. The steps that remained were broken and gappy, smashed and cracked by the fallen chunks of ice.

As they watched, a fat sinuous tentacle slid up onto the ice and back into the water, as though exploring the way up.

"We'll have to be fast," said Stella. "I think the Kraken's trying to get in there, too."

Magnus nodded, his face pale but determined. "Let's slow it down," he said. He scraped around in one of his pockets and launched a handful of seeds over-arm down the slope. "Briar!" His cloud chased the seeds across the ice, dropping a shower of summer rain wherever they fell. Stella watched anxiously. Could anything grow in ice and salt water?

Heather let loose another deafening scream and the huge tentacle changed direction, snaking up out of the water, wrinkled and slimy. It began to wrap itself around the base of the watchtower, seeking the source of the sound.

She cupped her hands around her mouth. "Nimbus!"

The little cloud skimmed towards her, just above the dark water, making her heart tremble that he might be snatched under. When he reached her, he threw himself at her chest and wrapped around her in a cloud hug.

"I know. I love you too," said Stella, tears trembling in her eyes. "But I need you to look after Heather. That's your job now."

Nimbus clung closer.

"Please? She's holding back the water, so she can't tell Fury what she needs. But you can, can't you? Look! She needs help!"

Nimbus finally peeled himself away from her. He darted towards the tentacle and fired a volley of lightning at its tip, making it shrink back. The sky overhead gave an echoing flicker and a triple fork of lightning flashed down, striking the base of the tentacle. It slithered rapidly back under the water.

"Yes, Nimbus! That's it! Get Fury to help!"

"There. That'll have to do," said Magnus. Stunted thorn trees now dotted the slope, their black roots winding into deep cracks in the ice. He started down the steps. "Watch the gaps."

It was a precarious climb, over tumbled chunks of ice and damaged steps. Stella's fingers burned with cold and her feet slipped and skidded on the broken edges.

Magnus reached the bottom first and began hammering at the narrow door. "Mum, it's me! Magnus!"

Stella pressed her back to the wall and kept an eye on the water. The deep pool in the courtyard below swirled with malevolent forms, circling impatiently, waiting for the water level to rise.

Another wave poured over the top of the castle wall and the ice creaked and shifted.

A muscular tentacle rose out of the water in the courtyard and snaked up the ice towards them. The thorn trees buckled and cracked under its weight.

"Oh, no!" breathed Stella. "It's heard you."

"Mum! Let me in!!"

Thirty-Six

THE FINAL RETREAT

A SERIES of firecracker pops ignited the gloom. Not just
Nimbus – three storm clouds were firing at the long
tentacle; inaccurate, but determined. The tentacle contracted, then
retreated. Thin lines of smoke rose from a series of scorches along
its length. It smelled like charred sardines; Grandpa's favourite
breakfast. Stella swallowed and tried not to think about that.

On the far wall, Tas raised an arm in salute. The novices were
lined up beside her. It was too far to shout, so Stella waved and
gave them a thumbs up: *Keep doing that! Buy us some time!*

But below Tas, at the edge of the ice, the water was beginning to froth with movement. A writhing mass of smaller tentacles, rising like eels; hundreds of them; lashing and swiping at the inexperienced storm clouds, sending them ducking and tumbling back to their novices.

Stella began to hammer on the door alongside Magnus. "Please!"

The water rushed away as the Kraken heaved itself up onto the ice. At the centre of the tentacles was a circle of teeth, all pointing inwards, sharp as hooks.

Stella screamed.

Magnus screamed too. "Muuuuum! Let us in!"

They both shrank back against the door, but there was nowhere to go, nowhere left to run, as the tentacles swarmed up the slope towards them.

With a sharp crack, the ice holding the door in place broke and they both fell inside.

Magnus leapt to his feet and slammed the door shut, running the bolts home.

"What happened? Did she let us in?" said Stella.

There was a huge boom as something heavy hit the door on the other side. It rattled in its frame.

"I don't know," said Magnus. "But we can't stay here." He grabbed Stella's sleeve and together they ran.

At the far end of the corridor was a cool glow. Stella bounded towards it, Magnus at her side. Behind them came the regular boom of the Kraken battering the door.

The corridor was a dead end. Stella skidded to a halt and stared around in dismay. The icy blue chamber was just like the winter cavern in the trials; surrounded on every side by a solid wall of glacial blue ice. They were trapped.

Frozen within one of the walls was a heavy iron-bound door. It had been completely swallowed by the ice; there, but unreachable.

"Told you!" said Magnus. "She's iced herself in. I tried talking to her earlier, but I doubt she can even hear me."

"She can," insisted Stella. "Otherwise, she wouldn't have opened that door for us, would she?"

"You think that was her?" retorted Magnus. "We were both hammering on it."

Stella huffed in frustration. "We've got to get in there somehow! It's not like we can go back." Another boom echoed down the corridor and Magnus's face paled.

Stella stared at the huge iron door. It looked as though it had been frozen there for centuries.

"Try calling to her again," she suggested.

"I did that already," said Magnus, crouching down and putting his head in his hands.

"Try again! Tell her about the Kraken! I can't believe she'd leave you out here."

Magnus shook his head and stood up. "I've got a better idea," he said, reaching for her collar. He hooked his finger under the sunshine scarf and pulled it out.

She'd forgotten she was wearing it. The scarf hung limply in his hand, a soft sandy beige; not even a hint of a glow. "You want me to find joy? Now?!"

Magnus shrugged. "Maybe if we both try?"

Stella and Magnus knelt facing one another, their hands gripped together, the sunshine scarf hanging limply between them.

"You start," said Stella. "You were good at this before. Tell me something happy."

Magnus closed his eyes and frowned in concentration. "Briar. Briar makes me happy."

The sunshine scarf paled to lemon yellow. Stella bit her lip, not wanting to hope. "More," she demanded. "When was the last time he made you laugh out loud?"

A smile twitched at the corner of Magnus's mouth. "When we first got here. He wanted to cheer me up, so he filled my room with roses – floor to ceiling, inside the council building. You should have seen the guards' faces when they saw!"

Stella smiled and squeezed his hands. Magnus opened his eyes and looked at the faint glow from the scarf. "Alright, your turn," he said. "Tell me a happy thought."

Stella closed her eyes and tried to think of something; anything. *Aaron,* she remembered. "Seeing the novices getting their clouds back," she said. "It made everything we went through at the Gathering worth it."

She pictured the delight on Aaron's face; the happy tears; the way his clouds had dived towards him. It was the best ever reunion.

"That'll do," said Magnus. She opened her eyes to find that they were kneeling in a puddle. She'd been concentrating so hard, she hadn't even realised. Between them, the scarf blazed glorious gold, radiating midsummer sunshine.

The ice around the hidden chamber had melted away. Not completely, but enough that the heavy iron door stood proud of the slick surface. She scrambled to her feet and put a hand to the cold metal.

She nodded hopefully at Magnus. "Try again."

Magnus leant against the door with both hands, his mouth close to the metal. "Mum? It's me, Magnus."

There was no response, but Stella nodded for him to keep going.

"Mum! If you *really* want to protect me, then let me in. I'm scared, Mum. Please."

There was a heavy clunk that made the iron door ring like a bell. Magnus and Stella stared at one another. "Go on!" she whispered.

Magnus turned the heavy handle and pulled. The door swung open with no resistance and Magnus stepped inside. Stella slipped in behind him.

Magnus's mum sat hunched in a huge throne of ice. Her clothes were rumpled and her hair stood out in odd spikes, as though she'd been running her fingers through it. Her hands were curled like claws around a large gem.

The master gem! It has to be!

Velda's eyes were soft with worry as Magnus stepped inside,

but went wide with horror the instant she spotted Stella.

"You brought *her*?!" she screeched, clutching the crystal closer to her chest.

Velda raised one hand and, with a swift gesture, drew an ice dagger out of the air. She raised it towards Stella, its slim blade glinting wickedly in the cool blue glow.

"Why did you bring *her*?"

Magnus raised both his hands. "I had to, Mum. There's a Kraken. It's inside the castle. Stella helped me escape from it."

Velda shakily lowered the blade and gestured around the small room. "I've got them here," she said. "All the most *violent* storms. They won't fall into the wrong hands."

Stella looked around. Trays of gems were stacked haphazardly on every surface.

Oh, for a Trowie hammer . . .

"Mum, we need to let them go. It's the only way to stop the Teran."

Velda leant towards Magnus, her eyes burning with betrayal. "Lies!" she spat. "You're too trusting, Magnus. Who are you going to believe? Some storm-weaving mongrel and her pet *sea witch*? Or your own *mother*!"

Stella didn't give Magnus the chance to answer. She sprang forward, deflecting the blade with the sunshine scarf and snatching the master gem.

Velda snarled in fury and grabbed Stella's wrist, trying to wrench the gem back.

"Magnus, help!" Stella's yelped, as Velda raised the blade of ice, ready to plunge.

Something skittered down Stella's arm and launched itself into the air. She barely had time to register that it was Sid before Velda yowled and clutched her neck, sending Stella tumbling backwards, the master gem clutched tight in both hands.

"Go!" said Magnus. "I'll keep her here."

Stella scrambled to her feet and ran for the door, as vines began to sprout from the walls and ceiling; an impenetrable net, pierced only by Velda's howls of frustration.

Thirty-Seven

BROONIE

IT was a simple plan, 'the best kind', Tamar always said: call Nimbus and every other storm cloud he could rally. Get them to distract the Kraken long enough that she could get to the castle keep and find the Trows.

That was it. That was her plan.

She'd already tried holding the gem tight and wishing all the storm clouds free. She'd even tried shouting at it: "Release the storm clouds!"

But nothing had happened. Not that she could tell.

Maybe only Velda could use it. Or perhaps there was a secret word to make it work?

Broonie would know. But first, she had to get out of here.

She edged her way along the corridor, the heavy crystal clasped to her chest, the other hand skimming the icy wall. She was pretty sure Nimbus must have heard her.

Certainly, the banging had stopped. Even so, when she got to the outside door, she was reluctant to open it. The hinges were askew and there were pale cracks in the heavy wood. What if the Kraken was waiting, right outside?

Trust Nimbus, she told herself and slowly slid back the bolts.

Outside, the weather still raged, the sky dark with storm clouds, the wind whipping spray and ice through the air. Beyond the twisted thorn trees that Briar had grown, there was a swift flash in the darkness.

Nimbus!

He was floating directly above the deep water.

Well done! Stay there. Keep watch.

The Kraken had retreated, but for how long she didn't know. The steep slope of ice blocks was empty now, but the water in the courtyard was higher – only a couple of metres below her.

Clutching the crystal tightly, Stella eased herself out through the gap, her eyes on the water. Huge shadowy forms moved beneath the surface. Quietly, carefully, she began to climb, wincing at the sound of the ice crunching under her boots.

She might have got away with it, if the novices hadn't spotted her. A cheer went up from the wall on the far side.

"Stella!"

"Look! She's okay!"

"Climb up, quick!"

She turned swiftly, her finger to her lips. Tamar and the Trows had joined Tas. Tamar was already shushing the excited novices, but it was too late. A long tentacle shot out of the water and coiled around her ankle. It yanked, and Stella fell hard, the ice driving the breath from her chest. She heard a series of cracks and sizzles as Nimbus began to fire, but the grip on her ankle didn't loosen. Instead, it tightened, dragging her back down the slope.

A stunted tree slid past Stella's face and she wrapped one arm around its gnarled trunk. Every muscle in her body stretched as she held on. It felt like she was going to be torn in half.

Another huge wave poured over the castle wall and the grip on her ankle loosened. Stella kicked herself free and held her breath. More and more water poured over her, until her lungs burned and she wondered if it would ever end. It felt like the whole ocean was pouring into Winter's Keep.

As the wave subsided, she stuck her head up and gasped for air, scrambling further up the slope. Something cold gripped her arm and she tugged away with a yelp, her eyes wide.

"Ssstay ssstill."

Stella blinked the salt out of her eyes.

A dark form crouched next to her, scaly and muscular, its face featureless but for a pair of dark eyes; black as midnight, hungry as a shark.

"Heather?"

"You've found it, haven't you?"

Stella nodded, though it turned into a shiver.

"Ssset them freeee!"

Heather stood, yanking Stella to her feet, just as the Kraken erupted out of the water in a huge coiling mass. Stella lurched up the slope in panic.

Heather whirled to face it, sending a volley of spines flying like needles through the air. The sea witch launched herself forward and sank her teeth deep into the nearest tentacle.

Stella gagged and turned away, hauling herself up the blocks of ice, spurred on by the thrashing and splashing behind her.

When she glanced back, she saw Heather slashing and biting, clawing and fighting. There were too many – a tide of monsters, all surging towards them full of hungry intent.

"Broonie!" screamed Stella.

There was a clatter and a crunch as the Trow landed next to her. She couldn't tell where he'd come from. She thrust the crystal towards him.

Everything slowed to a crawl as he took the gem; tentacles, swarming up the ice towards them like eels; Heather, arms outstretched, poison spines flying like a rain of arrows; Broonie, holding the gem to his lips, whispering words of release.

The rumble started almost immediately: a deep bass roar that shook everything. The ice cracked and settled; the walls shook; the water rippled.

Storm clouds poured up out of every crack and crevice of Winter's Keep – dark as peat smoke – as though a huge fire had been stoked in the heart of the castle. The Kraken slithered back down the slope. The sea witch stood poised at the water's edge. Broonie reached down and hauled Stella to her feet. His hand was startlingly warm around hers.

One of the Ice Weavers on top of the wall sent up a shout. "The water's retreating!"

Overhead, the sky boiled like an inky cloud; hundreds of storms, released and ready to blow.

"Go!" shouted Tamar from the high inner wall. For a moment, Stella thought the shout was meant for her – a warning – but Tamar was looking up, shouting at the sky. "You're free! Fly, now. Find your weather weavers!"

Help them, Nimbus. Calm them down. Tell them how much they're missed.

Nimbus flew straight up and was swallowed by the heavy mass of clouds.

"Open the sluice gates!"

The shout filled Stella's heart with dread. *No! Don't open them!*

But a glance down the slope and she immediately understood why. The sea outside might be retreating, but the castle courtyard was still full to the brim, isolated now, by the retreating sea. A nightmare aquarium of midnight-depth monsters.

The order passed all the way along the castle wall, shouted from one Ice Weaver to the next, until it reached the cluster of sentries on the far side of the breach. They immediately leapt into motion, clustering around a clunky piece of machinery. Three to a side, they grabbed its huge wheels and dug their feet in. There was a screech of metal on metal as ancient cogs ground into motion.

At first, nothing happened, but then the water in the courtyard began to turn. A belch of air bubbled up in the centre and a whirlpool started to form, dizzying to watch; like a huge plug had been pulled.

The monsters were surfacing now, exposed by the falling water. The blue flame of a marool circled the courtyard, its many eyes staring skyward. Loops of sea serpent arched and coiled. Beneath them all, the tentacles of the Kraken squirmed like a pit of eels. The Teran's army of midnight-depth monsters was being sucked back into the sea.

Heather stood at the bottom of the slope, a shadowy guard watching their retreat. Stella moved carefully down the slope towards her. She'd almost reached her when a slim tentacle whipped up out of the whirling water. Heather's eyes snapped wide as it twined around her ankles.

"No!"

Stella caught Heather's arm, just as her feet were snatched from under her, pulling them both to the ground. She hung on with both hands and hooked her feet in for grip, but the toes of her boots scraped forward over the ice.

Heather was pulled further and further into the churning black water; her feet, then her legs. She thrashed, trying to break free.

With every frantic kick, Stella's grip on Heather's arm slipped, until only their hands were joined. Broonie came thumping down the slope and grabbed Stella by the ankle.

For a moment, they were stretched; a long desperate line; then Heather was yanked away, leaving Stella lying on the ice, her arms outstretched, her hands empty.

Thirty-Eight

FLOTSAM AND JETSAM

DAY dawned quietly, revealing a heavy sky and choppy seas. Stella sat on the bench outside the Gate House, huddled in blankets, her hands wrapped around a scalding mug of hot chocolate. She hadn't taken a sip yet, but she knew it wasn't going to taste good; Grandpa hadn't made it.

Most of the released storms hadn't flown home as Stella had hoped. Instead, they remained: a towering whirlpool of cloud ominously circling the peaks and towers of Winter's Keep.

They're trapping Velda, like she trapped them, she thought, with a smidge of spiteful satisfaction. It was hard to feel any kind of happy, though. Especially given that there was no sign of Fury. He'd gone, along with Heather.

The early light had revealed a swathe of wreckage, bobbing gently on the waves. Stella could see the bright orange case of the life raft, empty as a shell, turning slowly in the current, way out beyond Winter's Keep. Mum and Dad's research vessel, reduced to flotsam and jetsam.

"You swear they're okay?"

Tamar plumped herself down next to Stella. "Cross my heart. They'll be here soon."

Stella nodded. At least they were safe.

She'd barely had a chance to focus on what was happening to them last night and in one way, she was glad of that. She wasn't sure if she'd have been able to carry on, if she'd seen their boat sink.

Stella heaved a sigh and Nimbus nestled closer, making the hairs on the back of her neck prickle. "I couldn't hold on to Heather. I did try."

Tamar closed her eyes and shook her head. "Of course you couldn't. I'm impressed you even tried."

"It was just like my nightmare! Only she *wasn't* trying to pull me down, at all. I was trying to hold on to her. Tamar, what if she's—"

"Heather is tough," interrupted Tamar, refusing to let Stella finish that thought. "Tougher than anyone gives her credit for. Besides, she's a creature of the sea!"

"Only because the Teran *made* her a sea witch. What if he takes it back?"

Worry settled heavily on Tamar's face and Stella waited.

"Let's just hope for the best," said Tamar. "That girl is a survivor."

It wasn't the reassurance Stella had been hoping for. Her lip began to tremble.

Tamar nudged her, making the hot chocolate slosh in the mug. "Hey! None of that! The storm clouds have been released. The Trows have their gems back. And we saw off the spirit of winter himself!"

Stella blinked hard. "I want Mum and Dad."

"I know."

Nimbus drifted away from Stella, then turned a swift loop and took off at speed.

"Hello," said Tamar. "Where's he off to?"

A tiny spark of hope flickered to life in Stella's chest. She put the mug down on the ground and shrugged off the blanket. As she reached the corner of the house, she gave a happy shout.

Grandpa was striding up the path, flapping his arms as Nimbus tried to hug him. Behind him trailed a very bedraggled Mum and Dad.

As soon as they saw her, they both broke into a run.

* * *

311

Now it felt more like they'd won. Stella was curled on Dad's lap on the sofa, Mum's hand warm in hers. Grandpa had occupied the armchair and was telling the story of his heroic rescue mission, with huge enthusiasm.

"A wave higher than you've ever seen!" he exclaimed, raising his arms in the air. Nimbus bobbed up and down, mimicking his every gesture. "It swamped *Arctic Star*, but not before they'd put the lifeboat out. So I got myself over there, fast as I could, and threw a tow line to them."

"That was the strangest part of it all," said Dad. "That patch of calm sea that came with you."

"Sea magic," said Grandpa, patting the tattered sea shawl. It was very damp and looking a bit ragged around the edges now, but he hadn't wanted to take it off. "Saved our bacon, this did, Stella!"

"You made that, did you Stella?" said Dad.

Stella nodded.

"Amazing!"

Mum squeezed her hand and Stella turned to look at her. All the fears of last night swept through her like a wave. She'd thought she'd lost them.

"I didn't mean what I said, before," said Stella, her voice wobbling. "I didn't want you to go away. I do need you, really."

Mum stroked her cheek. "I know you didn't mean it, love. And we're back now. We're not going anywhere."

"Why didn't you come *straight* back yesterday?" said Stella. "I was so worried about you!"

Dad tilted his head. "We tried, but even with our little patch of calm, the wind was against us. Your grandpa spotted a sheltered cove and we tucked in there, until the worst had blown through."

Stella thought back to the howling wind, filled with flecks of ice, the writhing tentacles rising out of the depths. She would not have wanted to be out on a boat in that. It must have been terrifying.

"What happened to the crew?" she asked.

"They're down in the town," said Grandpa. "The council found a place to put them up in fine style."

Tamar pursed her lips and shook her head. "Anyone *else* you'd like to invite to our most secret locations?"

"Oh, come on! What else was I supposed to do?" protested Grandpa, throwing his hands up. "We barely limped back to harbour as it was. I haven't *told* them anything. Anyway, there's always brain-fog – isn't that what you always say?"

"Grandpa! Don't encourage her!" exclaimed Stella.

Grandpa winked and shook his head. "They're just glad to be ashore. I doubt they'll be asking too many questions. We'll get them ferried across to the mainland before they even realise where they are."

Dad chuckled softly. "I hope you're going to tell *us* what happened?" he said.

Stella shook her head and buried her face in his neck. "Later," she said.

* * *

Around lunchtime, Mum and Dad went down to town to check on their crew. Tamar left soon after, muttering about 'council business'.

Mum had suggested Stella try and have a sleep.

It sounded like a good idea. She *was* tired. But she soon realised sleep was going to be impossible. Her head was still whirling with worry about Heather and when she closed her eyes, all she could see was swarming sea monsters.

After half an hour of uncomfortable tossing and turning, Stella gave up. She pulled on her raincoat and made her way down to the beach with Nimbus.

The sea was still rough and the wind unpredictable. The shore was littered with rope and food containers, boxes and bottles. It looked as though someone had emptied an entire truckload of random stuff into the sea.

Boat load, realised Stella.

Stella climbed cautiously along the rocks, heading for the spot where she'd practised before. It had the best view of the water. She'd got almost all the way out, when she spotted a familiar purple cardigan, topped by tufty white hair.

Tamar.

She was sitting right down at the water's edge, on her own. Stella climbed down, pulled off her rucksack and sat down next to her. "So you *are* worried about Heather."

Tamar snorted. "Force of habit. Been worrying about that girl for years. I'm not about to stop now."

Stella frowned. That didn't feel quite true. "If you were so worried about her, why wouldn't you help me set her cloud free?"

"Because I was worried about *me*, too! I thought she'd be out for revenge – I would be, in her place."

A prickle of anger woke in Stella's chest and Nimbus let out a low rumble. "Except she wasn't, was she," stated Stella. "In fact, she saved us."

Regret settled heavily on Tamar's face and she looked down. "It's not the first time I've been wrong about Heather."

Stella scowled out at the choppy waves, accusations bubbling in her mind. *All that time, you could have helped her! But you didn't. Because you were scared.*

Tamar sniffed and rubbed her temple. "What can I tell you? I'm a foolish old woman, who now and again makes gigantic mistakes. Unfortunately, Heather's caught more than her fair share of those."

Stella folded her arms. *That's a rubbish excuse for an apology!*

As though he'd heard Stella's thoughts, Sid scampered up Tamar's shoulder and extended one long leg to poke her in the cheek.

"Fine! I'm *sorry*!" said Tamar crossly. "Is that what you both want to hear?"

Stella nodded and Sid retracted his leg in approval. He lowered himself down on a shining thread and settled on the lapel of Tamar's cardigan.

"She can hate me if she likes," muttered Tamar. "I just need to know she's alright."

Stella undid the strap of her rucksack and pulled out the conch. Tamar's eyes settled on it and she raised her eyebrows. For a moment, hope circled in the air.

Thirty-Nine

AN OVERDUE APOLOGY

STELLA turned the shell over in her hands and licked her lips. She almost didn't want to try it, in case it didn't work. Then they'd *know* Heather wasn't coming back. And that would be worse. She heaved a brief sigh, then brought it to her lips.

The low note echoed against the high cliffs; a mournful tone, full of longing.

The waves rolled in, regular as breathing. Nimbus tracked to and fro over the water, but nothing broke the surface. The waves kept their secrets.

"Stella?"

Stella twisted round. Magnus was coming down the steep steps. She raised an arm, then stood up and climbed back across the rocks towards him.

"You two looking for Heather?" he asked.

Stella nodded and glanced out at the sea. Nimbus still patrolled back and forth.

"I heard what she did," said Magnus. "Good person to have on your side."

Person. It meant a lot. Especially coming from Magnus.

"You were a bit of a hero too," said Stella.

Magnus looked at his feet in embarrassment.

Stella gave him a friendly poke in the shoulder. "If you hadn't helped me get that gem out, we'd probably all be Kraken snacks by now."

"Kraken snacks?" Magnus chortled.

Stella smiled briefly and looked out to sea again, worry settling heavy in her heart.

Briar floated gracefully down from the clifftop and joined Nimbus. He settled over the surf in a misty haze.

"You think this weather's going to clear anytime soon?" said Magnus, nodding up at the hundreds of small storm clouds circling overhead.

Stella shrugged. "I hope so."

"Of course it will," called Tamar, confidently. "They just need a bit of time to reorientate themselves. That's all."

Magnus was easily reassured, but he didn't know Tamar like Stella did.

"The council are planning some kind of big celebration," he said, raising his eyebrows. "If Heather does turn up, tell her she's invited. The Ice Weavers are going to make a formal apology to everyone who had their clouds taken. That includes her."

Better late than never.

* * *

Stella re-joined Tamar after Magnus had gone. They sat there for a long time. Now and again, Stella blew the conch, but each time with less expectation of an answer. Eventually, Nimbus grew tired of sentry duty and swooped up to join the storm clouds, riding the wind around the cliffs of Winter's Keep.

Stella wrapped her arms round her legs and rested her head on her knees, humming the selkie song Gran had taught her. Heather's version would have been better – sadder – but she couldn't remember how it went.

"You expecting someone?"

Stella twisted, then leapt to her feet. Heather was floating lazily in the water, just beyond the breakers. With a swift smile, she ducked beneath the surface, gliding beneath the floating wreckage to the rocks. Stella held out her hands and hauled her up out of the water into a wet hug.

"You're alive!"

As she let go, she ran her fingers down the fine scales on Heather's arm, checking she was really real.

Heather grinned and flapped her gills. "You know I can breathe underwater, right?"

"Told you she'd be alright, didn't I?" said Tamar gruffly, climbing to her feet.

Heather stiffened and Stella stepped between them. She fixed Tamar with a pointed glare.

Tamar cleared her throat, steeling herself. "Heather, I've a few things I need to set straight with you. Skies above, I'm far from perfect, but—"

Heather face contorted in a snarl and Stella gasped. *Spit it out, Tamar!*

Tamar stood her ground and set her jaw. "I'm sorry," she said. "Sorry I did a rubbish job of training you. Sorry I let Velda take your cloud. Sorry I stood in the way of you getting him back. Most of all, I'm sorry I didn't listen to you. I let you down. I know that."

Heather watched her closely and flexed her hands. A row of spines appeared along her knuckles. She didn't say anything.

Tamar eyed Heather's hands and hitched her weather bag higher on her shoulder nervously. Sid seized his moment and darted onto her hand. He raised himself up and began a swift flurry of conversation, directing it at both Tamar and Heather.

Heather watched him closely and her face softened slightly. Tamar's face darkened as the leg-waving continued. Heather let out a short laugh and Stella looked at her in surprise.

"Right, Sid! That's quite enough from you." Tamar scooped him off her knuckles and dumped him unceremoniously into her weather bag, before striding away over the rocks.

"What did he say?"

Heather's eyes gleamed with humour. "That if Tamar ever does wrong by me again, he'll bite her in her sleep."

Stella gawped.

Heather shrugged. "I've always liked Sid."

* * *

Stella sat down on a broad rock. "So, what happened, after the Kraken pulled you down?" She'd spent all night trying to imagine it, then trying to un-imagine it again. It was like all her worst nightmares rolled into one.

She patted the space next to her and Heather sat down gingerly. Her movements were measured, cautious.

"Sorry! Do you need to be in the water?" said Stella. "I didn't think, just dragged you out! But it's okay. I can sit down by the edge."

Heather shook her head. "Something's changed. I'm . . . different, now. Look." She lifted up one foot and showed Stella the sole. "No more suckers!"

"So you can come ashore?!"

Heather shrugged. "Seems like it," she said. "I don't quite trust it yet. I hope it lasts. Imagine – dry land, whenever I want. No wincing, no limping, nothing!" She flexed her toes.

Stella took Heather's hand and smiled. "You finally get to choose."

Heather nodded. "I mean, I probably won't . . . come ashore. It's not like I'd be welcome. But at least I can find myself a quiet spot, somewhere out of the way; be with Fury, whenever we want."

"You'll always be welcome at my house."

Heather gave her a sideways look. "Don't want to scare the locals," she said.

"Trust me. When Mum and Dad hear you saved my life, you'll be lucky if they don't ask you to move in!"

Heather hurriedly shook her head.

"Visit, at least?" said Stella, seriously. "You know, whenever you fancy some food that's actually, er, cooked?"

Heather gave a slight smile and nodded. "Perhaps."

"Heather!" There was a loud whoop from the steps and they both looked up. Tas was hurrying down the steep stone steps at a speed that made Stella's stomach clench. She jumped off the bottom step and rushed towards them.

"You're alive!" she yelled joyfully at Heather. "We thought you'd drowned!

Heather stared at her. "I'm a sea witch . . ."

"Well, yeah, I know that. But still! Stella was scared the Teran might take your powers away?"

Heather nodded. "He did."

"So, how . . ." Tas shook her head in confusion.

"The Sea Mither saved me."

Stella gaped. "What? When were you going to mention that? You *saw* her?"

Heather nodded. "Kind of – I was way down deep when it happened."

"Tell us everything!" said Tas, her eyes wide.

Heather pulled her knees up and wrapped her arms around them. Her lips tightened for a moment, then she took a breath. "It's dark down there," she said. "Cold. The Teran waited until I was all the way down at midnight depth before he took my powers. I couldn't breathe. I couldn't tell which way was up. Even if I could have, it was too far to swim."

Stella leant her shoulder against Heather's. That was exactly what she been afraid would happen.

"And then?" prompted Tas.

Heather glanced seaward, remembering. "Everything went warm and bright – which is *not* normal at midnight depth. And I wasn't drowning any more – I could breathe. I'm still figuring out what's changed." She gave a cautious smile. "There's this."

She held out her arms and her scales rippled in a rainbow of colours, before fading to perfectly match the colour of the rocks. "That's how I escaped. I couldn't be seen. Though I didn't realise it at the time – I just swam as hard and fast as I could, back to the surface."

"Wow!" exclaimed Tas. "You can just choose the colour? Just like that?"

Heather nodded.

"Talk about accessorising!" Tas grinned broadly. "We are going to have so much fun picking you an outfit for the celebration."

Heather's eyes narrowed. "Celebration?"

Stella quickly took Heather's hand, in case she made a dive for the water. She widened her eyes at Tas: *Tone it down a bit!*

* * *

Heather looked at Stella seriously after Tas had gone. "I'm not coming ashore. If they want to apologise, they can come to me."

Stella nodded. "That's fair."

Heather grinned and Stella stared. "Your teeth are different."

Heather licked them and nodded. "Less masgoom, more orca," she agreed. "Still got a nasty bite." She snapped them together and Stella smiled.

"I don't doubt it. So? Where should I tell them to come?"

"They can meet me at the sea." Heather nodded at the towering sea stacks. "There."

Forty

A SKY-FULL
OF STORMS

I T took a lot of organising, but to Stella's relief, nobody objected. Shame hovered unspoken in the air. Suddenly nothing was too much trouble.

The council, it turned out, had an official barge for ceremonial occasions. Stella asked Grandpa if he could maybe take her and Tas on *Curlew*, but he shook his head.

"Took a bit of a battering the other night. I'd like to give her a good once over before setting out to sea in her again."

So that was how they came to be crushed against the rail of

the ceremonial barge, along with an entire crowd of excitable storm novices.

"Stop raining on me!"

"You fired hail at me!"

"Watch this, I've figured out lightning!"

"Enough! Or I'll drench the lot of you!" exclaimed Tas. "Honestly, I know you're enjoying having your clouds back, but give it a rest!" She was rewarded with a brief silence, though the novices' sideways glances suggested it wouldn't last long.

Stella looked back. The storm clouds still circled Winter's Keep, like a great dark whirlpool. They'd simmered down a bit now. The sparks of lightning and rumbles of thunder were fewer and further between. In contrast, the sea was mirror smooth – incongruous beneath the stormy skies.

Must be the council's doing, thought Stella, peering towards the upper deck. Sure enough, all the council elders she could see were wearing green sea shawls atop their ceremonial robes. *They're not taking any chances.*

A low shelf of rock stretched between the three sea stacks. It was barely above the water, but with the waves so still, it was exposed and drying rapidly. Heather stood in the centre of it, waiting.

The boat was manoeuvred alongside and tied up, then a wide gang plank was lowered. Stella shuffled to the front with Tamar, behind Ilana, the current leader of the council. Magnus and Silvan were right behind, along with some of the younger council members. They filed down onto the rock, fanning out under

Ilana's direction into a wide semi-circle facing the boat. There was an amount of nervous shuffling and throat-clearing amongst the council members as they took in the sea witch.

Heather waited silently, staring out at the glassy water.

She looked almost regal – like this was *her* kingdom and they were all just visitors – perhaps exactly what she'd intended when insisting the council meet her here.

The storm novices came next, hustled along by Tas. As she hopped off the gangplank, she caught Heather's attention with a quick wave and a double thumbs up.

Stella smiled. That was Tas all over – she could lighten up *any* situation.

As Tas passed Stella, she did their secret hand signal for 'Storm Sisters' and gave an almost imperceptible nod towards Heather. She was right! Heather was a Storm Weaver, too. A third storm sister.

After Tas disembarked, the remaining weather weavers moved to line the rails of the boat. Stella glanced up at the top deck. The council elders weren't coming ashore, it seemed. Apologetic maybe, but still mistrustful.

"Unprecedented threats call for unprecedented courage," said Ilana, her voice weighty with the sense of occasion. "Not in living memory has the Teran risen in the height of summer. Still less, threatened our own shores."

"Wouldn't have done, either, if it weren't for Velda's meddling," muttered Tamar.

Ilana shot her a sharp glance and spread her arms wide.

"We owe a debt of gratitude to the Trows, that will perhaps never be fully repaid."

"Where are they?" whispered Stella to Tamar. "Shouldn't they be part of this?"

"Daytime, isn't it." Tamar shook her head. "Besides, they've got no patience for council pageantry. They left last night. Took all their gems with them."

"I hope *someone* thanked them?" whispered Stella.

Tamar nodded. "I did."

Stella turned her attention back to Ilana. She'd moved to the centre of the rocky plateau to stand by Heather. In her hands were four long scarves. "Magnus, Stella, Tas, would you join us please?"

Heather flexed her shoulders and her scales rippled blue and white. Stella moved across to join her and took her hand in solidarity. Tas and Magnus joined them.

When they were all assembled, Ilana motioned for them to turn and face the barge. Stella's heart raced in her chest. So many people, all staring at them; though most eyes were on the sea witch.

Heather flexed her neck and spined fins rose like a collar, framing her face. A mutter of alarm rippled along the railing. Ilana turned and gave the assembled weather weavers a stern look. She stepped forward and draped a teal scarf around Heather's shoulders. Heather's scales immediately shaded to match and Ilana smiled in surprise. She took a step back and turned to face the barge.

"We honour Heather, our protector from the seas," she said loudly. "Wherever there are weather weavers, she will *always* be welcomed ashore, with warmth and gratitude."

The sea witch stared around at the assembled weather weavers, a stark challenge in her eyes. Stella was relieved to see people nodding.

She gave Heather's hand a quick squeeze. *You see?*

The hint of a smile played at the corner of Heather's mouth and her scales shifted to brightest gold, raising a soft murmur from the crowd.

Ilana moved along and placed a soft grey scarf around Stella's shoulders. "We honour Stella, protector of the skies. Your participation in the trials paved the way for this day, and you continue to exemplify the integrity and determination of a true Storm Weaver. Nine hundred storm clouds owe you their freedom," she said, nodding towards the maelstrom circling Winter's Keep. "They will not forget. Though we hope, in time, they will forgive."

Stella nodded, though she was by no means sure.

Heather leant towards her and whispered. "If Fury can, they will too."

Stella gave her a swift smile.

"Get the rest of the storm novices here," called Aaron from the far side. "They'll sort it for you!"

Ilana raised her eyebrows at the interruption, but nodded.

She moved on and draped a green scarf around Magnus. "We honour Magnus, protector of the land. Your Verdure skills

329

have come on apace since the Gathering! Without you, the defences of Winter's Keep would surely have fallen."

The last scarf was storm purple. Ilana draped it around Tas and nodded in the direction of the novices. "No mean feat, leading Storm Weavers," she said quietly. She raised her voice again. "We honour Tas, who not only helped reunite these novices with their storms, but also gave them a crash course in storm weaving! In time, we have no doubt that you will make a fine mentor."

The novices all whistled and whooped.

As Ilana turned away, Tas raised her eyebrows at Stella. "See? Leadership quality, me!" she whispered, with a wink.

Ilana spread her hands wide, presenting all four of them to the assembled weather weavers. The boat broke into noisy applause.

"What am I, then? Fish bait?" piped up Tamar from the side, though she was clapping as enthusiastically as the rest.

As the applause gradually died down, Ilana fixed Tamar with a smile and motioned her forward. Tamar moved closer, looking a lot less sure of herself now all eyes were on her. She was far more comfortable as a heckler than the centre of attention.

"What are you up to?" she growled at Ilana, out of the corner of her mouth. "I'm not joining the council again, if that's what you're after."

Ilana gave her a sly smile and patted her shoulder. "I don't think we could take the excitement," she murmured, then raised her hand for silence.

"The council have discussed this at length. For a renowned rule breaker, it seems only fitting to make an exception to the rules. Though she has refused our offer to re-join the council, Tamar has been named Leader of the Storm Weavers."

Tamar harumphed and nodded, but there was a sparkle in her eyes that Stella hadn't seen for a long time. "I might turn up at meetings from time to time. . ." she threatened, with a smile. "Just to make sure you're all awake."

Ilana shook her head in mock horror and Tamar smiled.

* * *

It was two days before the storm novices began to arrive.

Magnus was inside the Gate House with Tamar. She'd made it her personal task to tell him all the best tales about his dad's exploits as a Lightning Weaver. Magnus was an avid listener – often pressing her for more details, or querying anecdotes he'd heard from the Verdure Weavers. Velda's determination to protect him had deprived him of a whole chunk of his own history, and now he was hungry for it.

Stella was outside on the clifftop with Heather. She never took for granted that the sea witch would be there, but so far, each day she'd come back. Stella was beginning to hope that she might choose to stay for good.

Stella took Heather's hand. "You know you've got a home with us, if you want it?"

Heather looked out at the shining waves and shook her head,

her eyes full of calm certainty. "No. The sea is my home. It's where I belong."

Stella's heart fell, but she nodded. "I get it."

Heather nudged her shoulder. "You can always find me. You have the conch."

"We could picnic on the beach?" suggested Stella.

Heather's scales swirled mischievous orange before settling on silver. She nodded at the sea, a smile twitching the corner of her mouth. "Or you could come for a swim?"

Stella laughed nervously.

There was a shout of excitement from down the hill and Heather peered round the corner of the Gate House to see who was coming. She swiftly pulled up her hood.

"You don't have to do that," said Stella.

"It's a bunch of kids," said Heather. "I don't want to frighten them."

Stella stood up and moved forward. Tas was approaching, trailed by a long crocodile of small children, skipping along in pairs.

Wow, they're so little!

Most of them were pointing at Winter's Keep in excitement. The breeze carried snatches of high-pitched chatter and laughter.

Stella waved.

"Last year's storm novices," called Tas, by way of explanation. "The local ones, anyway. The council sent word out. This is just the first of them – there are more boats arriving all the time. You up for helping?"

Heather took a step back into the shadow of the house, but she needn't have worried. The legend of the sea witch had already spread. She soon found herself surrounded by a gaggle of curious youngsters.

"Can you breathe underwater?"

Heather flapped her gills.

"Cool!"

Heather's scales flushed rose gold at that, which was greeted by a coo of amazement.

"What! You can change colour?! Can you go invisible, too?"

Heather's bare feet darkened to green, until they were indistinguishable from the mossy grass.

"Epic! I wish I was a sea witch!"

Heather shook her head. "No," she said softly. "You don't."

"Right! Everybody, line ups!" yelled Tas. "Let's have some order here."

Not all of the novices were as confident as those clustered around Heather. Stella spotted one on the edge of the group, whose bottom lip was wobbling. She went over and crouched down next to her.

"Hi, I'm Stella. What's your name?"

"Abi."

"And what's your cloud's name?"

"Flash . . ."

Stella smiled. "A thundercloud, like mine."

The little girl nodded and looked up at the dark sky with

trepidation. "But I'm scared he won't remember me. I haven't seen him since last summer. And he was really new."

Stella looked up at Nimbus and raised an eyebrow. *You think you can find him?*

Nimbus bobbed once then shot straight up in the air. Briar dropped a shower of rain and launched himself skyward, following his friend. Arca and Drench weren't far behind.

"Oi! Where are you two off to?" shouted Tas at her departing clouds.

"They're helping Nimbus," said Stella.

"Oh. Alright then."

Stella turned back to Abi. "Don't worry," she reassured her. "Clouds don't forget. In fact, he's probably been missing you loads. So, when you're ready, I want you to shout his name. Loud as you can. Can you do that?"

Abi took a deep breath. "FLASH!!!"

Stella laughed. "Exactly like that."

Soon, all the novices were shouting their clouds' names in a joyful cacophony. Some of them jumped up and down and waved their arms too. Stella smiled and stepped back to join Heather and Tas.

"Got a whole storm family now!" said Tas, looking fondly at the small novices. "Here – Tamar, Magnus! Come and watch!"

Tamar emerged from the house, wincing slightly at the noise. Magnus appeared in the doorway behind her.

"Look . . ." breathed Stella and pointed.

High above Winter's Keep, Nimbus, Arca and Drench darted this way and that, herding the storms apart, nudging the spiral wider.

Gradually, the confusion of clouds began to separate and a small group of individual clouds became visible. The young novices squealed in delight and their shouts got louder as, one by one, their clouds left the huge storm circling overhead and dived towards them. Thunderclouds, flickering fierce and bright. Hailstorms, glittering like constellations of shooting stars. Blizzard clouds, their plumes of snow catching the light like prisms, painting the sky with rainbows.

Stella smiled at Heather, soaking up the joy shining in her face.

"Beautiful," breathed the sea witch. Her scales shone silver now, reflecting every colour of the rainbow in the sky above.

"A sky-full of storms!" said Stella, gazing at them happily as they approached.

Heather shook her head.

"From now on, let's call it a *freedom* of storms."

ACKNOWLEDGEMENTS

So, we've come full circle. The sea witch, the monstrous antagonist of the first *Weather Weaver* book, has finally had her story heard. I wonder what you think of her now?

When I first dreamt of *The Weather Weaver*, it was the Haken's story that kept nagging at me, refusing to leave me alone. I dreamt of deepest blue, of the strange and wondrous creatures at midnight depth, the freedom and peace to be found in the darkness, and wondered if she could find her way back.

My heartfelt thanks to Justine, Lauren, and all at Bell Lomax Moreton. Thank you for championing Stella and believing in me. I can't wait to share the next chapter with you.

The wondrous team at UCLan are small but mighty. A huge hug to Hazel – thanks to you, the *Weather Weaver* story has grown into a new Shetland myth – told and retold, constantly evolving, finding its way into playground games, sky-gazing dreams, and wind-whispered wishes. Tilda, my excellent editor, I treasure your insight and creativity – thank you for un-knotting my plotting and spotting every loose end. If this story is well woven, it's thanks in large part to you. Becky, just: wow! David's cover is rich with detail and packed with peril, and Hannah's illustrations are little gems all the way through. You have, yet again, created an irresistible-looking book. Charlotte, thank you for everything, including making me cry happy tears! And I'm super-grateful to the wonderful team who've spread the word – the book-loving team at Bounce, and Antonia for all her PR conjuring.

I had thought that being a writer would be solitary, but I'm overjoyed to discover that it's not. Much love to the ever-expanding circle of creative people who have egged me on from first spark to final edits. Anna Wilson (more peril!), Alison Powell and Write Club, the MAWYP alumni, the Gritty Critters, the Bathstol Writers, the Good Ship, the Twitter writing community, and so many more – in you, I have found my people.

This year has reminded me quite how wonderful librarians are – from putting the right book in the right hands, to organising events and school visits, to bringing whole communities together – you are amazing. Special thanks to Chloe and the team at Shetland Library for letting me swap words and ideas with a whole host of brilliantly creative young readers and writers.

I'm sending a blast of sunshine to all the independent and high street bookshops who've made shelf-space for lightning-bolt covers and filled your tables and windows with rainbows. You've greeted each book with a full-blown gale of enthusiasm and I am eternally grateful.

Much love to all my Shetland family and friends: Elizabeth and David, for the warmest welcome and giving me quiet space to dream in; Linda and Mary, for bookish adventures and excellent conversation; Jessamine, undefeated Scrabble Queen; Emily, Magnus, David and Hope – you are all a source of joy.

A shout out to Ben, you've turned my head inside out in

the most excellent way. And to my Glastonbury crew: keep asking the questions and discovering ever-better answers. You are all magical.

To Cath and Catherine, always there for emergency cups of tea and perfect harmonies: you are my sanctuary song – filling me with hope and courage.

Enormous thanks to Callen, whose uncommonly wise advice has seen me through many a passing squall. You deserve all the bright days ahead and you know I'll be there, cheering you on.

Cat, up with beetling, word-witchery and inventive re-sorcery. Your sense of humour is dark and your heart is a flame. I am so glad I have you.

Mum and Dad, thank you for proving that there are always new adventures around the corner. More story-time soon . . .

Boundless love to Leo, Isabella, and Louis too. These past few years have been filled with world-sized challenges and you've weathered them all. I am constantly in awe of your warmth, kindness, and imagination. Leo, thank you for excellent hugs and endless encouragement. Bella, your sass and fierce determination are an inspiration. Louis, you have main-character-level resilience. Keep finding those silver linings!

Bernardo, you lift me up. Here's to reinventing ourselves year on year, with plenty of laughter along the way. I love you, more than you can know.

And finally, dear reader, thank you. Yes, you! You are the reason that I write. Thank you for reading this wild and windswept adventure right to the very last page. I wonder what magic you'll conjure in your own life?

Whatever the weather, keep your head high and your eyes on the sky! You've got this. xxx

If you liked this, you'll love . . .

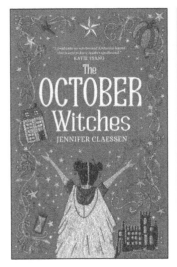

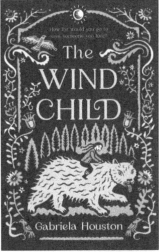

Have you read Stella's other adventures?

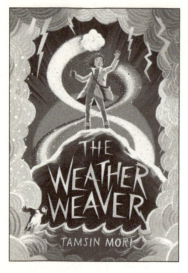

'A storm-swept adventure brimming with wild Shetland magic. I loved it!' ALEX ENGLISH

'A tender story of family with a whiplash of thunder.' JASBINDER BILAN

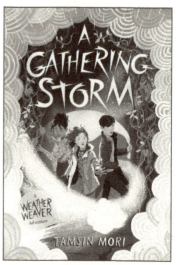